BRENDA COOPER

PUBLISHED BY
eSpec Books LLC
Danielle McPhail, Publisher
PO Box 493,
Stratford, New Jersey 08084
www.especbooks.com

ISBN: 978-1-942990-22-2
ISBN (ebook): 978-1-942990-23-9

Interior Graphic: Lily of the valley flowers © naddya, www.fotolia.com

Art Direction and Production: Mike McPhail, McP Digital Graphics

Copyeditor: Greg Schauer
Proofreader: Darragh Metzger

Interior Design: Sidhe na Daire Multimedia
www.sidhenadaire.com

Dedication

To teenagers everywhere.
We are trying to save the world for you,
and hope you will keep saving it from us.

Chapter One

THE AIRPLANE HANGS WHITE IN A PALE BLUE SKY ABOVE ME.

It has long wings, like the periodic stray gull that finds its way to us, and a body as thin and long as a bird's. There is almost no tail in the profile of the plane above me, although if I remember right from movies, airplane tails stick up instead of out like a bird's tail.

I want—no, I need—to know who is in it and where they are going.

I need to know if the airplane is hope.

It spends more time crossing the piece of sky I can see than I expect. As if it is calling me.

A branch snaps.

I have let my pursuers closer to me than I planned. Two men and a woman this time. One of the two men calls out, "Hey, girl!"

I know better than to answer. I'm perched on a rocky outcropping fifty feet above them, partially hidden by the dried carcasses of dead spruces.

It's possible they won't see me here, but if they do, the place is a trap.

I stand up a little too fast, part of my brain still shocked stupid by the airplane. I make a little too much noise, and the gruffer voice says, "There!" to his companions and then the woman shouts, "We won't hurt you!"

Right. You just want to feed me and ask me about the weather.

I had been too sure I'd lost them. Stupid.

I'm young and strong, and this time I don't get cocky.

I run up a series of switchbacks, pretending to be a doe bounding away from a coyote. My skin and mouth are dry. The afternoon sun has sucked all the water from me, and I haven't stopped to drink. The sole of my right boot is so thin that when I step hard on a stone, pain lances up from the ball of my foot through the long bones of my legs, but I keep going in spite of it. I run even though I don't hear anyone behind me. Not anymore.

I realize I haven't for a while; I got away.

I always get away.

So far.

Now if I can just get home and inside without being noticed.

I'm on our side of the place in the road where we threw dirt over it all and planted trees just after Before, and bits of the old road show through. It's not good to walk on since the eco-surface has been dissolving into black crumbs.

I crest a small hill and our wall rises up like a cracked egg, dirty white mottled with grey, the jagged glass we've glued to the top winking in the sun.

Between here and the wall, we'd removed all the dead wood. I stride across grey-green grass that Kelley had us plant in the moat of cleared ground around our walled garden. I don't like to admit it, but she picked well; the spiky, low growth has been alive for two years now, and it creeps back into the forest as we clear it further away. This is partly to keep our light, and partly to keep an open space so we can see animals or people coming.

Of course, the long drought is clearing up, too. Oskar still frets that there is not enough rain and not enough cold, but the hills and forests between us and the interstate are green and dotted with yellow and white flowers.

I trip over a log, going down hard on my right knee and my hands, scraping my palms near the black soil line from the fire we set five years ago to save the garden from a wildfire.

My breath breaks the silence. I sound like a rabbit before a thin coyote kills it, scared and breathing too hard. I make myself slow down and remember what Oskar taught me. Breathe through your nose. Breathe deep in your belly, so you can feel it going out and in.

Slowly.

S l o w l y.

I'm getting there. A cool spring breeze blows my hair against my chin and helps me feel better.

"Sagie."

I hate it when Kelley calls me that. My name's Sage.

She extends her left hand. There's dirt ground into the creases of her palm and stuck under her nails, and it smells wetter and stronger than the dry, cracked earth under my hands. A year or two ago, I would have apologized, but not now. Now I can look down on Kelley's graying dark hair, on her ponytail tied with a strip of bark. She holds her taser in her right hand, a black oblong that she protects as if it means her life. She leaves it out as we walk back, swinging in her hand, the arc of her movement precise.

My knee bleeds, but we both ignore that.

Kelley doesn't say anything, but I make up her feelings and words in my head anyway. *The walls are safe, but only as long as we're not noticed. If a mob finds us, we will all die. Besides, you aren't old enough for the world yet. It's dangerous. You might get hurt, or raped, and die all by yourself. There's men that would take you in and make you trade your body for water and food. It only takes three days to die without water.* If she was lecturing me instead of staring off, lost in her head, she'd look down at this point and see I have a small canteen clipped to my belt, one of the old ones where the metal's all banged up. *Well, maybe you'd live a week.* She'd look disgusted. *There's good people out there, but there're some that are as bad as bad can get.*

The only problem with a lecture in your head is you can't fight it. Kelley knows that, and it makes me even madder at her, but it's not like I'm going to be able to explain to the Board why I picked a fight with someone who doesn't say anything to me.

I hate living like everything is evil. Just this morning I talked to four women who had stopped just off the road to boil tea, and they said parts of Portland are safe. There's food and cars and order. Cars. I've never seen a car move, just cars rusted to blackberries and filled with junk or the bones of small animals.

The shape of the airplane sticks in my head.

Whether the world is still screwed up or not, I'll never amount to anything if I stay inside my whole life and work on little things that don't matter with little people who will die behind a wall. The wet, verdant world we live in is a bubble, and I want the real world.

Right before we get to the wall, Kelley turns and stares at me. I expect her to be yelling angry, but what I see in her dark blue eyes is just sadness.

I'm sorry she's sad. I don't tell her that; I can't show weakness.

The door in the wall is big and there's a whiter spot on the wall above it where my dad ripped the sign off in the second year of the drought, the second year after I was born. That was still Before. Barely.

Kelley palms the door pad, and it opens wide. Inside, it smells like dirt and water and frogs, and faintly, of flowers. We pass magenta azaleas whose bloom is just starting to wilt, and in spite of myself I smile when I see three bees on one plant. Kelley and Oskar both taught me to notice little things. Little things define the big things.

I stop smiling when I see that the Board of Directors is waiting. All of them. They're sitting in their formal place, on benches in a circle under the sign that used to be above the doors. "Oregon Botanical Gardens." The Board has run us since Before, and they still run us now. The three original members are gray and wrinkled.

There's four Board members. Kelley makes five adults staring at me. She says, "Sage, please sit," and gestures to the hot seat—the one for people who are in trouble.

I've been here before.

The Board's older than Kelley; they all spent most of their lives in the world I only see in movies. They all remember my dad, who's dead now, and they all remember they're the ones who make all the rules and I'm the girl who keeps breaking them.

I wait for them to speak first.

It takes a long time. I draw little circles in the dirt with my toes and pretend to be sorry.

Kelley clears her throat, and stares at me, her chin quivering. That's weird. I never saw her look weak. "Sage, we've done everything we know how to do to keep you in here. We can't bear to kill someone because you left tracks or got followed home. You may be only sixteen, but you're endangering us all." She pauses and takes a breath. "And more than us."

She means the whole saving-the-plants-to-return-them-to-the-world-someday thing.

Kelley forces the next words out. "I've told the security system not to open for you anymore."

So how am I supposed to help with the chores like gathering firewood and hunting rabbits? "Ever?"

Kelley ignores my question. "If you go out again, you will not be allowed back in."

She can't mean it. I'm her hope for the future. She wouldn't kick me out.

Tim and Li are the two old men of the Board. Li nods, telling me he supports Kelley. Tim looks impassive, but he would miss me. We play chess sometimes in the hour between dawn and breakfast. Sometimes I win, and he likes that.

He looks past me; his eyes don't meet mine.

Elise and Shell are the two women on the Board. They're both stone-faced, too, but they might mean it. They're scarier than Tim and Li.

Kelley keeps staring at me, sad. Usually when she's getting me in trouble she looks frustrated. "Do you understand?"

"Yes."

"Tell me what will happen if you leave again without permission."

"The door won't let me back in."

"And we will not let you back in," she adds.

Maybe she does mean it. Her eyes are all wet, even though she isn't crying. Kelley isn't done. I know because no one is moving, and they're all watching me. Kelley says, "Just so you don't do anything rash, you're confined to the Japanese Garden for a week. Report to Oskar in ten minutes."

She does mean this, except maybe the ten minutes part.

I nod at them all and walk away, keeping my head up. I hate it that they've made me feel small again. In my room, I sweep two changes of clothes into an old bag. I brush my hair and my teeth, and put those brushes in the bag, too. Ten minutes pass, then fifteen. I wait the minutes out, unwilling to be on time.

Oskar doesn't even notice I'm late. I walk in the glass box and close the outer door, and wait a moment, then open the inner door. I am inside walls, some glass, and under a plastic sheet roof. The air is heavy with water, cool. Oskar is nowhere to be seen. When he finished it, the Japanese garden was billed as the most authentic on the west coast. One of the first fully contained green energy buildings in Oregon, with solar cells on all the hard roofs and in the walls, and heat made by water that's warmed by the earth far under us. At first, the roof was to keep the garden from getting too wet, instead of too dry.

I negotiate the stepping-stone path, walking through pillows of pearlwort. The cinnamon fern that lines the right wall still has some tender, brownish fiddleheads so I pick them. Maybe it's a form of penance.

The very first of the wisteria blooms are showing purple. Oskar is on the other side of the flowers, between me and the waterfall.

He doesn't turn around for the space of two breaths. He's squatting, bent over, clipping the leaves of a Japanese holly. He is a small man, his skin pallid from the damp air he lives in, his long red hair caught back in a braid that falls down a freckled, white back. The top of his braid is grey. He is only wearing shorts; he likes to garden as naked as the Board will let him. Even his feet are bare. I have always suspected that at night he goes out with his flashlight and gardens more naked than that. Even though he is almost sixty years old, I think I would pull weeds beside him, with my nipples exposed to the cool night air.

He wouldn't let me, of course. They all treat me like glass.

He stands up and turns toward me. Even though the light is starting to grey to dusk, I can see that his eyes look like Kelley's did. "Why do you run away?"

I lean back against the big cedar column that holds up the wisteria arbor, breathing in the sweet air. "Why don't you ever leave this garden?"

I've never asked him this. Instead of looking startled, he smiles and his eyes twinkle a bit, full of mischief. "Because I'm saving the world."

He believes it, even though he's lying to himself. He is, at best, saving a tiny part of the world that I can walk across in five minutes. Everyone here thinks small.

I hold out my hand, the one with the fiddleheads in it, and he takes them and says, "See?"

He leads me to the kitchen, which is the only interior room with hard walls instead of waxed paper or bamboo or glass. He hands me back the fiddleheads, and I wash them in a bowl full of water and then pour the water into a bin so it can go into the waterfall, where it will be scrubbed clean by the filter plants.

We have everything ready, but before we start to cook, Oskar takes me up to the top of the rock wall at the center of the stroll garden, and we look out toward the ocean. It's too far away to see or hear, but the sun will set over it. He makes a temporary hole in the roof by pushing overlapping layers of water-capturing plastic aside, exposing the sunset. There are enough clouds to catch faint gold and orange, but most of the last rays leak up like spilled paint and fade into the blackening sky.

Maybe I can use the hole in the roof to climb all the way outside.

After the color starts to fade, Oskar speaks quietly. "I answered you. Will you answer me?"

So that's what he's been waiting for. I guess when you're sixty you have a lot of patience.

"We live in a bubble."

He laughs and pokes the plastic roof. It answers him by rippling, as if it were upside-down water.

I frown. "We do!" I wave my hand at all the roads and people we can't see from here. "In the real world out there, people are traveling and learning and meeting each other. They're struggling. They're taking back the world. This time..." I haven't really told anyone about this trip yet—I mean, no one had asked. Should I? "I walked the interstate and talked to people on it. Like always. I have my escape routes. They work."

He cocks an eyebrow at me but doesn't say anything.

"Eugene's coming back. There's thousands of people there now —they fixed the water system and they're growing greenhouse food. I met two families who were on their way there."

He clears his throat. "A year ago, you told me Eugene was empty."

"That's what I heard. But this time I heard different." I pause. "I don't *know* anything. How could I?"

"They don't have the right plants. That's what I'm saving for your generation. The bamboo and the bearberry, the astilbe and the peony." He says the names of plants like a prayer, and I imagine him naming the others in his head. The wisteria and the wild fuchsia, the fiddlehead and the mountain fern....

"I know what you're saving. You keep telling me about it." It's an old story, how we're saving the genome of the native plants in case the weather ever reverts to its magical past self. "It's good. I'm glad you're saving it. But that's *your* dream."

He pretends not to notice my tone of voice. "What your travelers see is the Mediterranean weeds that killed the native plants in California when Father Serra brought them on his donkey. Now that it's warm enough, dry enough, they come here and invade Oregon like they invaded California a long time ago." His face wears a stubborn look that makes him more handsome, wiping some of the wrinkles away with anger. He closes the hole in the roof and starts down the rock face as all of the colors of the garden begin to fade, and I hear him tell me, "It is your duty to the planet to help."

I can't keep my secret anymore. "I saw an airplane today."

He stares at me, and I know him well enough to know that he's surprised even though he is always slow to show emotion. "Tell me about it."

"It looked like a bird, but it wasn't. The wings never moved although the plane moved, straight. It was high up. It was white." I can't quite tell if he believes me. "It was beautiful, Oskar."

"Which way was it going?"

"North." I think about it. "Portland or Seattle, I guess."

He nods, but I'm pretty sure he thinks I'm making it up. He climbs down, but I stay and try and remember more details about the airplane until stars swim across the sky, diffused by the beads of water that gather there as the evening cools. After my eyes adjust enough to the dark, I come carefully to ground and Oskar and I share cinnamon fern fiddleheads and cattail roots and some jerky from a thin doe that jumped into our garden a few weeks ago and broke a leg.

After, I lie on my sleeping pallet, separated from Oskar by waxy paper and bamboo, and listen to the roof crinkle in the wind. If I don't get out, I'm going to die here in Oskar's Japanese stroll garden, walking the stone paths until there's not enough water left for the wisteria.

I can't bear being kept in a box as if I were a precious plant and not a real girl. I can't bear getting old without ever having a friend. But I can't imagine never coming home, either. Not seeing these people I've seen for every day of my life that I remember. Kelley and Oskar.

When I leave, I see people moving. Sometimes that's all I do, sit and watch people come and go, counting. Once I counted over a hundred in just a morning. They're going somewhere. They aren't living behind a wall and sitting in one place and waiting for everything to get better.

Oskar's breathing gets even and deep, and it's a comfort.

But not enough. I almost drift off, start thinking of other things, and then startle awake. Over and over.

When I give up, I sit up as silently as I can, strip off my sleeping clothes, and pull on my best jeans and most comfortable flannel before I roll up everything I brought and wrap it in an old blue Pendleton blanket so I can swing it over my shoulder. I fill two canteens with water, running it slowly so that I won't wake anyone.

I write Oskar and Kelley a note. I tell them I love them and I'm going to go save the world, and I'm sorry they won't ever let me back in. A tear drips onto the note but I manage not to sob out loud.

I carefully open the first of the two doors, trying to keep the rusty hinges from squeaking. Kelley is standing on the other side, a thin stick of a shadow that only moves when I'm through.

I'm caught.

Oskar comes up behind me.

I tense.

He leans forward and gives me a hug and he whispers in my ear. He says, "Good luck."

I blink at them both, stupid with surprise.

He says, "Me and Kelley both knew you'd go. It's time. The Board told us to keep you. They're scared that you'll tell someone about us, and they're scared they'll lose you. You're like a daughter to them."

No. I'm not. I know that. Mostly they say bad things about me.

Oskar keeps going. "We need you more than you need us."

Kelley thrusts a bag into my hands. It's heavy.

I feel thick in the throat and watery. I say, "I'll come back someday."

He says, "If you take long enough, we'll even let you back in."

I go before we all cry or laugh and wake the Board up. The stars look clearer out beyond the wall, and the moat of grass muffles my footsteps.

Chapter Two

I SHUFFLE THROUGH DARKNESS. THE BLANKET FEELS AWKWARD AND rubs against my shoulder and my things keep slipping out of it. I have to stop and grope the ground to retrieve a shirt and a pair of socks once, and my hairbrush another time. I count steps. A hundred. Two hundred. Two thousand and my back and shoulders burn. I look behind me a few times but see no one. We keep the gardens dark at night, sipping stored power to heat water for tea, a shared movie, or a game. I imagine Oskar and Kelley are still up, sitting side by side and whispering about me.

I trip over a rock and fall. Nothing is hurt except the scrape on my knee, which sends a warm runnel of blood down my shin. I am afraid of light here, afraid to show myself to whoever might be ten or two hundred feet from me in the dark. Before long, I stop and wait for dawn, flexing my knee from time to time to keep it from stiffening up. It's not really cold but a light wind makes it colder than the gardens.

Coyotes cry.

I am afraid. This is the right thing to do, but excitement has given way to the kind of fear that sticks inside my stomach like a cold ball. The fear drives me to pee on the ground, but I've done that before and it only bothers me a little. Something to get used to.

I have to do this. I will never grow up and bloom inside their garden, never meet other young people. I will never *matter* behind a wall. I want to save the world in my own way.

I already miss Oskar's breathing and the mint tea he hands me every morning in a cup that he made.

I keep listening for airplanes, watching for them to cross between me and the stars.

Light creeps over the Cascades and I spread the blanket out to see what Kelley has given me. Flatbread and dried apples. A knife: the small orange one with the plastic sheath. A roll of toilet paper and some women's things. Two clean pairs of underwear and two pairs of darned socks. A carefully labeled bag with precious aspirin and some bandages in it. A bottle of water purification tablets. A length of thick twine. The knife is the only thing people will notice is missing. Hopefully the Board will think I stole it and not that Kelley gave it to me. A note from Kelley. "Come back someday. Keep us secret. I love you."

"I love you, too." There are only birds and wind to hear me whisper it, but I say it like a prayer, the way Oskar taught me to talk to plants.

I tuck the note in my back pocket and put everything but the twine and a handful of the toilet paper neatly on the same side of the blanket, then fold the blanket over and roll it all up. It's a bit lumpy, but it balances better. The twine works to close up both sides so I can sling the whole thing over my back without leaking objects. As soon as I try walking I realize the twine hurts and re-do the whole thing, leaving a shirt out to wrap around the twine for padding. This works, which pleases me. The sun warms my face and shrinks the stone of fear in my belly.

I take a path I often use when I sneak out. It's thin and lined with baby black sage growing up through winter-killed bushes that a long freeze took out two years ago. Here and there, a wild rose puts out fresh light green leaves where it vines through the dead limbs.

Out of loss, fresh things.

Kelley would complain about the sage, which shouldn't grow here, but it is better than bare earth no matter what she thinks. The old world is gone, now. At least the new one has roses.

At the top of the last hill I can see home from, I stop for water. People know I'm gone by now. They are talking about me, and maybe some of them wish I were still there. For a fleeting second I want to go home and beg to be let back in.

But I have chosen. I wave at the botanical gardens, now small enough that they won't see me. No one will come looking for me. No one ever has, except Kelley, and she won't come today.

A hawk screeches above me, and I look up to see the hawk and a crow twisting in the bright morning sun. A small soft thud draws my eyes to a dying mouse that has been dropped during the chase, surely loosed from the talons of the hawk. I kneel, put my hand over it, and wish it good journey. A lesson from Oskar. I swear to myself that I'll remember his lessons as I wander in the world without him.

The path winds downhill in a series of switchbacks, toward the interstate. I-5. There are always people on the road, and the trick will be finding good ones. I have a place I wait, a spot where there are still living evergreens and vine maple. Steep cliffs protect the trees on two sides. A stream that threads down the middle of the cleft is mostly dry now, the bottom of the bed full of stream-moss colored shale. I sit on a tall, flat rock and look down onto the broken roadbed below. It's wide and gray with strips of grass grown up through cracks. These cracks are from neglect but I've seen two places where quakes separated the road so far that cars can't travel here. I've seen motorcycles twice, so noisy they shut the forest up and the people on the road move to the side and hide.

The interstate is almost empty now. A lone coyote slinks across it, followed by three wild dogs. All of them are spring-thin but strong. This winter the sky gave us a little rain and no snow. Only three nights of freeze.

I hear footsteps before I see the pack of men going south. Seven. I slide down out of sight and watch as they trudge by. Two carry rifles and one pulls a kid's wagon with supplies. Looks like blankets and water. Part of why I like this spot is that sound carries to me but these men are not talking. They look like trouble, so I keep my head down until they pass. Besides, I'm going north.

The next travelers are going my way, a group of twenty or so, five of them women and more than five children. I think there are seven. There might be an eighth in a big stroller pulled by one of the men on a bicycle. I almost stand up to walk down and tell them hello, but at the last minute, I don't feel right about it. I can wait.

I hesitate through three groups that have small warning signs for me. One has too many guns. A second is just adult couples and there's no place for me to fit. The third is mostly women, but they're lean and walk like predators.

I tell myself I don't want risks, not now when I'm free. But it tastes like a lie, and I guess I'm waiting for something perfect and that won't ever come. Maybe I'm too scared to really leave home, and that's not okay with me. I need to be brave. Besides, it's cool in my hiding place. There's sun on the road and none on me—the branches withhold it. Greedy branches.

Three couples walk together, pushing a cart—something big and silvery with tall wheels that work very well on the old road, maybe they were even made for it. They must have weapons since they've protected the cart, but they aren't holding them out in the open. They're talking between themselves in low tones and they sound pretty happy. They have a dog, a small white one that's riding in the cart. I don't see very many pets, except big dogs trained to guard or fight. One of the women talks to the dog from time to time, her voice rising and softening. Its name is Luke.

I use a technique I've used before to get to know people. I race a bit ahead, following a thin track up and down and across a flat, entering the road in front of the others. Nobody likes being come up on from behind; they feel better if they overtake me.

I slow down so they can catch me, keeping my breathing low and all my senses open.

They line up two by two and start walking faster.

"Good morning," I call out from just ahead of them.

One of the women waves. She's tall with red hair and green eyes and a touch of sunburn on her cheeks.

"Mind company?"

Her eyes widen.

"Yes." One of the men speaks for her and she lets him, dropping her eyes.

I fade backward, behind them. I don't want to be told what to do.

It's a good traveling day and soon another group catches up to me. This is a long train of people, even an old man being pushed in a squeaky wheelchair. I walk slow enough for them to engulf me, making me one of them by virtue of there being so many. There are a few teenagers like me. A girl who's maybe two years older comes up to me. Her voice is soft. "I'm Lelani. We're on our way to Seattle."

"Where did you come from?" I ask her.

"California." She spits the word out, like the state itself did something awful to her. "Southern California."

"I heard the quakes were bad there."

She sneers and shrugs. She is thin and wiry. Her hair is well-kept and clean, brown with highlights. "Do you hate people from California?"

"I don't hate anyone." I shift the blanket roll on my back so the slight pain cuts closer to my shoulder. "Did someone say they don't like you because you're from California?"

"There's a nice little town halfway up here. I wanted to stay but they won't take Californians."

"That's rude. What was the name of the town?"

"Wolf's Creek. They built it on a park. It's Post."

Post is the word people use for things that happened after the good times. Not like there was a single event. But Before things were all good, I guess. Then During there was bad weather and the quakes that were medium here but huge in California, and sickness here and everywhere, and Hurricane Nadiya that took out New Orleans for good, or so we heard before our satellite TV died. Oskar told me the worst wasn't the big things like quakes. He says it was the economy—the way money moves around. Money stopped working. Hyperinflation he calls it. People turned to trading stuff for stuff. The Board keeps a big stash of money, but Oskar said it isn't worth much, and I think it must not be or Kelley would have given me some.

"What was nice about Wolf's Creek?"

Lelani's voice softens, wistful. "They had a school. I miss having a school so bad I can taste it. We had one in California for a few years, even after the quakes. Parents ran it."

"What happened?"

"There's not enough water in California."

There's not enough water here anymore either. "Was it a big school? The one in Wolf's Creek?"

"It had every grade. I didn't get to go in and meet the teachers, because they said we couldn't stay. It's only for people from Oregon."

"Not a very good example of globalization," I say, meaning to be funny. Oskar and Kelley would have laughed, or said it themselves.

She looks at me like I'm speaking Greek. But then the garden is full of people with doctorates and a strange sense of humor. They did make me study every day.

A hand falls onto my shoulder and I feel startled and tipsy since the blanket affects my balance. “We’re not taking in anyone else.”

Lelani turns her face to him. “Please, pop. I want another girl.”

He gives her the kind of look that withers ripe fruit.

She takes my hand. Her hand is warm and grabby and a bit sweaty.

“Perhaps I’ll catch up with you later,” I say.

“I didn’t get your name,” she whines.

I pull my hand out of hers. “I’m Sage.” I speak to the man. “All right if I walk with you a bit? It’s a free road.”

He leans down and whispers in my ear, his breath smelling like toothpaste and orange juice, like the world before all of this. “I’m sorry,” he whispers. “My daughter gets ahead of herself. We don’t have enough for another kid.”

“I can feed myself. I know what plants are edible.”

“Look, you’d be trouble. I don’t want any trouble. It’s hard enough to keep Lelani safe.”

This I understand. “There’s been three people try to rape me and two try to steal from me in the last year. None of them succeeded. I can teach her to be safe.”

“You’re too pretty. Back off.”

I can tell he means it, so I jog over to Lelani and tell her, “When people try to hurt you, if you say you got AIDS, they’ll leave you alone.” She’s skinny enough this will work for her.

She looks at me and nods, her face all solemn. “I’m sorry. I hope I see you again.”

“Me, too.”

She whispers, “Be safe.”

“I will.”

I’ll have to keep trying, or else settle for walking on the side paths and having hope. But I know what it’s like to be chased, and already I’m so far away from home that there are trees and ravines and rusty signs I don’t recognize by the road.

I fall back, watching Lelani and wondering if she could have been a friend.

I let them all get ahead of me, and then drift down the road by myself. Four adults on bicycles pass the other way, then a pair of walkers. The walkers wave and I wave back.

Maybe I will walk to Portland by myself. It is only a few days from here. The bicycles probably came from there.

I turn a lot, looking behind me. The sun is up high now, and it's hot for spring. In the old days, this would probably be a rainy day. Two years ago, after the hard freeze, spring was filled with rain and rain and rain, flooding rain, and more rain, and more flooding rain.

The skies can't be trusted. After the spring full of rain they dried up for a year.

A knot of men come up behind me and I fade into the forest and let them pass. Any group that is all men of middle-age or less is dangerous. Kelley has told me this over and over. She has always said it like there was something real that happened to her, although she has never told me what it was. I have guesses. After all, her eyes narrow like she's angry when she says it, like she needs the anger. It's the kind of anger that hides failure and tears, that needs to be meditated out in the stroll garden. But she keeps this anger close in to her and doesn't let it out. Unlike Oskar, Kelley isn't the meditating type.

I nap on a rock hidden behind a thicket of vine maple.

I dream of being chased. My dream self is running when something pokes my shoulder hard enough to startle me awake.

Chapter Three

THE PAIN IN MY SHOULDER AND ADRENALINE FORCE ME OFF THE ROCK. As I grab the bedroll, I glimpse a boy, almost a man. Older than me by a few years. Something thin and deep left scars across his nose. "Up!" he commands me, brandishing a dry cedar branch.

My knees shake at the surprise of him and the nasty tone in his voice.

His free hand fists at his side. I don't see anyone else with him. "Give me the bedroll," he demands.

Anger drives up my spine. I sway, trying to look weak, using a breath to check my footing and notice roots and rocks and bushes.

"Now!" he demands. He's checking me out, looking at my breasts and my waist and below that and I feel dirty and mad. But while he's wasting time looking at things he can't have, I'm still memorizing. I'm taking deep breaths and getting set.

He holds his hand out, stretching it toward me. He's confident.

He's also off-balance. Oskar has taught me about balance.

I wave my bedroll at him, as if he is a bull and I'm a matador.

I grab it back just as he reaches for it. In the second he is overextended, I turn and leap. I hold my belongings up above my head and race, making sure not to get caught in the underbrush.

The branch hits me in the back, bouncing, doing no damage.

Twigs and bushes scratch my face, stinging.

The man follows, and there must be another person behind him. I hear two sets of footsteps. They are oafs crashing through bushes like bears. One of them falls and curses, but the other one keeps coming. I am faster, and lighter, and even though I don't know this exact ground, I will outrun them if I don't fall.

I lead them up over a rise, back down. Find a deer path.

My breath is coming fast now, in short, sharp rasps that stab my lungs. The man behind me is even more labored, his breath like a whistle, his feet pounding hard and heavy.

I go into my deer mode, light on my feet. A good runner.

Like a deer, I am prey in this instant.

They stay behind me, one close, one further back. Danger and maybe death. I'm gaining.

I lose the ground under my right foot and land on the same damned knee. I am afraid to look back. They sound closer. Fear drives me back up, away. A few more steps and I feel ahead again.

"Stop!"

The voice is in front of me, close. It has so much authority I hesitate before I put my head up, check the ground, and leap forward again.

"Go back the way you came."

The voice has power. The footsteps stop, and I stop. My breathing and their breathing are the only sounds I hear. Even the birds are shocked silent.

I take another step away, slower, still not sure where the man with the voice is standing. He isn't speaking to me, but to my pursuers.

"She's my sister," scar-face screams, angry.

"I don't care if she's your wife. No man chases a woman past me." I don't see a weapon but I imagine my savior is holding one. He almost has to be, because the man turns around without another word.

After a cuss and a grunt, both sets of footsteps fade until there is just quiet.

I have gone past the voice, and I could just keep going, keep my head down and go on to freedom, but I owe a thanks. I turn, shaky. A man stands next to a tree, one foot on a flat basalt rock. He is tall and broad, clothed in the greens and browns of the forest. Maybe he didn't have a weapon. If he did, I don't see it now. Just his hands, which are as big as my feet, and wide shoulders. He wears survival gear like it belongs on him: camouflage pants and a camouflage shirt and a canteen and outdoor boots that look almost new. He is probably thirty or thirty-five, blue eyes under dark hair.

I maintain my distance, keep my bedroll near me. There are twigs caught in my hair and I comb them out slowly to calm my shaking hands and say, "Thank you."

"Are you his sister?"

"No."

"I didn't think so." He stands still, like he can see how ready I am to just run again. "I'm Justice."

"You got that right." I know he means that's his name.

"You're the girl from the gardens."

I nod, surprised. Of course, I'm not far from home yet. My instinct to protect Kelley and Oskar and the plants remains. "What gardens? What do you know?"

"I know there's good going on at the old place. I know I don't have to be afraid of people from there."

"You don't have to afraid of me."

"Do you have a name?"

I consider lying to him. But he's been decent. "Sage."

"Sage. That's pretty."

I can't tell how wary to be. "Thank you."

He takes a step toward me, and I take a step back. He could catch me. Probably. I still have some lead, but I'm winded and he is fresh.

"I don't mean you harm. Have you eaten today?"

I shake my head, realizing I haven't. I have been so busy trying to find travelers to go with that I haven't thought about food. But now that he mentions it...

"You can eat with us, but you can't stay with us."

That's the deal I want anyway. "Who is 'us'?"

"Follow me." He steps toward me and I flinch but he passes me and keeps going, and I follow. It's work to stay up with him; I have to maintain a fast pace over ground I don't know and keep my feet. It could be a trap, but I don't see another choice and why is he so kind if he means me harm? Eventually we walk on a path. At one point he stops and points toward the ground. "Step high here."

A silvery trip wire sits a few inches above of the path, and then beyond it another and another. A normal stride would encounter at least one of them. They are in a spot that is probably always shaded so the sun never gives the wires away. I don't see any sticks or nets or other traps. There must be bells or maybe even electronics on the wires. "What happens if I trip on one?"

"Someone comes. But don't."

It feels mysterious and dangerous, like I'm in an adventure book. We're in a thick patch of forest, half dead and half green. A few places are dense enough to hide sentries. If they are there, they are good enough to be invisible.

Two more sets of trip wires and then we're in a copse of trees that appears to be far healthier than the forest we just passed through. They must be cared for, the way we care for our plants. Light glints off of a mirror and I realize we've been spotted and word is going ahead of us.

We pass a clump of native rhododendrons blooming pink and pale purple, the flowers bigger than my fist. Oskar and Tim would love to see this. The blooms distract me enough that I have to run a few steps to catch up.

I expect a camp, maybe some lean-to's with blue tarps over them. Instead there is a village with log houses and a central well. Trees have been cleared to make room for sunshine to wink on solar panels. They probably have as much power as we do at home. Stone walkways and a wooden bridge lie over a stream bed—dry now—that has been carefully lined with rocks. Six houses are visible. There are surely more in the trees or nearby. A huge building stands to the side in a clearing. A faded American flag hangs from a pole near the roof. The area around the building is fenced, and an open doorway shows stacks of raw material in neat piles. Wood for fires and wood that has been shaped into boards for building.

I increase my estimate of the electricity they must have. Everything is clean and tidy. A line of clothes hangs in the sun between two houses.

They started with less than we did at the garden but they have built more.

A woman comes out of a house big enough that there are probably three rooms. She has black skin and black hair, braided thick. She's wearing jeans and a blue t-shirt with a picture of the ocean on it. She waves, and Justice waves back, and then people start coming out of the other houses and out from around the back of them.

They waited for him. Discipline.

There are a lot of kids, maybe one kid for every two adults. Mostly they're younger than me.

People come up one by one and Justice introduces me.

The black woman is very pretty up close; high cheekbones and gorgeous green eyes that suggest mixed heritage. A slight Asian cant to her eyes makes her like an anime character, almost too beautiful to exist. Her name is Robyn, and her hand is warm as she shakes mine.

A tall young woman comes up to me next. Her eyes are also a bit oriental, her skin a light brown, her hair Pacific Northwest native black, which is and thick and straight. Her flat facial features look part Salish, like Tim. Mixed-up looking but exotic and pretty. She's wide and strong but not fat, only a little older than me. "I'm Monday," she says with a serious look on her face and laughter in her eyes.

"So you get a good start on every week?" I respond.

She laughs out loud, even though she must have heard that a lot of times. It's the kind of name one gets teased for. Her laughter releases something in me and I feel good about being here, like leaving home might work out after all.

"I'm Sage," I tell her.

"So you're well-seasoned?"

I shake my head. "More like just-picked."

She's my age. I've never had a friend my age. Now I can't imagine going on right after dinner. I want to stay and talk to her.

She steps away and more people come up. Names and faces flow in and out without me doing a good job of remembering them. A dark man named Steven who has the body of a twenty-year-old and the face of a great-grandfather. A small girl, maybe five, with blonde hair and blue eyes and the name "Colette," that I remember because I have a doll at home named Colette.

They are not one family or even one type of people, except that they all feel strong and warm.

They look better fed than most of the people on the road. Healthy. Clean. Like us in the garden, I guess.

I forget everything else as Robyn shoves a sandwich into my hand. It's flatbread with carrots and sprouts and chicken, and tastes like heaven. Only a greenhouse and some kind of farming could make all this fresh food be so easily at hand.

Robyn and Justice confer. When they come back, Robyn says that it will be all right for me to spend one night.

It's only late afternoon now, but I have been awake for a long time and I'm curious. I'll stay. "Can I help with anything?"

I can tell that was the right thing to say since Robyn looks like she won a bet. She takes Monday and me to the greenhouses, which are a little ways distant and stand in a row. Five of them. We go into the biggest, which has four rooms and running water. Robyn puts me to work harvesting radishes and carrots and cleaning out beds that have been exhausted and washing them. The work feels good and steady. Dirt coats my hands and gets under my nails and it reminds me of home. Monday and I do a lot together. She works quietly and steadily. I catch her looking at me like she is evaluating, but whatever question she is trying to answer never comes up in conversation. I imagine Kelley and Oskar watching me work with my hands in soil and water and roots before I've even been gone a day. I tell Robyn the things Oskar would have told me about taking care of the plants. How to talk to them when pushing the soil around the roots and which ones like some rocks and sticks mixed into their dirt.

We close the greenhouse door behind us and walk back down a wide path. Thin layers of stratus clouds have formed, and the sky is a fabulous red-orange with hints of yellow. Prettier than last night's sunset. The little town smells like chickens and food cooking and I hear low barks from dogs as I pass. The Board would not let me have a dog no matter how many times I asked.

They're probably glad I'm gone.

A real dog might have improved their lives, made them smile or laugh sometimes. They missed their chance. I don't miss anyone, not even Oskar or Kelley. It's too soon to miss anyone. But I wonder what they would think, and if they know about this place that is so close. If they did, why didn't they tell me about it?

About twenty people have gathered around six picnic tables that have been pulled into a big circle. There is no fire. In the middle, two bright silvery orbs encircle black cooking pots. The pots are big enough to feed the crowd and the silver tucked around them would be as tall as me if it were pulled up into a straight line rather than folded into a half-round and tilted toward where the sun just set.

Oskar has told me about these. "Solar cookers?"

Justice looks pleased. "Maybe we *should* keep you."

Robyn gives him a look that shuts him up. I sit near enough to one of the cookers to feel heat. Except it's not warm, not very. The pot inside is dull black and I can hear something bubbling softly in it, so there is heat on the pot, and my fingers feel warmer when I hold them toward the metal. The silver substance reflects the colors of the sky as if there were a small fire in it, and I am entranced.

Justice breaks the companionable silence. "Where are you going?" he asks me.

"Portland, I think."

"Why?"

I'm following an airplane sounds dumb. "I need..." What to say? "I need to learn about the world."

"Kelley told me once that she watches out for a girl that sneaks out all the time. I bet that's you."

"You know Kelley?"

"We check on each other once a month or so. We're defense for each other."

That answers my questions, and it stings that Kelley hid this. "She never told me about you."

"I made her promise. This is a secret you'll have to keep, too. That we exist." He's looking so hard at me that I fidget.

"You can trust me."

"How do we know for sure?" a tall man whose name I forgot asks.

There could be a wrong answer here. But I shouldn't hesitate either so I just spill out the first few sentences that come across my brain. "You might protect my own people. How could I hurt you if you help them?"

No one answers me, and Robyn is still looking at me quietly, encouraging something more.

"You helped me. I owe you a favor for that. Justice kept me safe this afternoon."

Robyn smiles and she and Monday and a boy named Rye hand around bowls of soup. Vegetables and cattail roots and fresh herbs all cooked together. It tastes of chicken bones and there's a little bit of meat. The other cooker holds flatbread with a soft texture on one side and a hard crust on the other, perfect for dipping into the soup.

Quiet falls as we eat.

After we finish, Justice and Robyn take me back to their house and we sit outside. The chairs are simple unpainted wood with wood dowels instead of nails, sturdy chairs that feel new. A soft breeze blows through the camp, cool against my cheek. A half a moon sheds light on the whole town. Justice asks, "Does Kelley know you're out on your own?"

"Yeah."

"Do you want to go all that way alone?"

And suddenly I don't, not really. The only reason I'm sitting here is the guy with the stick didn't know how fast I can move. I have a lump in my throat that shouldn't be there so I just shrug to answer him.

He speaks softly. "Can I give you advice?"

I nod.

"You were on the wrong road. I know it's closest, but tomorrow I can take you to a different one and give you a map. It's dangerous, too. All roads are dangerous. But I-5 is the worst."

He sounds like Kelley. "I've met good people on the interstate. I go there to get news."

"Can you tell your directions? North from south?" he asks.

I demonstrate. I am good at directions, even in the dark.

"Excellent. Then you can follow the map. I watched you for a while today. Did you know I was there?"

"No." My cheeks grow hot and I turn my face away. I should have known if I was being watched. Feeling weak makes me want to squirm and talk back, but this is no time for that. With effort, my hands stay still and I sit quietly.

"You should always know exactly what is going on around you." His voice has a touch of sharpness to it, like a warning, but not unkind. Just important. "If I give you an exercise to do, do you promise to do it every day, for fifteen minutes?"

"Sure." What's fifteen minutes?

"And if you can't do it for fifteen minutes, then you need to do it again until you can do it that long."

"I can do anything for fifteen minutes."

He laughs. "Sit completely still and listen to *everything* outside of you. Hear the trees moving, the squirrels jumping through the trees, the wind in the air. Feel everything—heat and cold. Know what belongs. When you know what is supposed to be there, you'll know what isn't supposed to be there."

"That sounds like meditation."

He laughs. "Figures they would meditate at the gardens. Listening to your breathing?"

"Or watching a flower grow, or a candle at night." Oskar meditated all the time, even gardening near-naked, but I only had to do it three days a week for a half hour. They were long half hours, and I argued about it, but secretly I liked it.

Robyn speaks up from beside Justice. "It's not like meditation at all. The only thing that is the same is your silence. Meditation is listening to the inside of yourself and shutting out the world. Call what Justice is asking of you 'Being Now.' It's being part of the world around you. You learn what to trust."

"I knew to trust Justice."

"And we know you're no threat and we even trust you to leave. We don't let everyone leave."

I swallow. It's an implied threat.

"Try it now," Robyn said. "I'll time you. Being Now."

I shut my eyes and go still, and immediately tell myself off inside for not finding a more comfortable position. My right foot demands some of my attention. I move it, wondering if the fifteen minutes has to start over. At least I don't ask. I hear people washing dishes and people talking and feel a slight wind. A dog whines. Some small prey hops through bushes to our right. The back of the chair is hard and I feel a knot in the wood.

"Tell us what you hear," Robyn asks me.

"Washing dishes."

Justice whispers, "I hear Rye stacking dishes he gets from Joy, and I hear Joy singing as the water falls onto the dirty ones in the tub and her right foot tapping to her song."

"What's on your right?" Robyn asks.

"Someone walking."

"Are they a threat?"

"No."

"Why not?"

"They are walking away."

"What do you smell?"

"Dish soap. Sweat. Beer. Wind. A damp dog, behind me."

"Okay," Justice says, sounding like he's not really pleased. "That was only a few minutes. I want you to do that for fifteen minutes every day."

"All right."

"We meet a lot of people. Try to help them. Trade food for information if people are honest." He is musing and lecturing, both. "Most of the people we meet are good. But there are some truly bad ones out there, and you have to be able to tell them by small things. The real crazies look friendly at first."

"I've been out a lot. Met all kinds." I've survived, too.

"When I was watching you earlier, you were looking for someone to travel with."

"Safer," I blurt out. Then, "I like meeting people."

He shakes his head. "You look like a liability to the best groups. Strangers out there who will want you will be looking for a girl, and maybe sex." He looks at me to be sure I understand. "Some might want more people to believe like them. Religious nuts, mostly, a few libertarians."

"Libertarians should be happy right now."

Justice laughs, warm and soft. "I see you're education has not been neglected." His voice gets serious again. "There's government coming back. Especially in the cities. It's not all good." He stops and looks far off, as if he is seeing a city in his mind. "You've got to be careful, even in Portland." He shakes as if he is coming back to the moment and Robyn puts her hand on his knee. He pulls her closer before he adds, "You don't have anything obvious to offer anyone that's not a predator."

I'm a little offended. "Then what do you want from me?"

I expect him to say that he doesn't want anything, that he's just willing to help. Like he says he does with people on the road from time to time. But he doesn't say that. "We came from Portland. I'd like to know what's going on there now." He's gruff about this, as if he doesn't want me to know he cares about the city. "You were going to come back and tell Kelley what you saw anyway. So tell me, too."

"Sure." Maybe I'm an advance scout for our whole region, a cool idea, and a little scary.

"I want to send someone with you."

"Who?"

"Who do you think?" Everything is a test with him. I can see how the place got to be so orderly. He forces it that way.

Justice isn't going to go to Portland. It can't be Robyn because she is his partner or wife or whatever and seems to do as much running things as he does. "Monday?"

"Yes."

That explains the question in her eyes earlier. She was deciding if I would be a good traveling companion. "Good. I like her."

"She'll help keep you safe. She's a fighter."

"Does she want to go with me?"

Robyn speaks. "It doesn't matter. She's not welcome here right now."

This startles me. "Why?"

Robyn shakes her head, and before she can speak, Justice gives her a look that suggests there are arguments behind this decision. He says, "She needs to leave. She knows why. She can tell you, or not." His mouth thins and his eyes narrow a bit and he seems both far away and annoyed. "She tries. Sending her on a quest may settle her enough to come back. We'll feel better if there are two of you."

"A quest?"

He grunts. "Same one you already told me you're on. Find out what's happening in Portland. I'd go, but I can't."

"Why?"

Robyn interrupts. "Leave it be." Her eyes are intense, protective. Of Justice. And hard. She's like Kelley; she can make decisions. "You don't know us. You shouldn't talk about us. We're your secret. So's the garden. Just go, stay awhile, and report back." There are more secrets in her eyes than the ones she's mentioned, but I don't even try to get them out of her.

If I want to know why Monday has to leave, I'll have to find out from her. At least I didn't—quite—get kicked out. "Does she want to go?"

A sharp laugh escapes Robyn's lips. "No."

Chapter Four

GUNSHOTS. MY EYES OPEN TO DARKNESS. ROBYN'S VOICE WHISPERS TO me from the other room. "It's all right. Stay still. They aren't near."

"They sound close."

"It's a trick of the way one of the ridges funnels sound."

I shiver, cold and fully awake. "Is that one of your sentry points? Are we being attacked?"

Another shot.

Robyn keeps her voice low and soothing. "Maybe. I haven't heard the signal for help." She gets up and adjusts the covers over me, and starts singing softly. Her voice makes me think of Oskar, not in timbre but in quality. It's soothing and comes from a well of peace that lives somewhere inside of her. I don't know the song, but it calms me enough that my breathing slows.

She breaks off singing. "Do the exercise. Being Now. I'll do it with you."

There is not much to hear. Robyn's breath. My breath. Someone walking by outside quietly but with purpose. I realize that none of the dogs are barking and suspect they have masters sitting with them. But that's my mind wandering away from the immediate since I can't hear the people, and I only hear the silence of the dogs. I am supposed to notice what's real, not what's in my head. I go back to the sound of the house creaking and a bit of wind blowing a tree branch against another branch outside. A coyote far off. Always coyotes in the night now. This wilder world must be good for coyotes. Coyotes and wild dogs.

Re-focus.

Robyn's breathing. She moves, maybe stretching her legs.

The shift of my own weight as I move a foot in response.

Steps coming our way.

The door creaks open.

I sit up, blinking as Robyn turns on a low light. It is Justice. Mud smears his cheeks and he looks grim.

Robyn asks him a question. "Was it organized?"

"No. Just opportunity failing someone." He sees I am awake and says, "Go back to sleep, Sage. You'll need your energy in the morning."

I close my eyes and listen carefully to the details as he washes up and climbs into bed beside Robyn, even hearing their skin touch skin. It is the caress of a man and a woman who are completely comfortable with each other.

I feel alone in a new way. I usually like being alone, but their touch and their whispers isolate.

Sleeping someplace that isn't home feels wrong. Sounds and smells startle me and it's colder than I'm used to.

It takes a long time before I don't hear them breathe anymore. Surely way more than fifteen minutes.

Bright sun makes me wince. The air is bitter with coffee. Even though I don't like it, I take a cup. It is a fortune I'm offered, a cup of coffee. Kelley almost swoons any time she gets coffee. We grow it and roast our own beans, but there is not enough space in the garden to satisfy the coffee drinkers every day. It is a treat.

These people probably grow it, too.

Breakfast, like dinner, is communal. The light must be wrong for the solar cookers because eggs are made over a low fire in big skillets. The leftover soup from last night has been thickened and poured like dressing over the eggs. It tastes better than it looks, peppery and thick and warm against the chill of the morning.

Monday is not at breakfast.

Back in the house, Justice and Robyn ask to help with my belongings. They produce a canvas pack with good straps for my shoulders and hips, and help me use my twine to tie the blanket below it. The pack is full of food and a better medical kit, but when Robyn packs, it still holds all of my stuff, too. This makes me feel less like a runaway.

She leaves an empty pocket. Justice rummages in a drawer and takes out three phones and three chargers. They are all dead, and one is very scratched up. "These work in the city. Sometimes, anyway. They're all unlocked, and they all have time on every account, enough for a month or two, or more if you use them sparingly. Monday has three also. You can keep in touch with each other. We can connect from here sometimes. Not often. Don't count on us. There's a satellite we can hack but it's not always overhead and we're not always listening."

I must look confused because he asks, "Ever used a smartphone? They'll connect you to everyone else who's connected, all over the world. The data part. There's no way to really make a call any more. Monday knows enough to show you how."

We have some back at the gardens but they are as dead as these are and no one even takes them out of the junk drawer any more. I have heard stories about how they changed the world, once. Of course, they couldn't keep cold or heat or earthquakes or Tibetan flu away. So they weren't enough. Still, I say, "Thank you," and shove them in the empty pocket.

"Listen up," Justice says. "Portland is dangerous. But there are good people there. You have to find them. Don't tell them you're from here, or about us, but you'll know who's good by what they share and how they talk. How they treat you."

"I understand," I say.

Justice asks, "Ready?"

We stop at the last house. This one is small, probably one room, and looks new. A small woman with narrow eyes and long arms stands on the porch. She says something I can't hear, and then Monday comes out. Her backpack dangles from one shoulder, like mine but camouflage where mine is forest-green. Military. She is dressed like me in jeans and a flannel shirt and a coat with low boots. As we get closer I see that her eyes are red and her face is tight. The woman on the porch reeks of silent anger. She doesn't return Justice's greeting.

Justice doesn't force it, just nods quietly at Monday. Funny how the littlest things are commands from Justice, and no one thinks of disobeying. At least Monday does not. She throws the pack all the way onto her back and buckles it, everything slow and measured as if she's trying very hard not to lose control.

Whatever she's fighting inside, she wins and walks out to us with her head up. Robyn hugs us all and wishes us luck, Monday stiff in her arms.

Justice takes us on a long hike up a ridge, down a gentle slope on the other side, and then across farmland, careful to avoid the houses. We see a few people at a distance, but there is no contact. We cross one wide road, and then get to another one, which looks fresh and black and new. "This is the last road they built in Oregon," he says. He sounds a little bittersweet. "Stay off of it for now."

He takes out a paper map that he's drawn. Points to where this road is—just calls it "Toll." Past it there is another road. "That's the old one," he says. "It never went all the way through, but it will take you quite a way. It's not on the big interstate maps, so there are fewer people. But don't relax." He looks us both in the face. "Ever."

Monday blinks at him, and I see the tears again, and I realize there is something personal between them. He doesn't cry, but he crushes her to him for a moment and whispers in her ear. "Stay safe, Monday. Come back to us if you can."

When he pushes her away the look on her face tells me there is more she wants to say to him. I'm a barrier.

I step away, but it doesn't do her any good.

He turns abruptly and steps in between the two of us, keeping his distance from Monday. Whatever words she had for him don't come out. She doesn't look back, just starts off. Justice looks at me and says, "She'll be all right. Take care of her, and she'll take care of you." Then he nods after her and I scramble to follow, feeling the weight of her.

I don't like leaving Justice behind. He is the strongest man I've ever met, strong as Kelley, and he feels good to be around. But he didn't keep me, or Monday. Instead, he's sent me to keep Monday. This bears thinking about, but I have to catch her before I can take time to think.

Monday is fast. She doesn't look fast—she's heavier and blockier than me—but she's fast anyway. I have to work to keep up. My pack is heavy. She doesn't talk to me, not a word. She walks with her feet set far apart and takes long strides. The walk of someone who's mad.

I try to think. It felt like Justice was telling me to take care of Monday, and I've never taken care of anybody. I've just been taken care of. After all, nobody back at the gardens was even close to my age. I feel her ignoring me like a lump in my heart, and I understand something I didn't before. I left to see the world, but I also left to find others like me. I want to like Monday, but even more, I want Monday to like me.

But it doesn't feel like she likes me at all. It barely feels like she knows I'm with her.

The sun is high now, almost noon. Even though it's cool and a bit breezy, sweat pours down my shoulders and the pack straps cut into them, the pack heavy on my waist. I start singing but Monday turns around and gives me a look that uses silence to scream *shut up.*

I take her quiet for a while. Then she stops in the shade and pulls out a water bottle and I say, "Hey."

She gives me a long hard look. "I'm out here because of you. I didn't want to leave. I didn't ask for you."

I stand up straight, feeling the pack. I'm shorter than Monday. It's empty here—just fields and a stand of trees and us, and two farmhouses near each other but far away from us. A few fences. "I didn't ask for you either."

"You don't know anything," she says. "Probably get me killed."

"I won't. I sneak out on my own all the time. I got kicked out for sneaking out."

She sighs deep, like the whole world is against her. Like I'm the stupidest person she's ever met. It stings.

"Look. I have the map." I hold it out to her. "I'll make you a copy and you can go your own way."

She doesn't answer me.

"Do you have any paper?"

"No." Sullen.

"All right. We'll go together until we find some paper and then you go on by yourself."

"That's not what Justice wants."

He's something to her. But I can't believe he is. I mean not really. He has Robyn. So she has a crush on an immovable heart. I get that. I had a crush on Oskar when I was twelve. For a whole year I followed him everywhere and dreamed of him at night. "Do you have to do what Justice wants out here?"

She gives a half a nod, then stops, maybe thinking. She doesn't answer, just drinks some water and goes into the trees to relieve herself, comes back out. As she's picking up her pack, I tell her, "I don't` want to be alone out here. It's better to travel with someone. Safer."

“Nothing is safe out here. You left safety when you left Just Robyn.”

“Just Robyn?”

“That’s what they call the little town Justice and Robyn built. Just Robyn. Too cute would be more appropriate, but it’s safe. He runs it good.”

“How long were you there?”

“Six months.”

“Where were you before?”

“Fucked.”

Well, then. I pick up my pack and start off, figuring maybe she’ll talk more later. I liked her when I met her, but it’s like she’s someone else now.

Just Robyn. It makes me laugh. Too cute is right.

Three hours later we’ve stopped for lunch, climbed a few formidable fences and stepped over some that have fallen down, and almost tripped twice over barbed wire that curls through dirt and grass. We’ve hidden from one crowd of twenty or so behind a moldy pile of old grass hay that made me sneeze, and she hasn’t said anything to me that’s not like, “Watch out for those people,” or “The road is going to turn soon,” or “I gotta pee.”

I wish I’d found a traveling group that first day before I met Justice. He and Robyn were nice and strong, and I liked seeing Just Robyn. We should be like that in the garden instead of so afraid. But Monday is a pain in the ass. I don’t feel safer with her around anyway, and I’m certainly not taking care of her or her of me. It’s another pair of eyes, but we’re not working together. Worse, I feel like Justice laid a responsibility on me to stick with her.

Or maybe a curse.

As the sunset starts—pale with no clouds for the sun to paint—I check the map. If I’m right, we’re near where we turn off the road Justice started us down. We’ve kept it to the west of us, which is to our left, rather than walk right on it like targets. “We should stop before we get to the toll road,” I tell Monday’s back, which is square to me as she looks away from the sun, across the fields, and back toward the Cascades. “Find a place to sleep before it’s dark.”

"We can see for a while longer," she tells the mountains.

"I'm tired," I admit. I also haven't done the exercise Justice wants me to. Being Now. I want to do it, if just because it means sitting down until dark and then we won't be able to keep going. I don't tell her that. But I don't move either. Surely her legs also feel like weights.

She turns and looks through me. "We'll be around people tomorrow." Her voice is flat and hard, harder than it needs to be for this conversation.

I nod. I point to some trees by the road, a thick group of them, mostly alive. "We might as well sleep there. It will be shelter."

Monday sneers. "Animals." She walks away from the road toward a pile of rocks where a farmer has cleared his field. There are a couple of trees and a lot of rocks, rocks as high as my head and pooled around a central pile that looks like it's been added to and taken from. Easy place for *her* to choose. She has more padding than me. But if she'll stop, I'll stop where she wants. A compromise.

We eat cold sandwiches quietly, watching the light go golden and then grey. A light wind smells of fertilizer and old hay. I pull on my extra shirt so I'm layered up for the night and snug down into the blanket on a spot that's mostly dirt. The old Pendleton only provides a little padding.

"Use your backpack for a pillow," she suggests. "Keep a hand through the strap. That way nobody can take it from you."

It's the first thing she's offered all day, so I say, "Thank you."

I close my eyes, shivering a little already. I can't imagine how I will sleep in the cold with rocks poking me in the thigh and shoulder. I listen, trying the exercise. Wind. We're out of it here, but it blows through the few trees with a lonely whistle. Rodents scurry between rocks on small feet. The night wings of something big fly above us. An owl or a hawk...probably an owl since they fly lower. Coyotes. Monday shifts in her sleeping bag. The roll of a rock down a pile, the call of a night hunting bird far off and the answer of another one.

The last thing I hear is Monday, sobbing softly.

I startle awake, feeling the absence of Kelley and Oskar and Robyn. It's still dark, but the jagged tops of the Cascades are darker than the sky as the sun stalks them. I have to pee so bad I stumble out of my blanket and step just a little bit away. As soon as I finish I realize I'm alone.

Monday is gone. So is her pack.

Chapter Five

My first instinct is to scramble after Monday, but as I'm shaking the dirt from the blanket and rolling it up I realize she could have left right after I fell asleep. So I sit and eat a few pieces of dried jerky that Justice gave us and watch the day come in. More sun. The air smells dry and I am dry with it, so thirsty I finish half my water. We should have found more water yesterday. I should have figured out how to get Monday to like me. I should have woken up when she was getting ready to leave and known the right thing to say to her.

I'm no more than a few hundred feet from the rock pile when five wild dogs come out of the bushes and trot parallel to me, pacing me. A big black one still wears a collar and tags jingle as he walks. The others are medium-sized. Too big to be prey for eagles, small enough for mountain lions or a pack of coyotes. The big black one eyes me.

I stand straighter and walk slower, showing I am in command.

The big dog whines.

"Shoo!" I tell it. "Leave." I use my firmest voice. I like dogs, love dogs. But wild ones can be dangerous. I have encountered packs before, driven them off. The black dog has serious scars on his ears, and one is torn and healed, flapping oddly. He's a fighter. He takes a step closer and I lunge toward him. "Go!"

He stares. Growls. A moment passes between us. Then his tail falls and he turns, the rest of the pack turning with him.

The little encounter makes me feel braver and more capable. The day is nice except for the dryness at the back of my throat.

There is no sign of Monday, no footsteps on the earth, no snags of her clothes. Bitch. But that word won't stick to her, not after I heard her sobbing.

I use the end of the road we have been following to find the "T" intersection that branches off a mile or so before the toll road. There are two men and two women walking the same way I'm going. I wait until they're across from me and say, "Good morning."

They stop, gathering close, and one of the men shows me he has a gun but doesn't point it at me. They are Kelley's and Justice's age, a little ragged but not starving. One of the women has her left arm in a homemade sling. They don't say anything, so I ask, "Can I walk with you a bit? I won't hurt you."

The woman with the bad arm says something to the man with the gun. He's bald and skin hangs around his jowls, evidence that he was fat once, but his eyes are a friendly blue. He whispers back to the woman and says, "We won't hurt you either."

I join them and we make it to the toll road in a group, which lets me relax some. I tell them I'm from California, adopting Lelani's story to protect the garden. They tell me they're from Klamath Falls. We exchange names.

I ask if they have seen a girl with dark hair and eyes and old jeans and a pack a lot like mine. They haven't.

We mostly fall silent and walk. The four of them are two couples and the women are confident enough to be friendly. I avoid talking to the men much although they are friendly, too. I feel even luckier when we find water—a hose has been run to the side of the road and a sign set out telling travelers to take the water but leave the hose. The sign also says, "No Trespassing."

Must be from a spring-fed well or something that has power like we do.

A car comes down the road, old and creaky, with three men in it. I'm fascinated by the bulk of it, the heavy purr of the engine that is different than the high whine of the motorcycles I've seen.

Rifles stick out of the windows, pointing up at the sky. We step aside and it passes us with no incident. This road is in much better shape than the interstate. The cracks are thinner and mostly filled with dirt and grass and the car rolls easily. It makes the air smell funny, and all the birds go quiet. The women look wistful as they watch it rattle and shake away from us.

For a while we are the only ones on the road, and we keep a friendly silence.

We pass a big group going the opposite way. An old man in a long brown coat with tattered edges stops in the middle of the road, blocking our way. "Pray with us. Save your souls. It is the Lord's need to hear from us all to keep the road safe until the end of days."

He sounds like that might be tomorrow.

To my relief, Samuel—the bald man—says, "No thank you, my friend. We have already prayed today and we need to press on." Samuel is very formal in how he says this, matching the old man's demeanor. It makes me want to laugh but I manage to look serious while the other group steps aside and lets us pass. They all keep looking down like they don't want to see us, and they are so thin they must be eating prayer.

I look at Samuel after we pass them, and he says, "Be polite. Always be polite until you can't be." He lifts the gun, which he always keeps visible. "Then don't miss." He means it, but his eyes are dancing as he says it, too, like the whole thing is a joke and tomorrow he will wake up and be a businessman or a computer geek or whatever he was Before. He's the kind of guy that doesn't let things get him down.

He reminds me of Kelley and her taser.

I keep searching the side of the road for any sign of Monday.

Just before the toll road, a moss-covered sign with bullet holes in it reads "Happy Acres RV and Tent Campground." A man in a blue uniform sits on a Harley by the sign. A grey dog with a studded collar sits beside him, its tail twitching from time to time. The chain-link fence on both sides is tangled with blackberry bushes just leafing out, forcing anyone who wants in to pass the man in the uniform.

Samuel crosses toward the other side of the road, keeping us well away from the man on the bike. The man watches us, assessing. He reminds me of the black dog from this morning. But surely he sees Samuel's gun since he stays still, legs wide over a red tank painted with flames. It looks new, the bike. Newness is strange to me and I stare at the tank, marveling at how the paint shines in the sun.

Bike and biker look like statues, stuck to the bit of gravel they inhabit. They make me shiver.

We're past when I realize that the biker knows everything, watches everything.

"Samuel," I call out. "I have to go ask the biker a question."

He looks at his group. The other man, Ellis, shakes his head. "It's not safe," Samuel says.

It's not and I should have been thinking clearly enough to ask him about Monday earlier. But I have to do this. "I'm looking for my friend. I'll catch back up to you if I can."

Samuel's gun wavers far enough toward me that I can almost see down the barrel. I frown at him and he notices, shifts it. "Sorry."

"Look, thanks." I'm stammering. "I...I'll come back and find you. Unless I find my friend. I need to look for her. D...don't wait." My stomach is sour with fear of the biker, especially since Samuel is looking at me like I've grown three heads. I back away, and they watch me for a few steps and then turn and keep going. I feel the separation from them, but it is in keeping with Samuel's politeness to let me go.

I walk back toward the biker, feeling small and alone. Maybe he will have an easy answer for me and I can catch back up to them. He says nothing as I walk up and the dog says nothing either, just sits quietly by its master.

A glance back toward Samuel shows he's standing and watching. They actually haven't gone far.

This makes me feel braver.

The biker is sun-brown with long dark hair secured to his head with a filthy bandana that might have once been light blue. His stained blue uniform says "Las Vegas PD" on it. His eyes are rock hard. He is waiting for me to say something, like I need a secret code.

"Did you see a girl go by here?" I ask him. "She has a camouflage backpack and dark hair, long like yours."

He doesn't say anything but his eyes narrow.

"Please? I'm supposed to protect her."

He laughs then and the stupid sound of my words comes to me and I laugh a little too, high and nervous.

"You should not pay to go in there," he says. "It's not safe." It's a weird warning from a guy who seems to exist to take payment to pass him. His voice says he doesn't really care, although he's giving me a very strange look, like a warning and an appraisal all at once. The whole time he is tracking Samuel and the others with occasional glances.

"I need to find her."

Now he looks a little sad, if still fierce. "Everyone pays."

Even though it feels like he is warning me, it also feels like Monday is in there. I can't explain this, even to myself. I just know. I swing my pack off of my shoulders and dig out a single piece of dried venison jerky. It must be the right thing, or a good enough thing, since he takes it from me and gives half to the dog. He lets me pass him.

There is a winding dirt road. Sun doesn't reach past the dying and dead trees and the thick underbrush except in little patches, so I shiver. Dead branches and old pine needles on the ground muffle my footsteps. The tracks of more than just the bike show in broken lines, most not thick enough to belong to cars.

It takes a long time to walk down the rutted road, and I have to watch my footing and look back at the biker from time to time. He and the dog remain statues. My stomach is tight and balled up and it feels like a mistake to be here.

Eventually I almost run into a faded square sign that shows a circle walkway and some paths. Deep laughter comes from a distance away, men making fun of something or of each other.

I decide to use the paths instead of the way that cars would have gone. The forest in the campground proper is thin and mostly dead brown, with a hardy deep green here and there on a branch or at the top of a tree, or on the bottom. A nature trail circles the camping spots. It's only a little overgrown and there are boot prints in the soft dust. A rabbit freezes when I round a corner and only moves when I wave at it. "I am not a hunter today," I tell it. "I won't hurt you." Its presence tells me no one else is nearby. Careful not to step on dry sticks, I go quite a long way with no incident.

The laughter of men bounces through the trees and it's hard to tell where they are until I catch a glimpse of a head through some branches. I drop the backpack and slide down slowly until I'm on my knees. I crawl forward under some bushes, dirt on my lips and in my hair.

Five men stand in a circle. Monday is sitting on a bench staring at the ground while they tease her. One of them comes in and pulls her head up and kisses her.

She spits.

Her feet are tied. Not her hands, and she is not using them to keep the men away. Perhaps she has already exhausted herself with this. She is using sneers and silence. I am sure she is only winning because they aren't ready to take her yet, like a cruel game. It feels like a lead-in to real danger but like they won't do any more than taunt her for now. I realize I can't know this. It's just the way the group feels.

I breathe as lightly as I can with my blood racing. Part of me wants to just back away, but I don't like that part at all and don't listen to it. Instead, I lie there on the ground smelling dirt and listening to the men talk trash at Monday. I take a slow breath and then another, and begin to notice details.

The biggest man is smaller than the biker near the entrance, but dressed a little like him: a dirty bandana over a long greasy ponytail and a shirt that hasn't been white in a long time. His pants belong to a uniform, with a white stripe down the sides. The other four are average-size men, not fat but fed. One is bald, but all resemblance to Samuel ends there. His voice and manner are cruel and he threatens Monday, holding up a knife. "We're all going to ride you," he says. "Right in a row. We'll tear you apart." This is blacker than the other teasing, a direct threat. He sounds like he'll do it, the edge in his voice so cold I shiver harder.

One of the others doesn't like this, and looks a bit sick at it, even looks at Monday with an apology on his face. But he doesn't say anything to the bald one.

There are motorcycles. One is big, matte black, and greasy with a raked out front. Kind of like the one at the gate, but old. The other two are low and have fat tires.

Coolers and tents litter the ground. The tents are set up, but there's no real logic. I would have set the camp up differently, like a fence like we lived in at the garden.

It can't even be two in the afternoon, but the men are drinking beer out of brown bottles with no labels on them. The wind sends the smell of the beer mixed with stale urine my way.

I can't be caught. I wish Monday was sitting so that she can see me, but she's turned away and she's not looking around except to watch the men.

I back away, afraid the dust will make me sneeze and I'll be caught. I remain alert, listening to them but not able to see them, cramped as small as possible behind some rocks and a spruce tree with some good branches. I am still enough that rabbits come out and nibble. They are prey but not my prey. I am like them. I feel like they do when they tremble at a passing shadow from a bird. I don't eat. I only sip a little water, enough to rinse the dust from my mouth.

Kelley would tell me to run away and not look behind me. Oskar would tell me to trust myself, and Justice would expect me to save Monday. I know Justice the least, but he has become my new conscience. He would not abandon Monday and neither will I.

I try to practice Being Now two times, but the things the men say keep me edgy.

I feel frozen, like a rabbit about to be skewered through the heart. I've decided not to run but I have no idea how to go forward. I have to think like a rescuer. It is not something I have ever been.

A motorcycle rumbles up, low and throaty, so deep the spruce needles around me quiver in response. What will I do if this gets worse and there are more of them? I'm already both afraid to try anything and afraid to leave.

There is friendly shouting, a voice demanding help. It sounds like the biker I talked to, but I can't see and I'm afraid to move. Then the motorcycle starts up again. It takes three tries, and then the other Harley that was in the camp starts, its engine rattling and whining. The men talk and yell at each other but I can't hear the words over the noise of the machines.

When the bikes are gone, I crawl back to my first spot. There are only two men left. One is the guy who looked sick at the way they were threatening Monday and the other one is the bald man. They don't like each other; they sit on opposite sides of the littered camp and glare. The bald one finishes a whole bottle of beer in three swallows and belches.

Monday watches them, still and silent.

Even though I'm shaking like a beaten drum and my blood sings loud in my ears, I feel around for two rocks, and take one in each fist. I push myself to crouching, wincing as my boots scrape across dry ground. No one notices. Baldy is swaying in his seat and Sad-Face looks like he might let Monday go without my help.

I stick my knife in my pocket and inch forward, staying low.

I wonder if I can just walk over to Monday and untie her feet, if it's that easy. But Baldy is awake and he is the first one who notices, his square head turning toward me. I leap and yell as loud as I can, throwing both rocks at Baldy. One misses. One hits him just above the eyebrow and draws blood. He's like a refrigerator lunging at me, or a tractor. Big. I duck under his arm and he has so much momentum he keeps going the wrong way long enough for me to grab a dirty pot full of something congealed and heavy. I swing it at him, yelling at Monday to untie her feet.

"I can't!" she hisses.

The pot connects with Baldy's forehead and he looks like a cartoon character, falling, reaching toward me but not even close. I twirl around and see Sad-Face is heading toward Monday, carrying a knife. It surprises me, but I bowl into him, head down.

His stomach is hard.

Monday is struggling with the rope, grunting, trying to watch everything and get herself free all at once.

The man slices at me, tearing my shirt.

I get a second and pull out the knife, feint toward Monday.

Sad-Face pushes me and I stumble into the table, cracking my head.

Monday grabs the knife from me.

I fall and roll and stand back up, hot with fear and a bit of adrenaline. Sad-Face's eyes are on me and Baldy is on his knees now, puking.

Thank god they're drunk. Sad-Face lunges at me, but he has no direction. I snarl at him.

He waves his knife at me. He looks confused.

I step backward.

He lunges toward me.

I dodge. But his shoulder still hits mine, and we fall, legs tangled.

I can't let him get on top of me; he's too heavy. My breath is fast and hard in my chest and I kick at him, hit his balls with my knee, and he grabs for me and misses. I'm standing over him looking down, not sure how I even managed to stand up.

"Let's go!" Monday screeches.

She grabs her pack, which is open and almost empty but near her. With her other hand she grabs me, heading for the road. I pull the other way, the way I came, so I can grab my pack, too. We race fast down the path toward the big sign, breathing hard, breaking sticks under our feet. We probably sound like five people.

As we get near the sign I realize the narrow road in is not a good idea, and I take off down a deer track I see, hoping like hell the whole place isn't fenced. The deer can jump higher than we can.

We almost run right into the thicket of berries that covers the fence, and I don't think about it hard. I scramble up, grabbing the vines coming over from the other side, the thorns drawing blood right away. Thorns won't kill me. Behind me Monday hisses, "You're crazy," and she's right but I don't stop. I will not get caught. I am the rabbit running and running. When I feel the top of the fence I go over and roll, the thick ugly vines cracking and swaying under me. They clutch at my feet and arms and I keep my eyes closed and one hand over my face and the vines pull and pull, giving ground in inches at a time, ripping. Then they don't. I'm lying in dirt and rocks and all of the vines under me are new and soft. This spring's growth.

I stand, shaking and stinging. The men aren't behind us. Not yet.

Monday is stuck, a little too heavy to have rolled free like I did, or maybe just too slow. After a deep breath, I wade back into the pile, the going much harder this way, like sweating uphill. I help her pull free.

We both bleed from a ton of small scratches but I still have my pack and she has hers. There is no sound of pursuit. Still, we run a while before we stop. We aren't near any road as far as I can tell. Woods give way to cropland. Uncared for, overgrown. We know it's from a farm because the only trees are tiny and one of those big metal waterers is overgrown with berries and grass, stuck forever. Its wheels are bigger than we are tall, the pipe running broken between them above our heads. There, by the big watering tool, I realize I can't go any further, and that we really got away. My legs give out, suddenly, and I fall to the ground shaking and breathing hard.

Nothing has ever scared me so hard.

Monday sits close to me, her face in profile. Blood runs down it from the blackberry bushes, and I reach up and pluck a thorn free, starting a fresh rivulet.

"Thank you," she says. Her face is all one color except the blood, a pale brown framed by her dark hair, which falls over one cheek. She turns so she's looking straight on to me. "I love you for that. I didn't deserve it. Not you helping me."

I don't know what to say so I wipe some of the blood from my hands with grass and then dig into my pack, lifting things out carefully with two fingers so I don't stain them. "They ruined my shirt."

Suddenly she's all tears, a mess of them, her shoulders heaving. Thin, awful wails come up through the sobs from time to time, as if she's watching someone die.

I take off the torn shirt, turn it inside out, and hand it to her. She clutches it to her face, blowing her nose into the dirty thing and crying some more.

It takes a long time for her to stop. By the time she's done, I have all of the first aid gear laid out in front of us on my next-to-last clean shirt and I've gotten my face and hands and arms pretty well cleaned up and have smeared ointment on the few scratches that feel at all deep.

When Monday's in good enough condition to fold the wrecked shirt up to find a clean place to wipe her face, she's still dry-heaving a little. She starts to hand me the shirt, but drops it in the dirt at our feet. It's worth nothing now. "You haven't been raped, have you?"

I shake my head. I haven't even been kissed. The worst that's happened to me is being chased by men who probably want to rape me, but I always got away. Clearly she's had worse. "You have."

She nods, once. She stares at three crows that have landed nearby and are looking at us with cocked heads.

"I'm sorry."

She swallows and says, "Me, too. I told Justice not to make me go."

"So why did he do it?"

"He told me I have to face the things I'm scared of."

I'm not sure about teenaged girls facing rape, but I bite my tongue. Instead, I ask, "Do you love him?"

"He saved my life," she says. Her voice has both pain and awe in it, and other emotions I can't name but they're deep in her.

Maybe that's why he sent her away. He has Robyn, and he's not going to trade Robyn for a broken teenager.

I have no idea how to say that to Monday, so I shut up.

Monday asks, "How did you get out here? You look like you've been taken care of."

"I left home. On purpose. I've seen the planes flying to Portland and I want to follow them."

"That's a really stupid reason to leave someplace safe," she says.

"The only people there were old. I wanted to have friends my age."

She turns to face me and sticks out her hand. "You have one now. You earned it."

I take her hand, which is cool and damp. We're both shaking, and it cracks us both up at once, and we sit there in the late afternoon under the falling down farm-water thingy and laugh like there's no tomorrow.

Chapter Six

I WAKE UP TO THE SOFT PATTER OF RAINDROPS ON MY CHEEKS AND louder pings as water hits the cross-pole of the metal farm machinery above us. Rain. I should get up and dance my happiness to see it. Oskar is doing that back home. I have no doubt.

Of course, I'm stiff and cold and my back hurts so I settle for smiling at the weather change.

This morning Monday is snoring beside me.

I sit up, cross my arms around my knees, and stare at the lightening sky. It's only been one day. Monday might have been killed, and really, me too. If I'd failed. If the men hadn't been drunk. But I did what Justice asked, and I was brave and it worked. I shiver a little at the responsibility of it, at the danger, and also just because it's cold. There are no walls around me and I can see across the broken fields bright with spring growth, and the English blackberry brambles. The sky looks bigger than usual.

Monday stirs, moaning.

"It's morning," I tell her, since she hasn't opened her eyes yet. "How are you?"

She takes a while to answer. "Headache."

"I have aspirin," I tell her.

"Really?" She sounds both hopeful and dubious. An eye opens and then closes again. "Where'd you get them?"

I rummage around in my pack. "People at the place I lived stored weird things leftover from Before. A case of aspirin was one of them. That's thousands of pills."

"They're still good?"

"Yeah." I find some, uncap the bottle, and peel off the little silver freshness foil. "Bottle doesn't say so, but they just lose strength, so we take three instead of two." I pour three into my hand, and from there into her open palm. "They work. I got two bottles." I hand her water.

"You're full of surprises."

Maybe I am. "Lie down until you feel better."

"What else did they have? Where you came from?"

"A whole case of cat food. No cats."

She laughs. Her eyes are closed again and her right arm is thrown over her face.

"And no, we never ate it. Never had to."

"Anything else good?"

"That we have left? About a thousand band aids and more blankets than we've ever needed. It's getting warmer, not colder."

"But you had coffee?"

"We grow it. Vegetables. One of the guys makes beer." But that's enough. I don't want anyone to know where the garden is. Not even Monday. "I left 'cause I didn't want to be there."

"No one leaves coffee."

My turn to laugh. Having somebody to laugh at silly things with is heaven. "They never let me have any."

Fifteen minutes later, we're both packed and the color is coming back to Monday's face and she looks better. "Which way?" she asks me.

I don't know where the toll road is after all that running, but I know north by instinct. "We've got to go around Happy Acres. So west first, then north."

"Okay."

We swing really wide of Happy Acres, miles wide, going deep into low hills where there are a few greenhouse farms that look well-kept and at least one place that smells like chemicals. When I wrinkle my nose, Monday says, "Biodiesel for old cars."

"Really?"

"There's a farm on the coast that makes it. They trade it for food. They don't have to make much to eat. The cars drive on the beach."

"I'd like to see that." We keep walking, and after a while I ask her, "Have you been to Portland?"

"Not for years. I was a kid there. We stayed until it got bad. I think I was five."

"Do you remember it?"

"Not like I remember the coast where we went after that."

The rain stops. We find an empty house and sit on the cracked driveway to go through Monday's pack to see what they stole. The electronics are still there, as well as a book and her clothes. No food. No tools, no first aid stuff. They stole her underwear.

I try to picture Baldy prancing around in Monday's underwear, which he wouldn't have gotten over his hips. In my head he tries anyway and falls down, comical. I tell Monday about that, and she giggles. "At least it was all clean."

We avoid people. We hide or stop or detour around them. Once, it's a whole town, complete with stores that all look closed or bashed in, one with no roof. There are people there, and I hear hammers on wood. Hopefully they're rebuilding, but the small hill we're peering at them from isn't close enough to tell.

I don't want to meet anyone else today.

We don't talk much. We walk, and look, and try to remember songs but don't do it very well. My feet hurt and my back hurts and I think Monday is feeling the same. She is pretty deep inside herself. It's all right though. We're together and I don't need her to talk.

We find a stream and fill our canteens and plop in water purification tablets.

Before it's even dark we give up for the day. Good thing since my legs are heavy and I've started stumbling. We spend a quiet night in a row of trees between houses, taking turns shivering and keeping watch and sleeping under all the blankets we have. Finally, it's too cold, and we both get under the blankets, swearing to stay awake. She's warm, and I'm warm, and it feels like heaven to be so warm even with the rough ground.

Dawn doesn't wake us, and I bet it's ten in the morning before I open my eyes and see Monday looking at me contemplatively.

"What?"

"Just thinking you're tougher than you look."

I don't know what to say, so I tell her I'm hungry and we eat stale bread and dried apples and Monday says, "I wish I had coffee."

Eventually, the houses are closer together, and Monday tells me, "This is the suburbs. The part outside Portland that butts up to the city. We need to be watchful."

She insists we stay in the middle of these streets, which are a checkerboard of tumbledowns with chimneys wrecked by quakes and houses with bashed-out windows and houses where people still live. Twice, dogs bark and lunge at us from inside fences.

Even though it's late morning, no one comes out of anywhere to talk to us, and we see no one. There's spring rain, which isn't really very hard but soaks us as if we're walking through mist. I always think of Oskar in the rain, and I suddenly wish for him. He could tell what all of the new plants I see are.

We can't see Portland even from the top of the hills, but houses and streets cling to the heights past us, houses almost next to each other, cars parked on the sides of the road. Here and there, a broken-down string of stores share a roof.

I scrape my knee again scrambling over a concrete wall between two dead houses, and Monday gets a spider web caught in her hair.

We count our blessings.

We're still timid so we don't look for useful things in any of the houses. We stick to water from two hoses and use the purification pills before we drink it. We will have to be braver soon since we're almost out of food, but today we can just coast and be alone together.

It feels like that now, like we're friends. We stop for each other when we need to, walk side by side, make up stories about the stray cats and dogs that shy away from our approach. We laugh at each other's jokes even when they aren't funny. There is no more talk of rape or even of boys or men.

I point out the plants I recognize and she seems interested in learning about them. She talks about comics and manga books and a big bookstore she remembers named Powell's from when she was a kid, from Before. I don't remember anything that specific about Before, but when I was little we lived out near the gardens, and my dad worked there. We moved inside as soon as the diseases started coming through. Monday's yearning for books makes me wish we had raided the library at Just Robyn.

Later that afternoon the rain picks up, soaking the dry shirts we'd put on earlier. "We need a place to spend the night," I say.

"I know."

She sounds a little afraid so I volunteer to go into empty houses while Monday keeps watch.

The first one is home to about twenty cats and desiccated bird parts have been shoved into the corners. It stinks of cat urine. I hold my nose and look in the kitchen cupboards but there's only bare wood.

The second house is locked and the windows are unbroken. Monday notices the hedges out front are square and neat. We decide to leave it; no need to steal like we were stolen from. We'll forage, but taking from a place people live feels wrong.

The third house stands half-built and the roof has let water and mildew in. I don't even have to go in—I just look through the framed walls and see the piles of waterlogged wallboard that are almost reduced to goo. No one lives here.

We go into more houses. No luck anywhere. Unless you count not getting jumped as luck.

It's almost dark, and we're standing outside a big, gated house that feels empty. Yard gone to hell, last fall's grass waist high, roses with black rose hips hanging from withered, broken stems. The house itself is bright yellow and it doesn't look damaged. We go over the fence and sidle up to the house side by side, careful to come in from a direction that no windows face directly.

The front door is unlocked. There are two rifles by the door but no one in sight. "Maybe they guarded this until after the worst looting was over," Monday muses. She's come with me this time since we've had her watching outside twenty houses and she didn't need to, but her mind is still on guarding.

Her theory looks like it fits so I say, "Maybe." and then, partway down the huge hallway my stomach growls. "Let's check out the kitchen."

It's stocked. Really stocked. A pantry full of canned goods and bottled water and even sodas. A few of the cans are popped but most are still good. Monday grins. "Home for a day!"

I try the faucet in the kitchen sink but it's dry.

"Must be on city water," Monday says as she flicks a switch and no light comes on. She heads into the dining room.

The place is so big I can't imagine that just one family lived here. Eventually we figure out it was just two people. There's a note on a dining table meant for eight. The writing is neat and precise.

"We've gone to Portland to look for a hospital. If you find the place, please help yourself to what you need but leave it neat in case we get back."

The note is signed Jessica and Thomas White.

"Wow, sweet." I say after I read it. There's pictures on the wall that must be them. Older couple. Grey hair. Dressed up neat. I don't see any pictures of kids or other family or even dogs.

"Let's explore," Monday says, looking more relaxed than I've seen her all day. Of course just being dry and warm feels good. Funny how we wanted rain so bad, and now that we have it, it's no fun.

We find clothes upstairs that are designed for old people and are too big in the legs and across the shoulders for either of us, but we pull them on anyway while we wash the worst stains out of our own clothes in the sinks with one bottle of water each—no soap—and hang them up in the bathrooms to dry. Monday finds underwear that almost fits her to replace the ones she lost. Old-lady underwear; better than no underwear. Maybe.

We spend the rest of the daylight going through the house carefully. We finish the kitchen and the study before it gets too dark to see. We pick ten cans of food out: soups mostly and four cans of chili. Monday calls it 'dead food' which makes me laugh. Oskar would have said the same thing.

We also find two knives, a can opener, a set of silverware each. Monday spends a long time looking through about six shelves of real books and chooses two. There are pens and paper in the study. I have no idea how to carry everything, but we want it all. Monday brings one of the rifles from the door upstairs. She fiddles with it and pulls out a brass clip. It's empty, but if it weren't empty it would have long, skinny bullets. She points it at the fading light from the window and squints. "Nothing in the chamber, either. It's useless."

"Maybe there's bullets in the garage or even in here."

"It's a twenty-two," she says with authority.

"Do you know how to use it?" I ask her. The closest I've come is touching Kelley's Taser, although we do have real guns locked up in a safe at the garden. Tim cleans them once in a while but I'm not allowed to touch them.

"If it had bullets I could use it. Justice makes everybody practice on Saturdays."

"Show me how?"

She shows me the safety and the trigger and what to do to fire the gun, and I hold it and pretend I'm firing it while the safety is still on. The light is almost entirely gone now, and Monday says, "I'll show you how to clean it tomorrow. And we'll look for ammunition."

I don't like the feel of the rifle, and I hope we don't find any bullets, although it would have been handy to have at Happy Acres.

"Aren't these too big to carry?" I ask dubiously. I can't picture myself walking up the street with a rifle on my shoulder.

"Yeah," she sounds regretful. "But if we find a handgun we're taking that."

I'm not sure that's smart either, but then I'm not the one who's been raped so I hold my tongue.

We lie down side by side on the big king bed. Monday uses a candle to read a book she finds on the bedside table, something about German history and the concentration camps. She reads me a few paragraphs out loud and the descriptions are so vivid and awful it makes our own situation feel better.

As I'm falling asleep in the borrowed clothes I realize I've forgotten to practice Being Now, and I try to do it but the bed and the quiet are too much for me, and I hear Monday turn three pages and I don't know anything else until Monday is shaking me awake.

"There's someone downstairs," she whispers. It's the barest beginning of dawn and there's enough light to see that her eyes are wide and her face flushed. When I start to sit up, shaking, she pushes me down and hisses, "Be quiet."

Monday already has the rifle in her arms, cradling it, the business end pointing at the ceiling.

"We should have got both guns." Then I could have one, too.

"There's no ammunition," Monday whispers.

I roll over and close my eyes, listening. Being Now. My own heartbeat and Monday's breathing are all I hear, both louder than normal.

A can falls off the counter down below. It rolls for a ways and then stops. Then another one falls off the counter. Something scratches softly, but fast.

"Wait here." I say.

"No."

"I think it's okay."

Monday looks dubious.

She follows me into the bathroom, although we should go outside with no running water in here. We each use it while the other turns their back. Then I hold the gun while she shimmies into her own clothes and then we trade. The gun feels heavy and cold.

In the meantime, a few other cans fall. By now, I can feel the grin widening on my face. Monday doesn't get it yet, so I sneak to the stairs and scoot down. She stands at the top of the stairs, fully at attention, rifle pointed over my head. Part way down, I gesture to her to follow me.

We peer into the kitchen.

A thin raccoon sits on the cabinet, holding a can in its hands.

Monday giggles.

"They're pests," I tell her. "Kelley hates them." I realize what I am saying, and that I shouldn't use Kelley's name. "Someone I know. They stole a whole crop of blueberries one year." Kelley used to chase them with two pots, clanging them together, and everyone would yell at her to stop because the Board made rules about being quiet, but she never stopped until the raccoons were gone. She got all red in the face. The image makes me laugh and the raccoon drops another can and a second raccoon—too fat to get onto the cabinet, picks up the can and puts it in a stack. "They're robbing us, you know."

Monday is grinning. "Looters."

"We have to get them out of here." I say. "They'll wreck the place."

"Does that really matter?"

"Of course it does." Whoever Jessica and Thomas were, they don't deserve raccoons. "Be careful. They bite." I scoot down the stairs, which leads to the living room. The kitchen is off of that. All the rooms are big and there's no good funnel to force them outside. From here I can see that they've come in by the front door. It's open about a foot.

The raccoons see me and freeze, and for a minute I hope they will just leave, then the fat one sits up on its back haunches and hisses at me. It's so comical that I laugh, but I know the dangers. "They have diseases. Don't let them scratch or bite you."

Monday is laughing, too. "What do we do?"

"Give me the gun."

"There aren't any bullets."

"I'm not going to shoot anything."

I hold the gun stock and swing the barrel at the raccoon, back and forth, fast. It backs up, and I can get to the broom closet. I set the gun down and pick up a broom and a mop, tossing the broom to Monday. "Keep them from going up the stairs."

The kitchen is big. The thin raccoon sits in the sink and the big one waddles away from me, heading back to the stack of cans.

I run around and close doors so they can't get out of the kitchen the back way or into the broom closet or the pantry. They skitter around the room, keeping some distance, watching me with little brown eyes inside of their masks. They actually are cute, especially the fat one.

I swat at them with the broom, trying to push them toward the front door. They keep moving around the kitchen, avoiding me, watching, and not looking very concerned at all. It has to be funny because I hear Monday laughing.

I roll one of the cans toward the front door and the fat raccoon follows it.

Soon I have all of the cans rolling and both raccoons following.

I'm standing behind them with the mop in one hand and the gun in the other. They stop before they get to the door and they both sit up.

"Come on," I tell Monday, "Stand next to me."

She does, waving the broom.

The raccoons try to dart around us but I slam the broom down in front of the fat one.

It stops and stares at me.

Monday and I both make considerable noise, including hooting like owls and barking like dogs. We must finally sound formidable enough to the raccoons. They jog out the door like they always meant to leave.

"That's not the most common use for a gun," says a male voice from behind us.

We both twirl, clutching the upside-down guns. A tall young man in jeans and a clean white shirt stands in the kitchen doorframe—the door I had just closed.

Chapter Seven

THE MOP FALLS FROM MY HAND AND CLATTERS ON THE FLOOR. I BACK up, keeping my eyes on the man in the doorway. He is taller than us, dark-haired and blue-eyed with fair skin and freckles. An odd combination that looks good on him. He's maybe twenty-five. He came in quietly, or was always here.

He heard us acting like dogs.

My face is bright red. I grasp the gun with both hands. It shakes in front of me.

"No need for that," he says. "I won't hurt you."

"Who are you?" I ask.

"Jack. I'm a neighbor. I watch out for this place. I heard noises." His smile is almost apologetic, his voice slow and even. "I won't bite."

"How do we know?" I ask him. "That...that you won't hurt us." Surprise and adrenaline makes me stutter a little.

"How do I know you won't shoot me?"

"I didn't shoot the raccoons."

"That would've made an awful mess." He's laughing, although his eyes are still on the rifle.

I glance at Monday, surprised I'm doing all the talking. She's standing completely still with her eyes narrowed at Jack. She might as well be a Monday statue. I tell him, "We just....we needed a place to sleep."

"Okay."

"You're not mad at us?" Maybe he's a friend of Jessica and Thomas.

"No. You haven't wrecked the place."

"Of course not!"

"That's why I leave the door unlocked. One time a single mom stayed here for two days and I checked on her, and helped her tear up t-shirts to use for diapers."

"We're not staying." I say.

"Have you had breakfast?" He's looking back and forth between us. "I make a mean omelet."

"Why do you leave the guns here?" I ask. Empty guns by the front door have not made sense since the moment I saw them.

"Why carry them back and forth? I usually leave them in the garage, but a mob of people came through here yesterday and I stayed to be sure they wouldn't stop."

Maybe. I'm used to believing adults, but Justice said not to trust anybody and I don't trust this Jack.

Monday speaks for the first time. "People don't forget guns."

"I didn't forget them. I have more. Besides, I took the bullets out." He reaches behind his back and pulls out a small pistol, then puts it back, all of his movement casual like he is used to guns and to people breaking into the house. "Look, I've been listening. I wanted to see what you'd do about the raccoons. You didn't hurt them, so I figured you won't hurt me. And maybe you could use some help."

He sounds more like the people from the garden than the people we've met out here. His voice is cultured and even. He looks healthy. He's the perfect weight and he has muscles in his arms and his white shirt is clean.

If he takes a step toward us, I might run like a spooked doe.

Still, he's really not acting like a predator. He feels like one, but maybe I'm just dubious these days. He's friendly. "Do you have running water?" I ask him suddenly. I must look like crap. My last shower was at the garden and my hair is greasy and I probably smell bad.

He laughs again, something he does so easily and often, it's creepy. "I'll trade you two showers for the gun."

I glance at Monday. I've decided to trust him—a little—if she does.

Her eyes are narrowed and she's standing with her feet braced and the gun pointed down casually, aiming at a spot on the floor in front of Jack. She meets my gaze, her eyes white and lips thin, then nods, just a little. I hold the gun I have out to him. His gun.

"No," he says, "Stock first."

I turn it and have to work to hold it out like this with the heavy stock away from my body. But I'm not stepping close to him. Not yet. He takes it and walks around me and collects the rifle

Monday is already holding out stock first. "Wait here," he says. "I'm going to put these away."

While he's gone, Monday comes over and whispers to me. "Those might be expensive showers."

"There weren't any bullets anyway."

She gives me a look like I'm an idiot.

"There's two of us," I whisper as much to point it out to her as to reassure myself.

Her voice is low, too. "We don't know who's in his house."

I really, really want a shower. As much as I don't like the guns. And we can't mistrust everyone. "Let's check it out."

She shakes her head. "Okay." She hates it, which makes me all nerves, too. Maybe we should run.

We can't talk any more since he walks back in and says, "Follow me."

"Can we get our stuff?" I ask. Not that it should be a question. Of course we can, but I feel like he's in control. Must be the pistol I can't see.

He gives us a mock surprised look and says, "You could have been doing that while I was putting the guns away."

He must know we were talking about him. He managed to sneak in on us chasing the raccoons, after all. He probably heard us whispering.

We pick up the mess the raccoons made in the kitchen and take the things we scavenged the night before and two water bottles each. As we're filling Monday's pack with the canned soup, I glance at Jack, but he nods and says, "It'll go bad someday. Or there will be a mob I can't keep out. Take what you need."

I smooth the edges of the top of my pack. It's almost full.

He nods at us. "Got everything?"

"Can I take a shirt?" I ask. "I only have one left."

"Hurry."

I go upstairs and paw through drawers, all the time thinking I just left Monday with a man with a gun. I scavenge two plain T-shirts that are too big, but they have long sleeves and will be warm to sleep in.

The shirts aren't even folded into my pack when Jack says, "Let's go."

We follow him outside and around the back of the yellow house, where an overgrown gravel drive leads down a hill, winding through two turns. Tangled humps of blackberry bushes line the drive, green shoots fighting their way through old canes as thick as my forearm. It's raining again, or maybe misting would be a better description. Whatever, the trail is wet under our feet and water spangles our hair. Cedars crowd the path, mostly evergreen but every fourth or fifth one is dead.

At the end of the long drive there is a wooden house that looks like it was built to merge with the nature around it. Fences bend to avoid full-grown trees. Above-ground planter beds have been prepared for spring planting. Crocuses poke up at the edges of one of the beds, pale white and purple. There is good direct light falling onto the house even through the covering rain clouds, and clearly the plants get light all morning and the first part of the afternoon.

Chickens flutter around in a big wooden cage with wire walls, squawking at us.

Inside, the house is all wood, but of many different colors. Parts are rough and others smooth, as if the walls have been scavenged from a hundred houses.

When we stop and look closely, Jack offers, "Me and my dad built this. The whole roof is solar. Water comes from a spring-fed well that only uses the pump in the summer." He looks incredibly proud of the whole thing. "We have power and water all year as long as we're careful, and we grow most of our own food."

"So short showers?" I say.

"But hot ones."

"Who's we?" Monday's voice sounds almost too casual.

"Just me right now. My sister's out for a few days, foraging. Dad's up in Seattle helping with a new solar program at the U."

Really? The university is running that well? But I want a shower more than a long talk about power. Power obsesses everyone. "Where's the shower?"

It turns out to be a small, square room with tile walls and a fat showerhead that's wider than my shoulders. Jack shows me the controls, which are levers rather than what I'm used to.

I think about Jack while the water falls over me like heaven. He's oddly cavalier about us and the guns and what we took from the house up the hill. Kelley would be fingering her Taser if she were me, but I want to be more like Oskar, who says the climate and the depression scrape the veneer off people and expose what's underneath. He's told me that often it's just nice weirdness and fear. On the other hand, Kelley always told me things that are too good to be true are lies. Even this far away from them, I feel their advice like angels on my shoulders.

When I'm clean and scrubbed and deliciously warm, I follow the sound of voices to a big kitchen where Jack is washing mushrooms in the sink with real running water like at home. Monday leaves to shower and I'm alone with Jack.

As he cuts up red hothouse tomatoes, the knife makes disconcerting clicks over and over, the only sound. I'm not used to being alone with men I don't know. Up close, he smells wrong, like salt and sour milk. "You two could stay in the house up there until the White's get back. Help out down here."

"No thanks. We're just passing through."

"Is anyone expecting you?"

"No." Monday glares at me and I realize what a dumb thing I just said. "People expect us back soon," I add. He ignores this.

His hands are busy whisking eggs in a battered steel bowl. He has flatbread out on the counter. It looks fresh and soft, and so he must have gotten flour from somewhere. Or made it. "We're vegetarian. I hope you don't mind."

"No. I mostly am, too. I grew up in a botanical garden." I shouldn't have said that so I add the lie I'm getting used to. "In California."

He looks impressed. "Then you really could help."

"We have to keep going."

"Think of it as a job. I'll be filling it with someone. You could eat regularly." He pours water into real glass glasses and sets them on a clever little mosaic-topped table that looks handmade. As he sets the glasses on the table, his shirt lifts enough to show the butt of the gun. "I already talked to Monday about it. It's safe here, and pretty hidden. We don't get much trouble. Your friend likes the idea."

Monday has appeared behind his shoulder. He touches her on the cheek. She flinches, then smiles. "We can talk about it later." Her eyes are wide in a pale face and I'm sure she's trying to tell me she's scared.

"Sit down." Jack gestures toward the table.

We obey.

He heats a pan and spoons a little fat into it from a tin can. Eggs sizzle, and after a few minutes, he balances three plates with an omelet shared across them, sliced tomato, and a bit of the bread.

It smells better than anything we've had since we left Just Robyn. Fresh-picked tomato. Except it's all dry in my mouth because I feel more scared here than I felt in the campground. Monster-under-the-bed wrongness, but nothing overt, no way to be sure. Maybe I'm scared for no reason. Maybe Monday's fear is infecting me.

Jack smiles and says, "You can stay, and I'd like you to." His voice firms. "But you have to give up on Portland. It's not as safe as here, anyway."

The rain picks up and wind rattles the windowpanes.

"What do you know about Portland?" Monday asks.

He shrugs. "Some stuff works, some stuff doesn't. There's fighting in the city. You really would be better off with me. But you just can't come and go. We can't have people finding this place. I leave sometimes to check on the White's house, and Elsie trades some of what we grow for other things we need, but that's all."

I need to talk to Monday bad. He's kept us from having quiet time together since right after he found us chasing the raccoons. He's either been with one or both of us. He has apparently decided Monday is the one he needs to convince because he turns to her and says, "You'd be safe."

She glances at me, "We'll think about it."

"Why not spend the night?" he suggests. "You can tell me what you want to do in the morning."

I talk as calmly as I can. "I appreciate the shower and the food. But we have things to do in Portland, and we really should leave now."

"In the rain?" Jack makes the idea sound crazy.

"It's only early afternoon. We could still make it a ways."

"I'd rather you stayed."

"Alright." Monday's voice is flat and sounds different. She doesn't expect him to let us leave.

"Why don't you rest for the night?" Jack asks. "The weather might be better tomorrow and you must be tired." He grins again. "Besides, I still plan on talking you into staying."

I struggle to look relaxed even though I'm getting less calm by the minute. "Can we sleep up there? At the other house? I'm pretty sure I left my hairbrush there."

He hesitates, but not for long, like a flash of waiting. "Sure. There's enough bedrooms there. We can get to know each other."

"Great." Not. Not at all.

Monday nods and grins likes she's just been invited to a party. Her voice still sounds off and she doesn't look directly at me. She's pretending.

We help him clean up the kitchen and suffer through a tour of all the working parts of the house: a compost bin, a drying rack for vegetables, the entire water system. He goes into precise detail, and while a little of it is interesting, the way he talks like we're going to need to know what he's saying feels uncomfortable. It's all impressive—more complex than our systems in the garden, more homemade, but I feel like I'm doing Justice's exercise with all my being, and like it's making me shaking scared even though there's no clear reason for it.

Jack is smiling and being polite. He's cute and clean. He's clearly proud of the intricate water retention and delivery system that runs between planter beds, of the chicken coop strong enough to keep out wild dogs and the traps he has on the outside to keep the packs out, traps kind of like the ones Justice has outside of Just Robyn. "Be careful not to step on that," he says, pointing to ground glass glued onto a wide board. "Not even in shoes."

Eventually there's nothing left for him to show us.

He tucks a Scrabble game under his arm and grabs three dark bottles of liquid and we all walk back up to the yellow house together, him right behind us so we can't talk. He sets the game up on the kitchen table and we all draw letters. I will go first, then Jack, then Monday.

"Do you want a beer?" he asks. "I make some every fall."

Monday reaches her hand out and he uncaps the bottle. She sniffs it and takes a tiny taste and nods like she likes it, but she doesn't drink more.

In spite of the fact that he looks really proud of the beer, I shake my head and grab a can of warm soda from the kitchen and sip slowly from that. It doesn't sit really well in my stomach since it's so sweet and sticky, but I know alcohol makes people stupid. Maybe he'll get drunk like the bikers in Happy Acres.

Monday excuses herself to go outside and pee while I ponder the board. I take my time, mostly because I can't think straight and I feel like a victim in a horror movie and just as stupid as those people look, too. Here I am playing Scrabble while the handsome man across from me has a gun tucked into his pants and has been talking like he wants to turn us into garden slaves.

I play the word SALVIA.

"See," he says. "You do know your plants." He plays "BALANCE" using my A.

"Good job," I say, marking down the points carefully, focusing on being aware of my surroundings. The house is quiet and creaky. Jack is watching me thoughtfully, his eyes a little slitted, his body alert—I can see tense muscles in his neck and along his jaw. Tough to describe, but he feels like he's pretending to relax. Like me.

I've been in the garden all the life I remember. Maybe I just don't know how normal people act. Kelley likes to tease me about having a great imagination.

I wonder what Justice would do.

I wonder if Monday has left me here alone.

Her footsteps come around the corner and I'm ashamed of doubting her so I don't look up. I doodle on the scoring paper. Drawing Queen Anne's Lace, the fine white flowers black because I can't draw white on white paper.

A gun goes off, thundering through the house.

Jack jerks toward me.

I close my eyes as blood splatters on my lids. It's warm.

I open them right way, heart pounding, fingers wiping at the blood as if it burns.

There's blood in my hair and blood on the Scrabble set and blood on the floor and I want to scream but nothing comes out of my throat.

Monday is standing behind Jack, close, her eyes wide.

He slumps over the table. His hand curls around a scrabble tile, flexes.

The quiet is immense and unimaginable.

I have killed things with rocks. I know how hard it is, how the rabbits thump their feet even after it seems they must be dead. A squirrel pretended to be dead until I'd picked it up once, then jumped up in my hand and startled me so I dropped it and then it raced up a tree and was gone. So I watch Jack closely, horrified and fascinated.

Maybe guns *are* that much better than rocks.

He doesn't move any more, but his blood seeps a long time before it stops.

I'm glad he's dead but I've never seen a dead person. Just animals, and mostly small ones. Deer, sometimes. Once, a thin bobcat.

I can't look away until Monday drops the rifle onto the floor and the clatter breaks whatever spell I have been under.

Monday pulls the handgun out of the back of his pants with two fingers and then holds it in her open palm. It's really quite small, and from the way she holds it, not very heavy. She checks it for bullets. She puts the gun into her pack.

I don't argue.

At first we stand there like prey. Like rabbits. I wonder if a neighbor will come, or police, but nothing happens. No one comes to the door, not even the raccoons.

We use water bottles to wash the blood off of my face and out of my hair, and the whole time each action is like movement in a dream, slow and fuzzy and wrong.

There should not be blood in my hair.

Monday uses soap on the stock of the rifle, then frowns. "This probably isn't good enough."

"No."

We put the water bottles and the towels from our hair and everything else dangerous we can think of into a white plastic trash bag. The pen I was recording Scrabble scores with. A kitchen knife we touched. Monday goes into the garage and comes back with a small box and tucks it into her pack.

"What is that?"

"Bullets."

I don't like this, but I'm glad she shot Jack.

We shrug our backpacks onto our shoulders. I carry the broom and the mop and the white plastic bag and she carries the rifle and we walk behind the house and into a strip of woods. We follow a grown-over gravel path under towering power stanchions. It rains on us the whole walk, a thin, damp rain that gathers on my eyelashes and soaks my pack.

We should have taken extra plastic bags to cover our stuff.

We should never have gone in there at all.

We should not be here. I should not be here, carrying evidence of murder in my own two hands and shocked silent by it and yet sure it's the right outcome.

Jack would have killed us. Raped us and killed us. Maybe played with us along the way.

We throw everything into a mound of blackberry bushes and push it in with our feet, getting fresh scratches on our legs. In two weeks it will be overgrown and someone will have to be looking specifically for evidence, or I suppose, for berries.

We sit down on two fairly dry rocks under a healthy cedar and stare at each other.

"Sorry," she says. "I had to do it. I didn't trust him from the start but I didn't want him to know it." She swallows. "It's best to appear docile until you aren't."

Samuel said the same thing. I stay quiet, listening.

"I opened the door to the garage at the same time I opened the outside door so he wouldn't hear. I found the gun, and the clip. I was going to just make him let us go, make him give me the handgun and let us go." She's repeating herself a little and her hands are twisting in her lap.

"Why didn't you?"

"Jessica and Thomas? The Whites? I don't think they ever went anywhere. Their cars are in the garage. Two of them. There was blood on a hammer on the workbench, and stains on the floor." She pauses. "Did you see the labels? The ones on the valves and levers in the washroom he showed us? It was the same writing as on the note. It was fake. I bet he kept the house stocked so it would lure in stupid people. He would have killed us." Her hands are over her face. "I had to do it."

We are in a horror movie. The Board only let me start watching them a few years ago and now I'm in one. This is weird stuff to think about, but my brain isn't working quite right now. I stand completely still and the world around me is sharp while I feel so lost I don't know my name for the space of a breath.

Monday bolts out from under the tree and bends over in the rain, retching.

I stand by her and put a hand on her back. She doesn't shy away, but leans into me. Her body is warm and damp from the rain.

After a long time, I say, "Thank you," and then, "I'm sorry you had to kill him."

She straightens and steps away from me. "I killed the last man who raped me, too." Her voice has taken on an angry tone, like a wall. Defense.

She's daring me, so I speak as calmly as I can, knowing viscerally that she has a gun and I don't, that she is different from me, that being raped made her someone who can kill easily. "You saved me," I keep my voice soft, like I'm talking to a wild thing, "And I saved you once. And if we don't go, we'll be destroyed by all this bloody crap. Let's get away from here."

She stands and stares for a moment, and then her jaw clenches and she nods.

We duck back under the cedar and retrieve our packs and start walking. I feel like I'm walking through a dream, like the last few days aren't real and like Kelley was right and I should have stayed home and stayed a stupid little girl who didn't know about rape and death and men getting holes blown in their heads.

After about a half an hour of silence Monday says, "I'm still mad at Justice for making me come out here."

"Yeah, I understand."

"Just Robyn was the only safe place in the world."

"The world has other good places in it," I reply, thinking of the garden.

"Prove it."

Chapter Eight

THE RAIN STOPS AND A COOL WIND DRIES OUR WET CLOTHES AND HAIR. After walking hours past where we dumped the bloody clothes and gun, we find some almost dry ground under another cedar. The tree is on the property of a deserted house with berry bushes hugging the roof. The branches hang over us like walls, meeting the earth. It smells like heaven, the sticky cedar smell filling my nose with something so unlike blood that I am grateful to the tree and thank it silently. It shivers as if it heard me.

Oskar taught me to thank the plants. I imagine he is sitting on his cot now, making notes in his journal or maybe re-reading a book. Maybe Kelley is playing a game with the old men, Tim and Li. Maybe she's even playing Scrabble.

I'm shivering even though I shouldn't be cold.

The tree stops the wind from touching us, although we feel the trunk sway with it and hear it pluck at the thin outer branches, grabbing and releasing them like waves. There are rodents with us, but nothing big, and I don't care. I like hiding and I like being silent inside the safety of the big tree and listening for squirrels and field mice. Twice I hear cars drive by.

Monday is silent.

I whisper to her. "This tree is a good thing."

She whispers back, "Trees are never any trouble."

"What other nice people have you known?" I ask her.

She must not want to answer because she asks her own question. "Do you like traveling with me?"

"Yes. I like having a friend."

"Okay then."

Monday isn't a person who likes a lot of words, so I resume listening until I fall asleep.

I wake once in the middle of the night, and Monday has an arm thrown across me, heavy and warm. My feet are cold, and I tuck them near her legs and realize I only have vague memories of being so physically close to anyone while I'm sleeping. I dream of being home and waking in the garden, listening to Oskar and Kelley talking about how they miss me.

Later, when my eyes open to dawn, Monday has rolled away and I'm shivering. A squirrel scrambles through branches too high for me to see it, and knocks some dead needles down onto my face.

It's clear and crisp; good walking weather. The houses get even closer together and there are families in more of them. Most are breaking down or being torn down for materials, but some look partly restored and a few actually look good. Here and there, greenhouses have been cobbled onto yards, mostly with makeshift plastic and glass that looks scavenged from other houses.

A scooter passes us from behind. We jump because it makes no sound.

"Electric," Monday says.

It's an old woman riding. She has bags of food strapped on the back. It makes me think of the silent planes. Of stores. I would love to see a real store that's open and full of things for sale.

We see a few more people, mostly working in their own little scraps of yard. Some wave, but I don't want to talk to anybody else and Monday doesn't seem to, either. So we wave but don't slow down.

Even though we're going up a steep hill, three men in tights ride quiet bicycles past us. They have long legs and look like machines the way they ride, floating as if gravity has given them a free pass while it makes the hill drag on our feet and hurt our lungs. The riders are all wearing shirts the same deep green as the cedar we slept under last night.

We stop for lunch and keep going; I want to see Portland. I've seen New York and Los Angeles in movies, and Portland isn't as big as those, but it's going to be bigger than anything I've ever seen.

I hadn't really expected it to feel safer closer to the city, especially after Jack said there was fighting. But I no longer look over my shoulder all the time. We see more people, and they don't look scared or scary. Cautious maybe, and there are always more than one. Two middle-aged women out for a walk wave at us and three different family groups have dogs on leashes.

We ask a group of women for directions, and they tell us up and over; Portland is just on the other side of the hill. We climb, winding up and up and up. Others are climbing too, and some going down. Not enough people to make a river, but a slight stream, some faster than us, some slower. A few look like they came up the interstate. I watch for Samuel or Lelani, but I don't see them. The way up takes forever, works at my lungs and my lower back. I think each bend will be the top and then it isn't.

Cars pass from time to time, and once a big motorcycle like the ones from Happy Acres. We pass something I've never seen, a barricade across a street that's manned by men with guns. They're all wearing shirts the color of green that the guys on bicycles wore and two of them have helmets like the kind in war movies.

We don't have to cross the barricade to go straight on the road we've been on, so we ignore them and keep going. That's what other people are doing.

A little further on there is another road that's blocked off. A police car is next to this one with its engine off. There is a big blue cross sign that means a hospital. Oregon Health & Science University. Behind the barricade the hospital bulks bigger and wider than anything we've passed so far. Lights illuminate the grounds and forested hillside. Machines hum.

This is the top. Where the hospital is. The big building looks so strange I'm actually glad to leave it behind and start down. It's too big, it could hold too many people. It makes me feel like an ant.

The road is lined with trees and I can't see between them except for tiny slices that show water or building or a bit of bridge. Then the road bulges out and the trees are gone. Portland is below us.

The sun is low in the sky over the east hills and the skyscrapers are gold and red with its reflection in glass windows. A river bisects the city, cut over and over by bridges that each look different from the other, like history crossing and re-crossing the water. I count five from where we're standing and staring. One of them is broken in the middle and one side dips into the river. The rest are all there, all okay, as if nothing bad has touched them.

There are a few other people near us; this is a natural place to stop. We stand at the very edge of the road and look down, awed. "That's the Willamette River," Monday says.

"I've heard the name. I didn't know it was so big."

She seems excited, like finally being this near our goal has infused her with sunshine. "Wait until you see the Columbia."

Oskar used to tell me stories about racing boats on the Columbia. It's here too, the Columbia. But I only see one river from here. "Have you seen it?"

"Of course not. But I read a whole book about it."

Figures. Monday, the reader.

Evening sunlight glints off the windshields of cars and scooters crossing two of the bridges. They look tiny from here. Even smaller dots are people on bicycles and people on the bridge closest to us.

Portland is not hiding from the world the way the garden hides; it is bold and bright and it's beckoning me down. I will make a difference there, I know I will. How could I not?

The city pulses with activity. I can't quite face it, not yet. "Let's stay here. Go down tomorrow."

"Here? Right here?" Monday looks incredulous.

I shrug. The pavement will be hard, but we can manage that. "There's a lot of people here. Enough to be safe."

Monday looks around, her eyes narrow, bouncing up and down on the balls of her feet as if trying to see dangers she isn't quite tall enough for. She is full of energy, nervous.

I'm relieved when she finally says, "I guess this looks safe enough."

There are a few others doing the same thing, although it's still light and some of the people are almost jogging, as if trying to get down to the city by some specific time. There are no lights on the road, so maybe that's what they want. Light. Like moths.

Lights come on in the city. Not a lot of them, but five tall buildings light all the way up, their bright windows reflecting on dark buildings nearby. Here and there smaller lights shine on the streets. Small squares of light shine through a few other windows, including some nearer to us. It is dark enough to see headlights, but light enough to see the streets.

Monday points up at the sky almost behind us. Two planes fly in, the last of the sun brightening their small metal bellies. We watch them drift down to land somewhere north and east of the city. "That's a good sign," I tell Monday. "Airplanes." The airplanes make me feel bigger in the same way the huge hospital building made me feel smaller.

We sit side by side at the edge of the pavement, watching the city, hungry for it. Monday is still fidgeting, but I'm glad to be able to sit still.

"It looks like magic," she says.

"I almost wish we had gone in tonight."

"No." She shakes her head. "Everything is safer in the daylight."

We talk a bit, sifting through ideas about what to look for first. The airport. A store. A library. The bookstore Monday remembers: Powell's City of Books. A place to stay. People we like. Coffee. Power. We don't come to a conclusion. We have some money that Justice gave Monday, but we don't know if the bills are good for anything, if money works in the city. Justice warned Monday not to count on it.

It feels like the discovery part of my journey is really starting, like anything can happen.

We hear footsteps and voices, and sit still like rabbits. There is no light falling directly on us; we are probably almost invisible if we don't move.

About fifteen people settle on another part of the pavement, pretty close to us but still separated by at least ten feet. They came from the city, rather than from behind us. They start a fire, close enough for us to hear the murmur of their voices. Their forms are dark silhouettes against the bright yellows and reds of the fire, and they talk amongst themselves for a few minutes, settling things, choosing places. Drums start, a call to dance. Some of the people begin to move to the beat.

The drums are loud, filling the space, drawing others hapless enough to still be on the road in the dark to stop. The group grows as the noise swells, the drums echoing between the trees.

I can't imagine carrying drums up the hill, but I'm glad someone did.

The dancers start crowding us. "Come on," I say. "I'm cold."

Monday stands watching. I imagine she is afraid and I am too, a little. But we are going to a city and there will be a lot more people there than this. Besides, I need something that is not death or danger. I also need to not be afraid. I grab my pack and start walking and she follows.

We stay outside the circle until a guy who's about thirty invites us to come closer and we stand by the fire and warm our hands. Soon our fronts are warm and our backs cold, and we smell like wood smoke. I've not seen fire very often; the Board is afraid it will bring people to the garden. I love the way the flames are yellow and red and even blue and sometimes a bit green, and the way they play on each other. The wood makes sweet and sudden noises as it heats.

The faces illuminated by the fire are a mix of colors from pale to deep brown. Their energy pops like the burning wood, noisy and surprising and happy. Maybe it's the way everyone seems cheerful and unafraid, but I feel better than I have since I left the garden. There's a piece of me that has been frozen ever since Jack. The sight of Portland lifted some of it, and the airplanes lifted a little bit more, and now the fire is warming the rest of the cold out of my heart, filling it with what I left home to find. Hope.

There are a few children younger than us, and two boys our age. A tall blond one and a dark-haired slight one who looks East Indian, like the boys in the Bollywood movies Li and Oskar love. They watch us from across the fire. It feels like they want to talk to us, although they settle for watching us like we're watching them.

What must it be like to live so near a great city, to live where you can come outside and meet friends and make noise? Where you can sing and dance and drum instead of moving as silently as possible? Even though they liked singing, and we did sing in the garden, the Board would never have allowed us to be so noisy or so visible, or to have so much fun.

There is a guitar and three lap drums and a tambourine and a harmonica spread amongst the group. I know some of the songs. One of the leaders, a blonde woman, dances so fast I can barely see her feet, and she tells us, "Make a noise the city will hear. Sing for freedom!"

She is infectious, driving me to join in, to touch the bare wood and tight, dried leather of the instruments, to move my own body, to sing.

I can manage the drums and the guitar well enough to hear some scattered clapping after I play some Beatles songs (courtesy of a copy of an album Oskar loved and played while we picked weeds). Monday sticks close to me, and sings with a clear throaty alto that fills the air around us. She is so good that the others let her lead a few songs. I'm mildly surprised that she does lead, and while she's singing she looks breathtakingly beautiful, her eyes closed, her face lifted up, music coming from someplace deep inside her.

By the time the fire dies down, most of the lights have gone out in the city below us. No one invites us home, so we sleep near the group of people we've been singing with, wearing all the clothes we can get on so we don't freeze. I dream of the spangled city below us.

Chapter Nine

SUNLIGHT AND A COOL WIND WAKE US EARLY. IT SMELLS LIKE WEATHER changing, and it's colder than the previous morning. Of course, these days winter and spring seem to dance in and out, taking bows separately.

We pack up slowly. My back is sore from sleeping on hard ground. Moving around helps.

Monday touches my knee and I look up. Two people are coming our way, carrying a thermos and four cups. I recognize them as the two young men from the fire circle. I grab my brush and get it halfway through my hair by the time they're standing in front of us.

Monday remembers their names. She's says them like curses. "Bryce, Raj."

The little merry one, who must be Raj, responds to her tone by holding out a cup to Bryce, who pours coffee into it and hands it to Monday. She takes it, sips it, and a half-smile plays around her lips, although I'm close enough to her to know that she really isn't very happy to have company. She is happy to have the coffee though and I'm happy when they hand me a warm cup to curl my fingers around. I was curious about these two last night. Besides, I'm learning to appreciate coffee, if only as a hand-warmer. It's been sweetened with something that tastes a little bit exotic, like butter and cinnamon.

They sit opposite us and Raj says, "I liked your music last night."

Monday ignores the compliment so I say, "Thanks. Thanks for the coffee, too."

"Where are you from?" Bryce asks.

"Came up from California. We're hoping for work in Portland. Is there any?"

Monday looks at me like I'm an idiot, but then I never told her about Lelani or pretending to be from California. She doesn't say anything though, and I'm positive she would have agreed if I'd been smart enough to bring it up earlier.

Bryce answers my question. "In the city. On that side of the river." He points toward the west, where the biggest buildings stand between a hill and the river. "But you might not like it. It's run by a man named Storm, and a lot of people leave."

"Why?"

"They don't like being told what to do." Bryce sounds pretty passionate about it, like he's left Portland himself for the same reason.

"We need to eat," I muse. "And I want to learn about the city."

"What about the other side?" Monday asks.

Bryce shakes his head. "It's okay. But there's no work."

"So you've never been to Portland?" Raj asks me.

I shake my head. "Not once."

"I have," Monday offers. "Mostly Before, when I was little."

Bryce is pretty in an ad-photo kind of way with a broad chin and forehead and bright blue eyes. His voice is pretty, too. Deep and full-grown, while Raj sounds younger.

Portland doesn't glitter like it did at night, but it still seems like it's calling to me. It's also nice to sit here and talk to people who don't feel creepy. "We'll take advice," I tell Bryce.

"I'd stay out of the city," he says. "But that's up to you. We'd walk you down, but we're not going there today."

He seems to be holding back, like he wants to say more. It's just a feeling I get from him, and I don't know whether or not to trust it. I look directly at him, shocked again at how nice he looks. Clearly I haven't been around enough young men. "Someone we met told us there's fighting in Portland. Is there?"

His eyes get hard and he seems to be looking far away. "Some."

Raj is more forthcoming. "There's a man with too much power in the city. Storm—used to be the Public Works guy for the city, now he runs things. He has an army in green."

"Public Works?" I'm not sure what he means.

"Streets and sewers. That's why he's so strong. He can still do that."

"Well, that seems like a good thing," Monday says, her tone the kind that's meant to cut off conversation.

"So who's fighting who?" I ask.

Bryce shakes his head but doesn't offer any more information. Maybe he's reacting to Monday, but I still think he's not as willing to talk as Raj. Raj is sweeter and more open, even if he isn't as pretty.

"So what else do we need to know?" Monday asks. "Does money work?"

Bryce shrugs. "Sometimes."

"Is there enough food for everyone?" I ask.

Bryce laughs again. "Sometimes."

Monday raises an eyebrow at him. Her face is still set, and I can feel her wishing they'd go. She drains her coffee cup and hands it back to them.

Raj offers more information. "They grow a lot. And they bring in food from the working farms south of Beaverton, and trade them labor and protection. Besides, there's only about two hundred thousand people down there now. A lot less than there used to be."

I almost choke on the dregs of my coffee, and try to imagine two hundred thousand people in one place, and I can't really do that. All I can draw up in my mind is a hill of ants.

"Are you okay?" Raj asks as he takes my cup. His fingers brush mine, and they're warm. "Can we meet you down there tomorrow?"

I look at Monday, who shakes her head. But then I decide to pretend I didn't see her. "We can use friends. But how would we find you?"

Raj grins. "I bet we can find you."

Monday is standing up and putting on her pack. "Thanks for the coffee and the information."

It's a dismissal and they know it, since they stand up, too. Raj takes my hand to help me up. He keeps hold of it just a second too long. Then he smiles. "We'll see you around."

"Good luck," Bryce adds. "Watch out for the greens."

Then they're gone and we're heading down, the city in front of us like Oz. I know it's really Seattle that's called the Emerald City, but Portland looks like it and I feel like Dorothy in the old movie, although I'm pretty sure none of her traveling companions are killers. I guess Dorothy killed the wicked witch when her house landed on the witch, but Monday has a gun. She's not the scarecrow for sure. When I look over at her, Monday looks relaxed, smiling, with her arms swinging and dark hair blowing a bit in the wind. I remember how she looked singing last night.

I admire the hell out of her, but I'm still confused about whether she's good or bad or both. Real life is so much harder than the movies. There's not as many clues.

We walk in silence, as if the city and the coffee and the idea of being somewhere has stolen our voices. The crowd thickens a little, like a great glob of people started up the hill at dawn and they're catching up to us. I clutch the straps of my pack, needing to be careful. Less than half of the people around us look like people long on the road—thin or underfed or depressed or gathered in tight groups. The others seem to be on a day walk. Like they live out here and they're going down there.

For the first time in my life I see people talking on cell phones, or staring at them and punching buttons. Ours are still dead in our packs.

Men dressed in green spread across the center of the road, as if making sure the lines of people stay orderly. They don't say anything to anybody that I see.

Storm's people.

The crowd starts bunching a little, as if something is slowing it.

A pair of boys that can't be any older than ten bump into me and one of them snatches at my pack, pulling it down around my elbow, almost taking me off-balance.

I jerk back, keeping control.

Both boys run back the other way.

Monday and I exchange glances and tighten the strings and fastenings on each other's packs.

A wide line of people holding guns spans the road. Two large banners flutter above them, strung overhead on wires. They each have a picture of a man's face on them. He smiles down at us, the image of his head bigger than any of us are tall. He has dark hair and dark eyes. The words, "Safe Inside the Eye of the Storm" are printed above his picture in gold letters rimmed with the same green the guards are wearing.

We discover the reason the line is all bunched up. At a row of tables under the sign, there are people writing down the names of everyone who comes in. They're asking questions. It takes time.

I see them take two men away, the two surrounded by five people dressed in the color of the forest. I don't like it, but I can't really say why. Maybe the men they take away are dangerous.

Chapter Ten

AT THE END OF THE BRIDGE, THREE NARROW LANES HAVE BEEN MADE OF the same kind of concrete barriers that line whole portions of the interstate. A tall man stands before the barriers and assesses everyone who passes. Some show him a green paper, and he sends them to the far right lane. He sorts the others into the middle and the left.

A family with two small children is right in front of us. They wear ragged clothes and their hair hangs in strings. These he sends to the far left line, which is mostly not moving. The woman gasps as he does this, but she says nothing, scuttling to do what she's told.

We stop in front of him.

He looks us over with an impassive and clean-shaven face. His eyes are brown and his hair is brown and his cheeks a bit sunken with age. He takes a long time, and I stand and hold my ground, my knees locked, my back as straight as I can make it. He finally nods to send us to the middle line, which is smaller and full of healthy people.

I let out a breath that I hadn't realized was stuck in my throat.

There is another barrier. Green-shirted men pull two people out of line and over to a table where other men search their stuff. I can't tell what makes them choose people to search, or what makes the people let them do it. I think about the gun in Monday's bag and how skittish she is, and I do my very best to look innocent.

My inner dialogue is, *"Don't search us! Don't search us!"* and all the time I'm smiling as hard as I can.

The men eye us but don't send us over.

Another lucky break.

At the head of the line, people sit under tarps at desks with stacks of green paper, pens, and somewhat sour looks. Everyone is questioned; we shuffle forward slowly. They let most people in our line in, although one older woman and a fat old man with suspenders are escorted to the line of people going the other way while we wait. But most people ahead of us get passes.

Two girls our age question us, watched over by an older woman with a stern face. The woman looks us over pretty close. Her face is set and hard, like her life is one tough decision after another.

We just had a shower and two head-washes, and we're not too thin or anything. Monday manages to look almost bored although her right toe taps the pitted concrete.

The girls seem as bored as Monday is trying to look. They ask why we are coming (to explore Portland, and to look for work) and how long we'll be there (we don't know) and how old we are (We both lie when I say eighteen and Monday says twenty-one). I keep pretending to be from California and Monday says she's from Eugene. The girl closest to me is blonde and neat and very, very serious. She fills out a green pass with our names, genders, and the ages we gave her with a thick red pen. She adds in the date (February 18th) and writes "14" in numerals and circles it.

She is careful and polite; efficient.

She hands us the passes and says, "Don't lose these. You'll need them to get back out, and you need to check back here or at a bridge for an extension or leave before fourteen days are over. If you get caught with an expired pass, you can be arrested. If you get caught in a demonstration you will be thrown out of the city." She doesn't give any of the words particular emphasis so they all run together and sound like mush. But it makes me shiver a bit and I carefully fold the pass and put it in my front jeans pocket. I'm ready to step away from the table when sour-face holds up a hand to stop us. I swallow and smile at her, hoping we aren't about to be searched after all. She hands us each a small green card. "These will get you a place in line for the city work crews."

I have no idea what she means, but I'm not about to ask her. The little card gets tucked next to my pass. The woman looks like she expects something so I nod at her. "Thank you."

"You're welcome." She turns to the next person in line and we're free at last.

Except not really.

We've simply been turned loose in a passageway that's only for people in our line. It's a narrow street with the same concrete barriers. At the end of it, there are more people in green.

We're herded into a building where a clean-cut young man checks the number of days on our pass and lets us through. The air smells like sweat and mold. Dirt has piled into the corners. Pictures of well-dressed officials smile at us from cheap frames. The one closest to the front of the room is the same man we saw on pictures on the way in, and I don't doubt for a minute that this dark-haired and dark-eyed man is Alexis Storm.

Even though the chairs are hard, it feels good to sit down. Except that I really want to get into the city.

We sit for a long time. Monday pulls out her book and I fidget. There's a bathroom with real flushing toilets, and I clean up my face while Monday watches our stuff and our places, and then we trade. When Monday comes back, both of our canteens are full, too. She hands me mine, and the water tastes like chemicals but makes me feel more awake. After about an hour, the room is half-full and a young man closes the door.

Two women come and stand up at the front. They both look tired. "Thank you for coming to Portland," one says.

"There is no free food or free water here, nor free power," the other adds.

"But it can all be earned," the first one tells us. "Most of you have multi-day passes. If you work at least half the days you are here, you might get extension on those passes. You can get food. In the meantime, you're free to move about the city, but you must always carry your passes with you."

The second one chimes in. "You can expect safety here. And if you violate the rule of safety—if you harm anyone or you consort with rebels—you will leave or you will be locked up like an animal."

All of this is delivered with way more enthusiasm than the little version of it we got from the pale girl who gave us our passes. When she's done, she smiles and says, "Good luck."

The doors open and we file outside. A metal fence surrounds the building. Just outside, the two women point out a place with tables and chairs like the ones by the bridge entrance. They tell us to come there to report to work. She says, "We'll see most of you tomorrow," in a too-friendly voice.

We're finally able to walk into the city.

The sun is straight overhead now, and it's hot and the sky is clear. Maybe that's a good sign after all the rain. Maybe we are where we're supposed to be.

We say nothing until we feel like we've left the gauntlet of entry behind. A block or two from the bridges, Monday says, "I don't like it that we have to work."

I shrug. We may have to work, but maybe we won't have to hide and worry about being prey. "I had chores every day. I bet Justice made you work, too."

She doesn't say anything to that.

"I bet we don't meet anybody we have to kill, either. I think maybe that's okay." Then, "So, now what?"

"We walk."

Up close, bright light isn't kind to the city. The buildings are dirty and the streets have holes in them. Yellow tape surrounds a few holes that are so deep they're dangerous. Sidewalks are root-cracked or quake-cracked and every square leans a bit. The street-level is mostly boarded-up storefronts, so we follow some music that we hear and stop in awe when we round a corner and see everything is open and bright in the bottom level of a whole big building. Power. Running water in a fountain that people use to fill empty jars and pots. Crowds of people gather there, some of them smiling and laughing together like all is right with the world.

Green shirts patrol the middle of the streets and people are buying secondhand stuff from tables that line the sidewalk and what looks like new things from inside stores. There are lines of people in all directions that we push through, surrounded briefly by chatter and the calls of women to their bored children. The air smells like grease and pancakes, like toast and honey.

The smells wake my stomach up. We stop in a doorway that has been boarded shut and chew on some jerky and share a can of clammy cold chicken soup. We could probably buy food, but I don't know how and I suspect Monday doesn't either.

It's hard to feel brave here. The city is so different from anyplace I've ever seen and I don't know how to act. I don't want people to know I'm afraid.

I tug on Monday's arm so we get away from all the people. There's too many of them. I'll get used to it—I'm sure I will. I like it. A few streets over, the sounds have faded and we're walking by boarded windows again. I don't feel as crowded as I did by the stores, but there are still a lot of people. Almost everyone walking past us seems to be going somewhere specific and mostly they move faster than we do. Every tenth person or so is wearing a green shirt or has on a green bandana or something else green.

I wish for Bryce and Raj, particularly Raj. There are so many people here I can't imagine how we will ever find them again.

Monday's not afraid. She's more relaxed than I've seen her since that first day at Just Robyn. "This isn't so bad," she says. "I bet all the green shirts keep things pretty safe."

"Do you want to go to the bookstore?"

Given the way Monday's face lights up, I must have said the right thing. She starts walking faster. She seems to know where she's going since she heads back toward the bridges, but turns just before we get to them so we're walking north along the river. There's a park, with walls and paths and grass that someone mows. "The river used to be lower," she comments.

"How do you know?"

"I remember," she says. "I remember this all. We used to bicycle here and the river was far below the wall. Now it's almost at the top. It must be sea level rise."

At first, I'm thrown since this isn't a sea. "Tides?"

"Wouldn't they be higher since the sea is higher?"

"Probably."

Two tugboats pass us, pulling barges full of grain, and in one case, of people. Smaller boats dart between the bigger boats and the bridge pilings, the people on the boats call out to one another. Some boats have fish in them and some are so full of people they ride low. A fresh wind blows our hair sideways.

The walk is crowded. We find restrooms that work in a building that must have been designed just to be a bathroom. A wonder. Small things like bathrooms we can use make Portland seem civilized in spite of all the boarded windows and slanted sidewalks.

We pass another bridge. Monday squints at the street sign and says, "Keep going."

We pass more bridges. There are barricades to keep us from the one that's fallen in the water. We get to a low bridge with cars going through lines like we just finished, with the same green passes, only bigger and wedged inside the windows. A short, fat man in green pants and a blue shirt waves cars that already have the passes through. Monday grins. “Burnside. We go up here.” She’s almost like a little kid, like the Monday who was bouncing around the park last night. We’ve only gone a block or two when she points down a street with bright red buildings lining each side. “Chinatown,” she says.

“What’s that?”

“Chinese people live there.” Then she stops. “That’s how it used to be anyway. I guess they still do, but it’s also a tourist thing.”

“There’s no tourists now,” I point out.

She laughs. “What are we?”

Most of the signs are in Chinese. It smells like grease and frying food and while there are boarded-up stores, more than half of the buildings are open, people ducking in and out of doors, talking in singsong, sometimes yelling. The crowds are thick enough I’m glad Monday isn’t leading us there. It startles me when three red chickens race across the road. Two boys chase them. One of the boys is definitely Asian, although the other one is too black to be very Chinese. We’re walking past Chinatown and not through it, but I feel like I’ve glimpsed another world.

Two other worlds. Portland itself and now, inside it, Chinatown. It’s disorienting and exciting all at once, like being awake inside a dream.

Then it’s my turn to tug on Monday’s arm. Hanging on a wall beside an open door with people standing nearby and talking is a hand-lettered sign with gold curlicue flourishes that says, “Electricity and wi-fi.”

The open door leads to a big room with power sockets all around it, and chairs in front of the sockets, facing out. In the middle of the room, there are carpets and some kids’ toys, although there aren’t any kids there right now. Over half the chairs are full. The sign on the wall says, “$10.00 a half hour per plug.” Taped just below it is a sign that says, “One work chit per hour.”

Neither of us has whatever a work chit is, but Monday has the money Justice gave her. I glance at her and she’s digging in her heels a little. “The bookstore’s right up there. Ten minutes.”

“But we don’t know where another one of these is!” I say. “Or how long it’s open. Justice gave us the phones for a reason.” It feels like getting the phones to work will mean we aren’t so alone in the middle of all these people.

She brightens at Justice’s name and gives in. We pull out all the phones and decide to plug in a matching set that are square and thin, and about the size of my palm. The only difference is mine is a dull black and Monday’s is bright blue, and has a scratch up the back where silver shows.

We do like everyone else, and sit. A boy who can’t be much more than ten comes by. Monday hands him twenty dollars. He puts it in his pocket but sticks his hand out again. Monday shakes her head at him. “That’s what the sign says.”

He shrugs and says, “Boss said twenty per phone.”

Monday’s jaw is tight and her eyes flash like she might argue, but she digs out another bill and gives it to him.

We plug our chargers in. At first the phones don’t turn on, but Monday says, “It takes time.” It feels damned good to just lean back in a chair someplace safe and have nothing we can or should do. “We made it,” I whisper just loud enough for Monday to hear.

Monday mutters, “Barely,” and of course she’s right and then we have to not look at each other or we’ll break out laughing and that seems wrong in here where it’s mostly a place of quiet and waiting. After a moment Monday looks down at her screen and whispers, “It works.”

I don’t think mine does, but she reaches over and pushes a button and the screen glows a bright empty blue and then comes up black with little pictures on it. “Ever used one?” she asks.

“No.”

“Me either. Though I’ve seen people with them.” I realize that I hold something new to me in my hand, something as common in movies and books as cars and washing machines and neat neighborhoods and mass transportation. It feels like magic, like suddenly becoming part of the old movies that seemed completely different from my life.

Monday shows me how to bring up internet pages and social networks, including one called ConnectU that’s global and another one called PDXNET that we decide must be unique to Portland. Messages from people I’ve never met scroll down the screen. I learn to jump from item to item. Lots of things we try don't load and a lot of links are broken, so it's like searching through a half-dead world for life, but still I feel like I have distant places in my hand, and the voices and pictures of people I will never see.

"So how do we get in touch with Justice?" I ask her. "Or Bryce and Raj?"

Monday frowns. "Justice told me he has nicknames I'll recognize. I guess we have to give some to ourselves."

Before we can figure that out, the money boy comes by and tells us to get along or pay up. The phones aren't fully charged yet, but Monday puts hers away and stands up.

My legs are stiff and I'm hungry again, but Monday is on a mission. Her strides are long as she heads up Burnside, away from the bridges. The sun is low enough for tall buildings to throw shadows on us, but there is enough light that all of the buildings of Portland are still full of dark windows like hundreds or thousands of eyes above us.

Monday's long black hair bounces up and down, tangling with her backpack, as she actually breaks into a jog. We come in sight of the sign that proclaims Powell's Books. It's a big square brick building, at least on this side. Two stories all around, or a bit more.

The windows are boarded up.

Chapter Eleven

PLYWOOD COVERS THE STREET-LEVEL WALLS OF THE BOOKSTORE. A spray-painted white background is nearly invisible, hidden behind swirls of colored paint, notes written with marker and pen, drawings of people and trees and sunsets. Some of the work is so detailed it creates forests and bookshelves and bicycles.

A lot of people loved this store. That's what the pictures say to me. Love. Admiration. It's beautiful, Powell's City of Books. But in an empty, aching way.

Monday stares the building down. Her chin quivers. She reaches a hand out and takes my hand and stares at the empty building.

"Look at the art," I whisper, a bit awed.

After more silence than I can stand comes from Monday, I remind her, "You have a few books to read. We should go find a place to sleep before it's too late."

"Okay."

She doesn't move until I tug on her hand.

"I don't know what I expected." She is finally walking away from the bookstore. "Maybe that there would be someplace here for us."

"It's our first night." I withdraw my hand from hers to adjust the straps of my pack. "They said we should check in before dark if we want to sleep in one of the common areas. We're almost out of water. I'm sure they'll have water."

A slight sigh escapes her lips, but she gives Powell's one more glance and we head away from it. We walk fast enough to keep the worst of the cooling night from biting more than our cheeks.

Three green-shirts step in front of us.

We startle.

The biggest is a tall man with a mustache and long, greasy hair. "See your pass?"

We pull out the passes and hand them over.

"Newbies." The man takes a long time to stare at very little information on the pass. "Do you have any food?"

I don't want it taken. "We ate it already."

"Work chits?"

We show him the small green cards, but it turns out those are just the right to work, not anything that says we did work. He frowns. "You can sleep with these. Since it's your first day." He is wearing an old, scratched watch, which he glances down at. "Except you're going to be late."

Monday's eyes narrow and her whole body stiffens. Either fear or anger or a bit of both. "If you give us back our passes maybe we can make it on time."

"If you run." But he's still just standing there. He looks at his two fellows, who are cleaner than he is, one bald and one with a short haircut and glasses that have been glued together badly. "Shall we watch them run?"

The bald one grins but broken-glasses shakes his head. "Give them back. We don't want trouble with Storm."

Greasy-hair stares at the passes in his hand. "Which one of you is *Monday*?"

When she nods, he hands her the pass and says, "Pick a real name next time."

She takes it, her face a mask of silent rebellion.

He looks at me. "You must be Cathy, or Julie or something. Don't be too full of yourselves."

He probably thinks he's funny, but I'm shaky and getting as mad as Monday. I need the pathetic piece of paper so I wait, trying to look as polite as I can. He crumples it in his hand.

Broken-glasses says, "Luke," in a way that's threatening, and the paper gets thrown to me. I catch it and smooth it and put it back in my pocket.

Luke gestures at us and says, "Run, now."

We turn away from them. Monday leans down near me. "Don't run."

Of course not. Still, we walk fast and I don't relax until we get a whole block and they haven't followed.

Monday says, "I was in Eugene before I came to Just Robyn, and you don't have to prove anything to anybody there."

"What was Eugene like?"

"Poorer than this," she says. "But you could just get along."

We go back to the building we entered Portland through, taking two wrong turns. By the time we find it, the sun—already behind the hill that borders downtown to the west—is barely sending pale beams up to kiss the darkening sky goodnight.

There are no green shirts. It's already so dark we're throwing mush for shadows. The gate is clamped shut with a thick chain, a heavy lock pulling the links down.

Around us, the same smattering of lights we saw from the lookout last night begin to wink on, and the street becomes lines and pools of light and dark, with far more dark.

"We're too late."

"Come on," Monday says, heading away from the river. There are more people in the streets, menacing in the dark. Monday leans down and whispers, "Walk like you know where you're going. It's safer."

We turn away from groups a few times, although no one stops us now, not even green shirts. There is chanting and yelling in a few places, but we're not close enough to make out the words. Gunshots happen twice, making us jump.

I'm glad we have each other. The dark caverns between tall buildings are spooky and smell of grease and rot.

I realize we've passed the same places that we've passed before, and so I say, "Let's go up. We'll know which direction we're going that way. Up's verifiable."

Monday is holding her arms tight around her, teeth shivering. "Anything. Find us someplace warm."

She's right. Portland feels bad now. It isn't natural, all this concrete and brick and glass.

When we stop to catch our breath and look down, the river runs dark beyond downtown, visible as a shimmering blackness touched by the lights from the bridges.

The streets narrow, and instead of names they have numbers. We turn down one that has more light than dark, NW 23rd. Here, the street is lined with one- and two-story stores and houses, and people wander in and out of them, some with cups in their hands. It makes me thirsty, and reminds me I want water and to stop somewhere. There are no cars except some parked on the side streets. It feels safe enough, and it sounds nice, people talking in friendly tones. Still, we stick to the middle of the street, watching both sides.

We find a bathroom by following a sign into a wooden house with a red metal roof. There's a couple sitting outside on the steps and other voices in the house. We find the bathroom, use it, and fill our canteens from the sink. It's cleaner by far than the public bathrooms by the water or the ones in the big room where they gave us lectures. There are stacks of paper napkins on the sink that work for toilet paper, and a sign that tells us to use as little paper as possible.

Music comes from one of the stores, and we go in and see that empty shelves have been pushed against the walls and rugs are piled up on the floor for people to sit on. It's warm and people talk to each other in low, friendly voices. We find a sliver of wall to lean against near the back of the room.

In the front, three women sit on folding chairs. One has a drum, one a tambourine, and the third a guitar. They're singing songs I haven't heard, although I've heard the same kind of music back at the garden. I close my eyes, listening. Being Now.

The singers' voices are sweet and high, although one is slightly off on the highest notes. The drummer is good, very even, and regular like a heartbeat, although a little faster than my own heart is going.

A whispered conversation is close enough to me I hear a bit of it.

"—Sue on 20th has tomatoes. She'll trade for bread."

"Can we make it a party?"

"I only have three loaves."

"I heard there's flour coming to Saturday Market. I'd kill for a tomato."

"I'm not going down there. Too many damned greens."

"Hope the tomatoes aren't gone."

A string of silver bells over the door makes a soft sound whenever it opens.

The music soothes, and it's a struggle to stay awake even though I haven't yet done the exercise anywhere near Justice's fifteen minutes.

The entrance bells rattle softly and a voice hisses loud enough to stop the music. "Greens."

All sound stops.

The guitar and the drum get set down carefully.

A few whispers, short and curt.

The light goes out.

There is silence except the breathing of the thirty or so people in the room. Darkness. It smells like sweat and silence and fear.

Engines thrum by, three vehicles.

Monday puts a hand on my shoulder, pulls me closer to her. I smell her breath, which is a little sour.

The deep rumbly sound of the engines fades as the vehicles get further away. The bells go off again, and a voice cautions, "Wait," they whisper loud enough to hear in the silence and the darkness.

A few moments later, the door opens again. The voice is normal now. "Close your eyes." I do, and the light flicks back on, slapping at my closed lids. The music starts again, and the whispered conversations.

Monday looks deep in thought, and her face is pale. "I don't like it here," she says, low enough that I'm probably the only one who can hear.

"This place?"

"We should have gone east to Eugene. Or skipped Portland and gone to Seattle."

"The airplanes landed here." I'm happy with the idea that there are guards to warn us of danger. People here seem friendly. Not that anyone has talked to us, but then we're in the middle of a concert. That no one has bothered us is good enough.

Although I'm hungry, I make do with water while I wait to see what happens next.

It's probably a sign of how the room feels safe that I pass out before the next song finishes.

I blink to grey light shining in through the windows and illuminating the sleeping bodies of at least twenty people sprawled across the floor. Most are huddled together in groups of two or three, although a few sleep alone in the crowd. Monday is beside me, head pillowed on her pack, her mouth open. She's snoring little huffing snores, barely loud enough to notice. She looks relaxed and unafraid in sleep, young. Even though I really need to get up, I sit and watch her breathe for a few moments. She is beautiful with all of her anger gone.

I love seeing a place where so many people could feel safe together and not be behind walls.

Monday stirs and then her eyes close again. I get up and use a small toilet in a room in the back and brush my teeth and hair. When I return, Monday is sitting up and blinking. Ten minutes later, we're both cleanish and walking along the street outside. We find a cart with hot water and tea and some flat bread and cheese available to a small line of people. As we stand in line my fingers feel the cool of the morning and my belly rumbles.

The woman in front of us offers up a work chit in trade.

It's our turn.

The man with the tea holds his hand out. I remember the motorcycle man again and dig into my pack for the last can of soup that we took from the yellow house. The man looks dubious, but he hands us one cup of tea, one piece of bread and a very small bit of cheese that he cuts carefully. "You'll have to share," he says.

Perhaps the soup would have been better to share, or the last can of chili that's still in the bottom of my pack, but the tea smells so good I take it. Monday and I find a place to lean against a wall with our packs between our feet. We pass the tea back and forth and get three bites each of food.

Monday says nothing until it's all gone, and then she stares at the cup for a moment. "We best go report for work," she says.

We walk in front of a building with boards behind cracked windows. There is a big ratty corkboard stuck full of fliers and stickers and torn notes. I tug on Monday's arm and point.

Justice's face stares at us from a faded poster that looks like it was once yellow. There are words above and below it, and I can make out "Meeting" and "Freedom" and that's all —there are more but they are either covered by other paper or faded to nothing. "He's younger in the picture."

Monday stares at it, the edges of her chin quivering. While she spends time not answering, I think about Oskar and Kelley and realize Monday misses Justice fiercely, at least if the look on her face is truth. I wait, though, letting her answer.

"That's him."

Looking closely, we spot Justice's face in more places. He and Robyn stand next to each other, surrounded by people carrying signs. There's another one where he and a tall blond man are standing together on a rock, and it looks like they're talking to a crowd. In another picture near the top of the pile, one of the newest looking fliers, we see something about electing the blond man. We can make out his first name. Kevin. That's about it. Most of the posters have faded past reading or they talk about events long gone — concerts and meetings and potlucks and clothes swaps and donations for the hungry and the old and the sick. Of course, now that's everyone. Or almost everyone.

"We have to go," I whisper.

Monday holds her hand up to the picture, touching the dirty glass in front of Justice's face with one extended finger. Then she turns and leads, staying ahead of me so I have to work a bit to keep up.

Chapter Twelve

After we leave the window that displays Justice's picture, it takes us about half an hour of walking to get down the hill and go to the place where the greens hand out work. The city is busier in the morning, as if the light draws out people who have hidden through the whole dark time.

It's still cool as we stand around in bunches, warming in the early sun. Greens come by and pick people out.

They call out work and take people with them.

"Gardening."

"Street cleaning."

"Sewers."

"Food line."

I'm starved. I wonder what happens to people who don't get picked.

The woman with the sour face who let us in the gate yesterday calls out "Reclamation." She walks up and down the line signaling for people to follow her. In front of us, she stops and looks thoughtful, and then sends us to a growing knot of about twenty workers. Almost as many greens surround us. All of us—greens and everyone else alike—are strong. Not necessarily young, but no one is old or unable to walk or work. Most are men, but there are four other women; all greens. Two of the women are extra broad and tall twins, maybe five years older than us.

The other two women are older with stringy hair tied back in ponytails and sturdy but stained work clothes and boots. Practical. They walk beside us and ask us questions about where we came from. As soon as we tell them what we told the people at the gate, Monday starts asking them questions. Their names are Cheryl and Lyssa, and they have always lived in Portland. They like Storm and that the city is pretty safe, and they can't imagine what anyplace else must be like. They tell us the seawall has fallen in Seattle and there's no running water in southern California at all.

They're not like the men that stopped us last night. They are nice to us, maybe even friendly.

We stop in the middle of the street when we see where we're going. A mountain of junk shines in the sun. Truckloads and truckloads of it that have been piled onto a road. Maybe more like a mountain range of junk, complete with peaks and valleys. Some of the trash has fallen into a sinkhole behind the main mound, but most is stacked way taller than we are.

As we get closer, the junk pile resolves into distinct items. Broken picture frames, crushed toasters, chipped drinking glasses and plates. Bicycle wheels bent out of shape and tattered lampshades gone to mush from the weather. Ravens and smaller birds flit from shiny object to shiny object, collecting treasure for nests.

A few more steps and a puff of wind brings a great miasma of mold and bird shit and a faint whiff of dead things that makes us wrinkle our noses. The greens gather us in a circle, handing out scraps of material to tie over our faces and worn gloves for our hands. All of the greens have their own gloves; the ones we get are stiff with other people's sweat.

One man refuses the scarf and the gloves and turns and walks away.

The greens ignore him, except that one whispers under her breath, "Happy starving."

The smell has killed my hunger, but the idea of leaving with no way to buy more food keeps me listening as we get instructions which are very detailed but amount to "recycle this mountain of stuff."

Monday leads us gingerly up the pile, keeping us a little distant from everyone else, just close enough to hear the orders they give us.

We pull whole objects from the pile. We're looking for anything that might be mended and re-used, like garden rakes with broken handles. Metal is safeguarded and piled by type into big metal bins. Greens are the only ones allowed to sort metal. We put red marks on electronics that are past saving, and they all go into a special bin. Dry paper has a special holder. Just trash—like old, soiled clothing and soaked paper—ends up in a separate container as well. Most of the pile is trash. A truck comes four times and empties this bin, and two of the times the same truck brings new stuff.

Some of the junk brings up images of other lives I've made up from movies. Blue ribbons from a dog tournament in 2019 are folded up neatly in a wooden box with the name Charlie in dark letters on the lid. A broken camera lens as big as my hand. Monday has to tell me what it is since at first I think it's something to look at stars with. A single, tiny tennis shoe lights up when I flex it.

Monday finds a book that makes her smile, and she tucks it into her waistband and pulls her shirt over it.

By lunch, we've filled ten bins and started stacking goods beside other bins. Monday has a scratch all along one arm that bleeds intermittently and attracts flies. The smell worsens as the day warms.

My hunger gnaws at my belly in spite of the smell now, demanding my attention even more than the sharp edges and rats and dive-bombing birds. Hunger makes me slow.

I'd like rain. The heat is still and damp. Thick black clouds hover east and south, but above us the sun shines forcefully down on the mountain of shiny and dull things, on the sharp things and the old things and the hot and smelly things.

A line of five green jeeps drives up to the edge of the mountain.

A man hops out of the second one in line and walks toward us. I recognize him from the posters of his face on the bridge as we came in even though he's shorter than I expected.

Storm.

I stop, mesmerized at this first look at a stranger whose face I've seen in a hundred places. He's the reason I'm picking through junk. It's a brutal thing that has to be done. I understand that.

His hands are empty, but he's followed by two men with rifles. He talks to a few of our keepers and although I can't hear the words, his tone is demanding.

Everyone he's talking to stands straight, looks serious, and speaks back to him in low tones.

The men with the guns look around all the time. Their eyes never stop, their heads swivel like hawks. Back in the jeeps, I see more guns.

Perched near the top of the junk mountain, I feel like I'm in a weird movie, like none of this is real. But then I'm dizzy with the smell and the chasm in my belly and a thirst that tugs at my throat.

Storm looks up at me, and I think for a minute that he's going to climb the pile of crap himself, but he turns away and climbs into his jeep. After he leaves, there is a period of silence before we all start talking again.

Even though it smells worse than anything I've ever smelled, worse than sickness or rot or sickness and rot together, by the time a truck drives up with lunch I'm starved. We each get a whole plate of mixed-up stuff. Some stale crackers, cookies that taste like cinnamon and have real sugar on top, some tomatoes and bits of chewy meat jerky. I'm hungry enough it all disappears with almost no comment.

That's all the food we get, and even though our plates were full, I'm starved by the time we're allowed to knock off work. At the end of the day we trade the rags and gloves for work chits. Before that, one of the green women pats us down, and she takes the book away from Monday and throws it into a trash bin. When she gets near me, her hands are professional and perfunctory, but I still feel violated and a little pissed off. Not that I say anything, but I hate that, too. My silence.

Monday and I get three chits each. If I understand the system, we can't take a whole day off until we work another whole day. Not and eat.

Chapter Thirteen

MONDAY LOOKS LIKE SHE'S DRAGGING, AND I WONDER IF HER FEET ARE as hot and achy as mine. We buy cups of thin vegetable soup with two of our work chits, but that's like slapping the hunger so it only turns its face for a moment.

Early evening light stripes through buildings, giving an orange cast to faces in the busy street. "I want to go back to Powell's," Monday states.

"What do you think will be different?"

"I heard someone in the bathroom telling me they got a book from there."

"Did they say when?"

"No."

Funny. I expected her to want to go right back to 23rd and figure out what Justice's picture means. I want to know, and I'm pretty sure she doesn't know. We kind of have to pass Powell's on the way to 23rd anyway.

We're only partway there when we see out first demonstration. In my head, I'd expected something violent. Greens with guns, maybe with Storm in the lead, facing off protestors in some other specific color with guns, too.

It's not like that.

On one corner, three older women are dressed in purple with black hats, carrying signs. "Say No to the Storm," is painted on one sign. Another suggests, "Bring Back Portland's Sun," in bright blue. The women holding the signs stand and wave at people. They don't say a word, even when people talk to them. Some people stop to tell them things, some raise their arms or make a victory sign in support, and a man spits in one of the women's faces. She barely reacts until another man steps forward from the small crowd surrounding the women and uses a rag to wash the spit off. This makes her touch his cheek and smile.

A third woman—younger than the sign-holders but older than Kelley—hands out pieces of paper to the passers-by. She is also in purple, but she's done it up to an extreme with purple eye-make-up and purple nails and purple necklaces. There is a purple streak in her dark hair, hanging loosely below a purple scarf with fringe that frames her eyes. She is animated, smiling and occasionally speaking.

Looking at her makes me smile, too.

I go over to take one of the fliers and she looks at me with deeply determined eyes that are the same color as the sky. She hurries the paper into my hand.

Just after I close my fingers over the flier, men in green shirts surround us, enclosing Monday and me in a circle that includes the three women and one middle-aged man I didn't even notice until he's trapped with us. He's got a small brown dog with a white tail sticking to his feet, growling up at pretty much everybody.

The man is like us; caught in the wrong moment. Maybe more innocent. He has not taken one of the fliers.

I hadn't seen the green shirts. It feels like they came out of nothing and now they are everywhere. The warning from the bridge plays in my mind.

The greens make the circle tighter, standing shoulder to shoulder and we're so tight together we're shoulder to shoulder, too. There could be fifteen of them, maybe a few more. One of the greens, a woman, slugs the woman next to me in the shoulder so hard she stumbles back, pushing me off-balance. A man rips the paper out of my hand and another steps on my foot. His hand hits my chest so hard it brings tears to my eyes, unbidden, and drives anger up my spine.

Monday catches me as I reel back from the hit. She's braced herself and keeps me from falling.

A green kicks the dog, who gives out a high-pitched screech and rolls around our feet, tangled in its leash. This is even worse than touching me. The dog doesn't know anything about passes or green shirts, and it's small enough it could die if it gets stepped on.

The owner catches a bit of leash and pulls the dog to him. He falls to the ground and curls around the dog's tiny body so the green shirt kicks him instead of the dog. He is crying piteously, his cheek on the pavement, clutching the shaking dog and exposing his own back.

One of the women who has been caught with us steps over the man, forming a bit of shield.

The man who kicked the dog grabs a free bit of leash, pulling on it like he's going to steal the dog or hurt it more.

The owner calls the dog's name, "Alfie, Alfie."

I don't think. I grab the leash from the green shirt, pulling it free, and put my body between the green shirt and the man with the dog.

Monday stands beside me, looking pissed.

I pass the leash back to the man.

One of the green shirts reaches toward me.

Then Raj is suddenly there and Bryce and three or four others, then even more. A line is formed between the greens and us. Bryce and Raj separate us and the man with the dog, pulling us away from the ruckus. The man thanks me in a hurried sob and fades fast into the small crowd that remains, clutching Alfie to him like a child.

In a few moments we have been saved, moved away from the greens and the protestors.

I stand up on a bit of wall in front of an empty shop and try to see what's happening. The greens have the women with the signs, and the girl with the purple hair and the blue eyes. There are a lot of greens. More than the protestors, but not more than the passers-by. "What will happen to the old women?"

"Nothing good," Bryce says. He's stiff and full of energy, but the altercation is over now, the greens hurrying away with their captives and the rest of the street going back to normal already.

"How did you find us?" Monday asks.

Raj grins at her, looking a bit like a successful hunter. "I've been keeping an eye out for you. To be sure you're safe. I heard you worked Junk Mountain today. We spotted you a few streets back and were trying to catch up with you."

Bryce is looking at us like he's testing. "We needed to know what side you're on."

He's completely serious. My teeth bear down on my lower lip so I don't laugh.

He grins. "You just showed us."

"Don't follow us," Monday snaps.

"Good thing we did, don't you think?" Bryce has one eyebrow raised and looks serious.

"Yes," I say before Monday can say anything else. I'm happy to see them and I'm positive I don't want to tangle with the green shirts. I want to find the good news to bring home. Not the crap.

"We're going to Powell's," Monday proclaims, stubborn.

"Can you wait an hour?" Raj is almost pleading. "We have to leave then, anyway."

Monday looks as desperate as Raj. I'm not even sure which one to feel sorry for; maybe I feel sorry for both of them. But I'm rooting for Raj. I want to find out what's happening. "What do you want us for?" I ask.

"We need more people—"

Bryce cuts Raj off. "We want you to meet our friends," he says. "They can help keep you safe here."

Okay, now I'm curious. I hope they aren't all little old women in purple, but then, I'm already suspecting Bryce and Raj are rebels. They're talking about sides, after all. I try and look apologetic as I glance at Monday and ask her, "Do you mind?"

She looks like she's swallowed a bug. But she has the grace to nod.

The corner we're on is Burnside and Broadway. I can see the Powell's sign before we turn down a wide swath of park between two streets and go three blocks or so north. We turn on Everett (I'm trying to remember all this; Portland is big and scary, and we've already been lost twice).

Bryce leads us around the back of a place called the Devil's Distillery and Public House. He nods casually at a man who is clearly a door guard and waits for him to step back. The guard is quick about it and looks pleased to see Bryce.

Inside, Monday looks around and lets out a low, "Sweet," that's as much whisper as word.

There's beer on the walls, and pictures of beer, and little white lights. Some of the beer labels are old and some look homemade, which makes me think of Jack. Wooden tables half full of people. A lot of the faces are serious, but one table is telling jokes and laughing. Pitchers of amber liquid sit on most of the tabletops.

"I'm not old enough to be in a bar," Monday says.

“Neither are we,” Raj replies, laughing, almost bouncing on his feet. He appears to be looking for someone. I like the way he’s animated, always moving, always alert. Like Monday. He says, “No one cares here. Hell, probably no one cares at any bar in Portland any more. Most are dry, but the Devil’s Distillery is always stocked.”

A stack of fliers like the one I lost in the scuffle for the dog sits on a table by the door. I pick one up. It’s black and white and looks like it was done in a hurry—some words aren’t spelled the way I learned them. There are lists of people to follow on PDXNET and times and places for demonstrations against Storm and what they call “the storm clouds,” which I guess must be his people or his green shirts or something. The back of the flier has two articles on it. One is titled, “Storm Dictates” and the other one is “How to Stop the Storm.” I fold two copies into my pants pocket and look up to see Monday and the boys all sitting at a big round table with a man a few years older than Bryce. The man has a neatly trimmed brown beard and intense eyes. He feels like a small, compact force. When I walk up he holds out his hand. “Hi! I’m Andy. You must be Sage.”

I nod and squeeze in between him and Bryce. Andy smells likes paper and ink and the beer in his hand. A nearly-empty pitcher of beer sits on the table and everyone but me has a full glass in front of them.

Oskar and Kelley have both warned me against drinking.

Monday pours beer into my glass and pushes it into my hand. I take it in spite of the voices going off in my head. It’s sour and strong and it reminds me of the smell of the men who attacked Monday in the park.

But they all raise their glasses and Bryce says, “To new friends,” and Andy says, “To a better Portland.” We clink the glasses together and everyone, including me, takes a sip.

The beer tastes so bad it’s hard not to spit it out, but I manage. A few more people who vary from Bryce’s age to Andy’s squeeze around the table. All of them are men.

Monday is itchy. She’s never said it, but I’ve figured out she doesn’t like crowds or being around people. I can see the distress in her eyes, and I wish I had found a way to sit by her.

Andy and Bryce and the others talk about a friend of theirs who disappeared three days ago, about key messages for fliers, about feeding crowds of people, then about one of the old women in purple who was found in the river a week ago. Storm claimed she committed suicide but Andy claimed that's a lie.

A lot of the talk doesn't make complete sense to me, either because I don't recognize the names and places or because I'm halfway through the beer. It's angry talk, fierce talk. It draws me; it's passion. I want to feel things as deeply as these people. Nothing in my life has been hard enough to make me this angry.

Maybe I need to be part of a fight.

It has been a few hours since we ate and my stomach hates the beer as much as my taste buds hate it. But I manage to finish the whole glass.

Monday is on her second beer. I want to know what she thinks, but I can't ask her here in front of everyone. "Monday," I interrupt her listening to a story from Andy about using a crowd of people to stop a tractor from knocking down a building. "I have to go to the bathroom." I push myself up, leaning on the back of the chair and on Andy to stay upright. "Come with me?"

She gets up, and comes over to me and steadies me. "Take our packs," she says.

Bryce tells us which way to go, and we thread through tables to the restrooms at the back. Even though almost all of the tables are full now, the restroom is empty. But then there are probably five men to every woman in this place. After we do our business, I stand at the sink and throw cold water on my face, trying to feel better. The cold is good and cold, too, but in spite of that it only works a little to wake me up. "We need to eat," I say to the mirror, which shows that I look thin and my hair has gone to rats in the back. I dig out a comb and get to work.

"I want to leave," Monday says. "This isn't our fight."

"We're going to have to take sides." I'm thinking out loud. "I want to. This side." She's looking skeptical so I change the subject. "I want to play with the phones before they run out of battery." We still haven't done what Justice asked and sent messages.

Monday finishes brushing her teeth and puts everything away and settles the pack on her back. "I don't want to get caught here. I want to go back where we were last night."

"Maybe these guys have a better place."

She looks resolute. "Let's not even go back to the table."

I've just filled my chest with enough breath to argue with her when there is shouting and screaming outside the door.

We stare at each other, and the dizziness from the beer makes me hesitate. Then we back into different stalls, standing on toilets, trying not to breathe.

The thin door to the empty stall next to me thuds into the metal wall between the stalls. I try to scrunch so that fingers and feet and everything are invisible. I didn't lock the door. It slams open and then closed again, fast, just missing my nose. I hold completely still, back in rabbit mode, hoping not to be seen.

It works.

Monday's door slams open. She is fierce in her anger. Cussing. I hear her dragged from the stall, her feet bracing and re-bracing as she's pulled out the door. She doesn't say anything about me.

I hop off the toilet seat. I'm standing in the wrong place in my rush to get out and slam the door into my nose, adjust, catch my pack on the door, and then burst with inelegant gasps in the empty bathroom.

Monday' pack is in her stall. I grab it, so I have them both.

I swallow, scared and awake now, my stomach switched from sick to fluttery. I slip through the door.

No one is looking at me.

A big man in green has Monday by the arm. He's strong; he's holding her with just the one hand even though she's struggling.

She catches my eye and waves me back.

I barrel forward instead, head-butting the man. He steps sideways, off balance. Monday jerks away from him.

I toss her the pack and we're running.

We dodge a group of greens. They start yelling. We race through the door, inhale the fresher air of outside.

Hands grab us and throw us onto a truck. Two huge guys, maybe three, positioned outside the door. I land on the same knee and scrape the scab off, drawing out fresh blood. We bump into other people already in the truck, and then more come in behind us. Hands tug on my shoulders and my clothes until I can stand and then we're pushed toward the cab so others can be helped up. It takes a long time. "What's happening?" I ask a woman squished up next to me.

"They're throwing us out." She sounds pissed but not scared.

"Where?"

"Other side of the bridges. It sucks since I gotta be back tomorrow."

"Why?"

She gives me a look that suggests I'm clueless, and then we're separated as the crowd shifts to make room for more people.

One young man jumps off the truck, lands hard, and is boosted back up, favoring his ankle and wincing every time he puts weight on it. This is not a new routine.

The truck is full of whispers and curses but no one yells even though I can smell anger and fear and alcohol. These people are, in this moment, obedient. We act the same.

By the time the truck pulls away it's packed with people. The metal floor rattles and sways under our feet, like being in an earthquake, and we clutch each other to stay balanced while it makes a tight, slow turn. Monday and I stand with our feet wide and our packs around our stomachs so we can keep them safe. The truck reeks of trash and rotting vegetation and diesel, so it's not new, not Post.

I feel like a farm animal. But I cling to the woman's words. We're just being dropped somewhere else. Thrown out. But not hurt.

A splintery wooden fence surrounds the bed. I clutch it and watch us pass the park and then over Burnside and then turn left and then right, back onto the big street. It's still early in the year, so the light is already gold and long shadows fall onto the truck from the big buildings, moving us in and out of light so my eyes hurt and it's hard to focus well.

The beer is sour in my belly and I gulp cold air and try not to puke or fall down.

We rumble past Chinatown.

I get my balance down better and look for people I know. I don't see Bryce or Raj, and I hope they got away. There are probably more than fifty people jammed close in the truck, and I can only make out about twelve faces. Andy is one of them, but he's on the other side of the truck from us and he looks like he's laughing.

Monday's beside me, rustling in her pack. I hope to hell she's not pulling out the gun but of course she is. She tucks it into her jeans so it's against her stomach behind the pack, pulls her shirt over it.

I ask an older man with a missing finger, "Where are we going?"

He shakes his head and says, "It'll be okay." He sounds more scared than his words are.

I'm thirsty and confused.

The truck drives down Burnside and stops at the bridge, waiting. It inches forward and forward, slowly. A thin woman jumps over the cab and gets away, and then a man tries it and he's caught by three greens. They hit him in the face before they throw him back in with us.

Eventually the truck rattles over the Burnside bridge, the water blue and gold and green under us in the early evening sun. It's too bright to look at the city we've just left, so we look east where the sky is still pale blue.

We didn't even manage to stay in Portland for two whole days.

Chapter Fourteen

IT'S TRUE DARK BY THE TIME THE TRUCK STOPS ON THE FAR SIDE OF THE bridge. I want to be out of the crowd of people in the truck, but it's hard to see what's around us. The headlights are still on, and they show only an empty street with no other illumination. A few street lights shine dimly in the distance behind the truck. I look up and spot a few faint stars in a space between clouds. Monday whispers in my ear. "Go straight. Walk fast. We need to get away."

"Okay."

The back gate is lifted off and a man stands at the end of the truck with his hand out taking passes from people as they get off. He is fat and white with a white beard that hangs eight inches long under a wide, mean mouth. I consider lying and telling him I don't have one. But we don't want to be searched. He's big. People behind are pressing on me. I dig into my pocket and give the pass over to him, although I keep the two work chits.

Monday does the same.

He looks hard at us both. "No work chits?"

We earned those. Plus I imagine him finding Monday's gun. "No," and then I stumble over air and fall, drawing his attention to me so Monday can step past him.

Bless her, she understands what I'm doing and takes my arm and helps me up, pulling away from the man.

Something falls, clattering. Surely the gun. My breath catches in my throat and I'm grateful for the dark as Monday scoops it up.

We run.

Heavy footsteps follow us.

I glance backward. The fat man is already slowing. Behind him, people pour out of the truck and scatter. I smile at the idea that they kept their passes.

It doesn't seem smart to slow down. I pull ahead of Monday, grab her hand, and together we pelt down a street with only one street-light and yards and yards of dark. We fetch up against a brick wall, gasping for breath and shaking.

"That wasn't so bad," I say. "We have our stuff."

"We're still in Portland," she says. "This side of the river is Portland, too."

I'm bent over, trying to decide if I'm going to get sick after all. Beer and fear and running are all mixed up in my belly and I'm gasping. "Not. Storm's. Portland."

Monday puts a hand on my shoulder, and it reminds me of how we stood after we threw away the rifle and the broom, only we're reversed. I stand up and take deep breaths until I feel like myself. I try like hell not to look as scared as I feel. The street and buildings near us are all dark and shadowy. I can see people walking; no one is near us.

"This might be worse," Monday whispers.

"The planes land on this side of the river."

"You're obsessed with planes."

"You're obsessed with Powell's." And then I lose my straight face and giggle.

Steps echo behind us, at least three or four people. There aren't as many lights working on this side of the river, just the occasional pool of a streetlight with solar panels on the top. "Maybe we should go back and find the people from the truck."

"Did Bryce and Raj get caught?"

"I didn't see them." She's still whispering and now she's tugging on my sleeve. I follow her. The steps behind us sound closer.

We speed up. After a corner or two, we pause in a circle of brightness from a street light. Monday's face is shiny and she looks stubborn, which I'm learning to interpret as scared. Her eyes are big and dark.

"Can you run?" I whisper.

She answers by taking a longer stride and then another and then we're both running. Whoever is stalking us—it feels like stalkers now no matter who it is—follows.

We run as silently and fast as we can.

There are more lights and more people a few blocks down, and Monday leads us that way. As soon as we're in the crowd, we slow down and try to act like we're in control.

I keep expecting someone to tap me on the back from behind, but no one does.

Following other people leads us down Sandy Boulevard, which has empty tracks and a few more lights than the rest of the area. We walk for an hour or so, and there are people everywhere. I keep thinking we should come out of the crowds and the city but the same scenery goes on and on.

Men whistle at us and Monday whispers, "Ignore them."

"We should find someplace to sleep," I tell her.

"Soon." Monday sounds scared. "I want a place with more people, or less."

There are small crowds all around, four people, five, sometimes ten. A cold wind blows through our clothes, and I'm grateful when we get to a long block that's well lit.

We come to a block where the sidewalks are littered with tables: square and round and plastic and makeshift and fine. On the tables: candles in jars, a few battery-powered lights, live chickens in cages, fruit and vegetables that must have come from greenhouses, people with tiny improvised kitchens selling sausages and salads and homemade beer and filtered water. Used clothes. Used shoes. Used household stuff. Medicine past its sell-by date. People hawking all of it, chattering at us.

Rap blares from boom boxes and country and folk music spills out of real instruments played by shivering people.

I almost trip over a stray poodle with dried mud coating its fur and smart eyes that stare at me for a second and then look away.

I feel dizzy. The lights and the sounds might as well be inside my head trying to get out. I collapse onto a brick planter wall. I can feel all of the blood in my body and every breath I take.

Monday notices almost right away, and turns back and sits beside me.

"I can't do this much more," I tell her. "There's so many people. So much change. I learn one thing and then I need to learn two more."

She puts an arm around me, and I lean into her warmth. "Of course you can," she says. "If I can keep going, you can keep going."

I sit and breathe, in and out, in and out, focusing on that instead of all the sound and chaos. After a while the street stops spinning around me. "I think maybe....maybe I'm not used to so much danger."

"Different to be stuck with it."

"I can't go home from here."

"Sure you can," she's laughing. "Just start walking." Monday knows I won't do this as well as I know I won't. Danger and confusion is better than boredom.

There *are* a lot of people. Too many. Monday and I walk so close to each other we touch from time to time, and her touch is always like a spark to me, something bright and helpful in the middle of so many strangers. Light emanates from some windows, others are boarded up. None look welcoming. We walk a long time, staying in the lighted places, and close to each other.

Eventually the street starts to shut down for the night. Boxes come out. Surprisingly, most of the tables stay where they are, goods tucked under them, people pillowed among the boxes of stuff. Here and there, small bodies lie tucked under blankets. I spot children, two dogs, and once a cat on a leash.

A few trucks come by and pick up boxes of goods, and other are wheeled away on odd-looking trailers that people pull by hand. One whole table folds into a wooden box with wheels that can be pulled down the middle of the street by two bicycles. A thin man and a wide woman pedal hard up the street with chains attached to the table. It looks like it might fall over any moment, but it doesn't. The man is so tiny he has to stand up on the pedals to get any speed at all and his elbows and shoulders protrude from his body. She's stocky; a roll of muscle encased in a roll of fat. She doesn't need to stand up, doesn't really even look like she's working hard.

As the odd contraption makes its way down the street, I sit down in the place where it was.

"Hey," a spindly black man talks to us. "You need to crash there, you can. But you best be gone before Ray and Evie come back." He's pointing a finger at us and waving it as if we're kids. But his voice is kind enough and I'm nauseous and hungry both at once and my legs are out of strength.

"We won't bother you," I tell him. The concrete is hard but anything is better than more walking.

"I haven't seen you before," he says, lifting a silver flask to his lips and taking a long sip. "Where did you come from?"

"Other side of the bridge," Monday spits. "They kicked us out."

He nods. “Refugees from the Storm.”

I laugh, the situation suddenly funny. “Not exactly. We weren’t even there two days.”

“Lucky for you,” he says.

“How so?” Monday asks him.

“Pretty girls like you might have found themselves Storm Troopers.”

“What are Storm Troopers?”

“You’re not from around here.”

I’ve been told that a couple of times today. Maybe I should just wear it on my forehead. “No. We just got here from down south. I’ve never seen this many people in my life.”

“You’re shivering,” he says, and holds the silver flask out. “Have some. It’ll help.”

Monday is already reaching for the flask, which she wipes down with her shirt, and then sniffs at. Whatever she smells, she seems to think it’s all right, and so she takes a big swallow and holds it in her mouth, letting it come down slowly.

I accept the flask from her outstretched hand and sniff. Sour. The smell makes me feel a little sick and my tender stomach gurgles.

“Go on,” Monday says. “Just a little. It will make you warm on the inside.”

I’m dubious. I touch it to my lips and it burns a little.

“More,” she says. “Don’t wimp on it.”

I take a mouthful and I mean to hold it like she did but the whole inside of my mouth fires and I let the drink down my throat and it sits burning in my belly and makes me hot and then just warm. Sour medicine.

It feels good. “Thanks.”

His hand is out and I give him the silver cylinder, thinking I do and don’t want more. “What’s a Storm Trooper?” I repeat.

“Storm’s army of the young. The people he convinces should follow him, the ones too young to remember there was a life where government didn’t tell you when you could piss. He gets adults, too. People will trade their souls for power and water and a warm place to sleep.”

A warm place to sleep sounds good right now.

He takes another sip, much more than I did, and makes a face at it. "But the kids are the saddest. They don't know anything better. He gets some of the ones left behind, kids that come in curious and starved."

He means kids like us, but at least he doesn't say that.

"I'm Two Bit," he says. "'Cause I always got two bits to say. And you're?"

"Sage and Monday," I say.

"An herb and a day." He laughs and drinks more, but doesn't pass the flask around again. "Well, in case you haven't learned yet, don't trust Storm. He says he's going to take care of you, but he really means he's going to give you what he wants you to have, and make you work for it, too. You're better off over here. Keep to this side of the bridge."

Two Bit reaches into a box and pulls out a pillow and three thin blankets. He hands one over to us.

"We have one," I say.

"I expect you need two. Gonna rain, soon anyway. I can feel a storm coming, something that's nasty. The wind has forgotten it's spring."

All I feel is a light breeze. Monday shakes her head at him.

He's stubborn. "I can spare this. You get settled down. You both look like the devil's been chasing you for days."

"Thank you," Monday says. She's comfortable with him. I don't know why, but it makes me relax, too.

She and I sleep with our heads on our packs, cuddled together with her sleeping bag under us and my blanket and Two Bit's blanket on top. It's so comforting to curl up next to her heat that in just moments the world disappears.

The next thing I know, light is kissing my cold eyelids and painting the street bright. Everything looks much dirtier now, and here and there people begin to stir and shake off blankets and grumble. Trash from last night scrapes across the road in a light cold wind. I'd been warm, but even the two blankets isn't enough now.

"Weather's changing," Monday says unnecessarily.

Two Bit is still asleep, so we put his blanket back over him and walk off. A few times we see groups of people that look dangerous enough to avoid, but mostly we just trudge toward the airport. Or at least, I think that's the way we're going. It takes a long time. The sky above us is empty of planes and full of grey clouds, so the only thing I have to go on is my memory of where the planes have been landing. Cold reddens our cheeks and noses and I find paper-thin leaves from last fall to blow my nose on.

We keep each other's spirits up by making up stories about people we pass. This old man used to own a zoo and that young girl is a refugee from China and her brother is the head of a gang and the family that looks lost came from New Orleans and they'll be lost forever.

By noon I spot a plane, by accident, one of the times I'm looking behind me to be sure no one is stalking us. It's above us, flying low. I can hear the wind as it passes, but no engines. We need to go a little more east.

As if the plane were an omen, we come across some people trading coffee they make over a fire on a corner for other food. Monday asks them to sell her a cup. They laugh at the money she offers them but give us each a cup and a long piece of flat bread, which brightens our mood a lot. In fact, Monday is so much more cheerful I resolve to find some coffee and a way to make it, and carry that with us.

We follow another airplane in. It's small; maybe big enough for six people.

We get to where I can see the runways. There's a high chain-link fence all around. Twice, we go through parking lots looking for ways in but we don't find any that look safe. Then Monday spots a thin path behind a building and it leads to a hole in the fence.

We climb through the hole one at a time, pushing our packs through, and walk toward where I saw the plane glide down.

"Hey!" someone yells. A bicycle comes up behind us and a girl our age yells again. "Get off the runway."

I duck and look behind to see a plane coming right toward us.

Oh.

We stay low and race off the runway. The wind of the plane's passing mixes with the cold wind of the coming storm and threatens to rip the hair from my head.

The plane is long and silent and so beautiful it takes my breath away to watch it float in, tipping its nose up a very tiny bit before dropping to look like an elegant insect flying silently over the ground.

The bicyclist rides over by us, fast. Her wheels throw a spray of gravel at our ankles when she pulls into a sharp stop with a little skid. “Hi.” She is a bit breathless. “I’m Tamara. Call me Tam. I saw you in Devil’s. Glad you found us.”

Now I’m confused. I didn’t see her, but then the place was big. “Were you in the truck with us last night?” Monday asks.

Tam shakes her head. Her dark hair is in a tight, black bowl cut and it flies up around her ears. Her eyes are an improbable green and her skin the prettiest pale brown. She could be a mix of three or four races. She looks both sturdy and beautiful. “I never get caught.” She is teasing us, as if we should have known better.

“Hey, that was our first time in Portland.”

“I know,” she says, her expression becoming a bit contrite. “We usually know when they plan to raid. They surprised us.” She is sort of circling us with the bike, one foot dragging on the ground from time to time like a lazy brake.

“So who’s ‘us’?” Monday inquires.

“Why, the people who are going to take back Portland.” Tam exaggerates her words and winks. “Come on,” she says. “I bet you’re hungry.” Then she’s off, heading toward a big building that must be an airplane hangar, even though I’ve never seen one. It’s rectangular and tall and one whole wall is a set of metal rolling doors. Like a garage only on a whole different scale.

We have to jog to keep up. The wind pushes us toward the hangar with cold fingers. There is an incredible amount of space after the cramped truck and the night market, as if everything is empty and cold and full of wind and sun. It feels great to run after Tam, to feel like I’m running toward something instead of away from unknown enemies.

Airplanes line the side of the runway in neat rows. They shudder in the winds and the ropes that hold them sing and snap.

The airport sprawls around us, great big buildings and a tower on the far side of the runways. A few big jets sit forlornly on the far side, wind-blown debris piled against their wheels.

I don’t see anyone else moving in the whole area except Tam and the people climbing out of the small planes that just landed.

This is what I came to Portland for. The planes and the space and the promise of new things.

The airplanes came from somewhere; I want to know where.

A normal-sized door accentuates the height of the hangar doors. Faded blue paint peels from the metal of the walls. Tam holds the door open for us, and we enter.

To my left, two planes are parked at angles, noses toward the roll-up doors. The hangar dwarfs them; these would only seat about four people. They are maybe as tall as me and half of me again. Their wings remind me of birds. They only look a little like the planes in movies. Power tools rumble and sputter and someone gives orders and someone else answers questions.

On my right, the room has been turned into three sections. The closest to the door holds couches and chairs and a makeshift kitchen, with about six people lounging and talking. A row of cots lines the side wall, although no one is sleeping on them at the moment. Low shelves and cubbies behind the cots look like they were scavenged from five different houses. They hold books and personal belongings and potted plants. I spot chives and rosemary and basil, as well as two kinds of cherry tomatoes. Life, exerting itself inside of the sterile building.

A metal fence at the far-end of the hangar protects heavy-duty metal shelves that hold a jumble of cardboard boxes, sheets of metal and tools, and even blankets and cans of food.

The middle of the room appears to be work space, with tables and chairs and computers and posters and people painting more posters and attaching them to sticks. Another group is fussing with electronics, using small desk lights. I spot a few teenagers, and on the side of the table furthest away from us, a man who circles the workers in a wheelchair. He's moving fast, and occasionally I hear him give an order.

Tam is leading us there, and before we even get close Andy is up and heading toward us from an angle, cutting us off. "Monday, Sage. Glad you found us."

We hadn't been looking for them. "Thanks."

"You took off pretty fast after the drop."

I translate this as we ran away from the truck.

Monday says, "So."

Andy nods at Tam, dismissing her, and she gives him a pouty look but obeys. “So we were worried about you.” He leads us to an old brown leather couch that is nearly as comfortable as a bed. “Soup?”

“Yes.” Soon I’m holding a coffee mug of something that turns out to be potato soup with enough spices that it clears my sinuses just to smell it. Andy was worried about us. I like that.

A gust of wind rattles the metal walls but it feels safe and warm here on the couch. Andy smiles at the sound. “We’ve been waiting for a storm. That makes this our night.”

“Why?” Monday asks him.

“We want the city focused on something else while we go in.”

Clearly I should know what he’s talking about, so I nod and keep working on my soup. Andy’s attention is drawn by someone in the work area waving him over. Even though I don’t understand what’s going on, we’re warm and safe, and from the sound of the wind rising outside, this is a good thing. It’s cold enough we need our coats on, but we’re okay that way, almost comfortable.

At most, there are fifty people in the hangar. It’s hard to imagine how such a small group plans to unseat the greens. I want to walk over and look at the planes, but I’d have to cross a lot of empty space, and I’m not sure what the rules are here yet.

Monday and I both jump as staccato sounds slam us, something sharp smashing the walls. The first thing I think is that bullets are slamming into the side of the building. We look at each other. “Hail,” she says.

A loud crash and scrape announces that the wind has eaten something.

Chapter Fifteen

A GUST LIFTS A CORNER OF THE METAL ROOF OF THE HANGAR, BANGING IT back down, then does it again. Wind pounds the metal walls, the rush even louder than the voices of the people gathering at the door with ropes in hand.

One woman screams and everyone looks up.

Wind and cold air howl down inside the building from under the roof, cold eddies finding us and lifting our hair. The roof section falls back down and the wind stills.

Monday and I glance at each other, deciding without needing words. We leap up and follow the people out of the door.

Outside, the wind is a force with a cold bite. It tastes of rain. Our clothes and hair ripple. Gusts make me feel light. We lean into the storm and follow the people down to the airplanes just as big fat drops of rain start to stain the wind.

The planes are tied down with three ropes each, except one that has broken two of the lines and flipped so it's scudding on the top of its wings like an upside-down bug and pulling at the one remaining line. I doubt it will ever fly again, but half of the group ties the carcass tighter anyway.

A tall, thin woman pulls me and Monday over to one of the planes that's straining against its tie downs. "Help me out?"

She shows us how to thread the ends of the ropes through metal clips on the plane. There is already one rope there, so we have to force additional line through the eyebolt. While we're doing that she says something to us but the wind steals her words.

"What?" I yell.

"Thanks, I'm Alex."

"Sage!" I can't tell if she can hear me. She steps away and lashes the lines to metal circles set into the concrete. While she's tying, we lean into the ropes, making sure they're taut. I can feel them digging into me, twisting as the wind grabs and pulls at us.

The plane is small and soft, with rounded windows. I try to notice details in spite of the wind and the attention I need to pay to the ropes. I touch the plane every chance I get, as if it is a talisman. It does not feel like I thought it would; it feels heavy. Not at all like a bird. I expected the propellers in the front to be sharp and wicked, like knives. Instead, they're sweeping ovals with twists, so smooth I almost don't believe they're real.

The plane quivers in the wind as if alive. When we're done, Alex has us move with her to another one. While the three of us are repeating our actions, the wind plays this airplane's glassy surfaces like some kind of eerie instrument; the high-pitched thrum echoes in my bones.

Returning to the hangar, the wind blows hollows in our cheeks and pounds our chests so that walking is an exaggerated, slow-motion exercise. It blows my nose and ears freezing and once in a while it switches direction enough to slap hair into my slitted eyes.

"Where are you from, Alex?" I yell into the wind.

"Spokane."

I want to know. "Did you come in on a plane?"

She nods.

"Why?" Monday asks her.

"Reporter. I'm gathering news to take back."

I want to beg her to take me flying, but we reach the hanger in the midst of another group and after we struggle in and get the door closed, Alex thanks us and disappears into a crowd.

We can't have been outside more than an hour, but two big trucks have arrived and been parked in the lee of the hanger. Inside, there are at least twenty or thirty more people. Signs with various anti-green and anti-Storm slogans are being carried into the trucks and the whole hangar smells like soup and coffee. Cell phones and hand radios are all around, so common every third or fourth person seems to have one. There is a background buzz of people speaking slowly into them.

Someone grabs my shoulder from behind and spins me. Bryce. "We found you."

I stare at him. Pleased. I look around for Raj, spot him coming up from behind Bryce, grinning.

"What are you doing here?" Monday says over my shoulder.

"This is it." Raj is grinning like he just got a present. "We're going to take out Storm as soon as the wind dies. There's been protests for days, and now we're going to show that we mean it. They won't be guarding the bridges in the aftermath of this wind; they'll have to clean up snapped trees and unblock streets and stuff like that."

Monday is leading us back to the couch where our stuff is, and she's got a bit of challenge in her voice. "How are you going to take him out and who's going to replace him?"

No one answers her, although Bryce scowls.

"So you didn't get caught in the bar?" I ask, trying to lighten the conversation.

Raj has the good grace to blush. "No."

Bryce adds, "But you would have got away with us if you hadn't been in the bathroom."

A door bangs open, letting in a gust of cold air that draws goose bumps on my arms. Two people have to lean into the door to force it closed.

"Come on." Raj tugs on my arm. "Meet Bryce's dad." He's carrying a big secret that he's proud of, although Bryce looks away.

They lead us to the man in the wheelchair. Bryce stands awkwardly and gestures between us. "Sage and Monday, this is my father, Kevin Lord."

"Mr. Lord."

He ignores my outstretched hand. "Kevin."

The man on the flier we saw in the window, the one who had been standing next to Justice. Only he was walking in that picture. His limbs are pretty normal looking, and he's strong with wide shoulders and a tiny flat stomach. His feet are big. He nods, "Glad you could join us."

I want to ask him about Justice, except Robyn told me not to tell anyone we know them.

My first impression of Kevin is that if he didn't have the wheelchair he'd be like a cross between Justice and Oskar. Maybe he is anyway. I take his hand. "Nice to meet you." Kevin smiles, his teeth white and even and his eyes a bright blue that exudes friendship. "Bryce—why don't you and Raj go help Sal and Tim load the second truck?"

I know an order when I hear it. Bryce looks disappointed, but he's obedient, just like Tam was earlier. He and Raj leave.

When I turn back to Kevin after watching those two walk away, I don't like the look on Kevin's face. I have the distinct impression he's not happy we're here. But a glance at the airplanes inside the hangar reminds me why I'm here. I'm going to stay until I learn more about them. Somehow.

"Nice to meet you," I say sweetly, wanting to get back to our packs since the hangar has become so crowded. We should have grabbed them before we followed Raj and Bryce here.

"Tell me why you came here?" Kevin asks. He keeps me in front of him with a look even though he's in a wheelchair. "Bryce said you came from California."

I don't say anything, and neither does Monday. It's not like either of us is going to tell him where we really come from. There are enough people in this one hangar to swarm the garden or Just Robyn. If he knows anything about California he can trip me up fast, so I say, "We live in another part of Oregon. We came in for news and supplies. I didn't know about Storm or your plans or anything like that."

Kevin shakes his head. "California is one lie. I don't want to hear any more or we'll be sure you leave us."

Monday breaks in. "We're just protecting our own. You would lie to protect yours. We mean you no harm."

He acknowledges her position as understandable with a nod. "We can always use people to help us."

"So tell us what to do," I say. "We'll help."

"Why should I trust you?" he asks.

"Or we you?" Monday retorts.

They glare at each other, Monday looking down at him because of the wheelchair, but not very much. Kevin must be taller than six feet standing.

"We're here," I tell him. "With you. We just helped you tie down your planes. We'll help you empty the trash, if you want. Whatever." A gust of wind accentuates my next words. "We're glad to be someplace warm."

I feel someone behind us before I turn and see a tall, rangy man with a baseball cap pulled low over thinning hair. He's holding up my backpack. "They have six phones. Two have a little charge."

Monday bares her teeth and grabs for him. "Don't touch our things."

There are five men around us. Monday and I are crowded next to each other. "I think you better follow me," Kevin says, wheeling toward the couch we'd left our stuff on.

We follow. There's too many people to run away from, and besides, I haven't done anything wrong and outside it's all wind and rain and dark.

Our backpacks have been gone through. My knife and all of the other phones and chargers are in a pile on a little table. They even have our clothes in a pile, underwear on top.

Monday's face is shifting between red and pale, and she looks like she wants to hurt someone and like she wants to run.

Kevin tells us to sit on the couch and we obey. He can look at us at eye level now, or maybe he's even a little taller. "Why are you carrying so many phones here?"

"You have no right to right to search our stuff," Monday asserts, her arms crossed.

I feel like a kid brought in front of the Board at the garden, small and angry. "There are phones all over this hanger," I point out. In fact, I can see three or four people talking on them, and two more staring down at them, reading things from the screens.

"I know those people. I know everyone who knows about this hangar. Except you two. I can't have any spies telling Storm what we're about to do."

"I have no idea what you're about to do," I counter.

The tall man is staring down at the phones we have, punching buttons. At least somebody knows how to use them. I wish I'd found time to sit and play with mine. Maybe then I'd know what he's looking at.

Kevin sighs. "We're in a fight here. For Portland."

The man with the phones looks up. "One of the home accounts for PDXNET on this phone is JustinTime2."

Monday narrows her eyes and Kevin's get bigger. He wheels over to the thin man and holds out his hand. "Give me that, Clell." Monday's phone is dropped into his palm. He pokes at it, his fingers fast and precise even though the phone looks small in his hands.

He addresses Clell, who's now swiping his fingers expertly over my phone. "The account hasn't been used from this phone in months."

A grunt. "JustinTime1 posted a few months ago. Relaying information from Seattle and Chicago. Sat news we already had." Clell squints. "This one has the default account set to "SignsofSpring 2."

Clell has figured out more about these phones in two minutes than we did in half an hour.

Kevin has gone thoughtful. "Who did you steal these from?"

Monday has every limb crossed and her mouth is a thin line. "Someone gave them to us. To stay safe with."

"Six of them?"

"So we have spares," she says.

"You haven't used them much," Clell says.

"We haven't exactly had time. Ever since we left home we've been chased or walking or bundled up in a cold, crowded truck and dumped out just over a bridge." I hear my words coming out like the wind outside, fast and tumbling on each other, carrying my anger at them for going through our things, but also some of the weight of the whole journey. "There isn't exactly a lot of power outside of the city. The first time I ever saw Portland was two nights ago—from the overlook where we met Bryce and Raj."

Kevin is holding up a hand. "All right. So you're new in town. You didn't know we have a war on. You just happened to meet my son and his friend and decided to join our side."

The way he's saying it sounds silly. "I saw the planes and I wanted to follow them." It sounds weak even if it's true. "Besides, we didn't 'decide' anything. We followed the planes. I hoped they meant peace and science and good news about the world."

Monday adds, "And maybe that they meant a place where we'd be safe. Not have our shit searched."

I give her a look. This is not the moment to use words like that.

Kevin seems amused now. "And you're carrying around the phone of one of our leaders."

I chew at my lip, hoping we'll learn something. After all, we already know he knows Justice. From the flier.

Clell chimes in. “Ex-leaders. A guy we haven’t seen in person for three years and haven’t talked to in any way for one year. I was beginning to wonder if he was dead.”

I glance at Monday and she’s gone quiet and inward.

“Who is JustinTime to you?” he asks.

Monday shrugs. “A friend gave us those phones and said they might work in Portland.”

“What friend?”

She stares at him, her mouth shut.

I keep mine shut, too. She’s clearly decided to keep what she knows about Justice secret, and it’s her choice. I’ll go along.

If he could, I’m sure Kevin would stand up and loom over us. We tell them we don’t know who SignsofSpring is either. The names have to mean Justice and Robyn. Instinct tells me they and Kevin would be on the same side. But they told us not to mention them, and I’m not going to, not unless Monday does.

Kevin and Clell keep asking us questions we don’t know the answers to. They’re polite but firm, and they eventually stop poking at our phones. The tall guy goes to stick mine in his pocket and I get really mad. We’re trying to help these people, or at least we were. “Those are ours.”

“They’re almost out of power,” he says.

“Which we paid for.” I’m not about to lose those phones. “You don’t have any right to steal them from us.”

Kevin says, “We’ll give them back after tonight.”

“Look.” I close my eyes, take a deep breath, open them again. “We don’t own them. They were loaned to us.”

Monday adds, “We can’t use them against you with no power anyway.”

Clell hesitates and glances at Kevin.

I say, “Please.”

Both phones get dropped into my hands.

A small, round woman with grey hair and a limp waddles up and talks to Kevin in a low voice. He nods at her and says, “Give me a minute.” He looks at us for a long time, keeping us pinned on the couch. “I don’t know what to think about you two. I don’t know if my son found people that can help us, or if you’re spies, or if he just found two lost little girls. I don’t know how you’re related to the last people who used those phones. And I don't like it that you won't tell me."

We sit still and don't tell him anything.

He looks hard, determined. "Because I don't know, I've got to protect us. I'm not going to hurt you. Just sit here, quiet. Don't use any power. Don't use any phones: yours or ours. Help yourselves to food and to sleep, but we'd prefer you not leave us tonight."

He rolls away, his upper arms pumping his wheels fast enough that his followers have to take long strides to keep after him.

Chapter Sixteen

One of the men who had been watching Kevin grill us stays behind. He's an older man and we could overpower him if we wanted to. He doesn't look tough at all. He's got a bit of a baby-face in spite of a lean body, and his brown hair is touched with grey. His eyes are soft and he looks sorry for us, and maybe just sorry period.

I scoop my stuff back into my pack, pleased that nothing is missing. I'm happier as soon as my underwear isn't lying out for people to see. Not that anyone has looked. But still. As Monday finishes carefully repacking her own gear, I mouth a one-word question. "Gun?"

She nods. I laugh then, realizing she's been sitting a little forward during the whole awkward interview and that she could have shot them and didn't. It's good to figure out that she's not crazy enough to use the gun to solve problems it won't solve.

Monday and I spend an hour making up stories about what might be happening here. The rain and wind continue, the wind occasionally whistling through cracks in the hangar, banging metal against metal.

We see Bryce and Raj once. They wave at us, and we wave back, but they're on a mission and we're not allowed to move. Being stuck makes me chafe, but I can see it's getting to Monday more. She doesn't watch the movement in the hangar, she glares at it. I'm sure that it's only the wicked wind and rain outside that keeps her in here.

The man who was watching us is further away now, getting himself a cup of hot tea. I say, "That has to be Justice and Robyn. The names they mentioned."

"Of course." Monday answers.

"Do you know why Justice left here?"

"I didn't know he was ever here." She shakes her head, looking a little pissed, like a person left out of a secret. "I've never seen them leave Just Robyn."

"How long were you there?"

She's frowning. "Over a year."

"Do you know how old the town is?"

"No."

None of the buildings had looked any older than a few years. It all kinda fits. We'd been locked in the garden for fourteen years. Most of my life. Clearly, most people have been doing more than us all that time. The world outside—or at least Portland—is a lot more recovered than I'd expected. And the planes are a miracle.

It's more than the airplanes, too. Sure, there's only a few stores, and there's only a few cars, but I don't think Kelley thought there'd be any. But Justice knew. He was here. I glance over at our keeper, but he's in conversation with a younger man, and only watching us a little. Monday is picking at her nails, so I tap her knee to get her attention. "Do you think Justice sent us because he didn't want to see these people?"

She gets really quiet and tense and kicks one foot up and down. "He told me he sent me so I could get better." She fidgets on the couch, looks around, and then looks back at me. "I don't think they'd take me back."

"Ever?"

She shrugs. "He told me I get too angry, that I'm a danger to myself and I have to fix that. He told me warriors heal themselves, but I *was* getting better. Really. Just being there. I hate him for kicking me out."

"You don't hate him."

She purses her lips. "Him or me or Robyn. Maybe I hate all of us."

Something happened there. I remember how hard Monday clutched Justice when we left. I push her. "What did you do?"

Her face tightens. "They caught the man who raped me."

She told me she killed him earlier. "You killed him in Just Robyn? In town?"

She sniffs and gives a little nod. "It made me crazy for a little while."

I hold her hand for a few minutes, squeeze it. I'm a little mad at Justice, too. Except I saw how much he loved her. It makes me think of Kelley helping me leave.

Her eyes are shining with tears, and I don't want her to lose it here. We're being watched. I want to hold her, but that's probably not a good idea either, so I change the subject. "I think these are good people. I think they're trying to make Portland better."

"We're trapped."

The guy who was watching us comes back with two pieces of bread and a hunk of cheese. He looks almost apologetic as he hands them to us. He shouldn't feel that way; any food is fabulous. Mine is gone fast. He stays near us then, and so I start asking him questions. "What's your name?"

"Jim."

"Hi Jim, I'm Sage."

"That's a pretty name."

Monday takes out her book and makes a point of ignoring us. Her hands are still shaking a little from whatever she is remembering.

"What can you tell me about the airplanes?"

He glances over at them. "Not much. They make them in Boise, Idaho. There's a plant there that was built Before, runs on all solar and makes solar planes. They're doing okay. Guy that owns the planes thinks he's a newsman."

"A what?"

"Thinks he can fix the world if he knows enough, I guess. He wants to hook people who know stuff up with other people who know stuff."

"That sounds like a great idea." I want to fly in one even more if it can help the world.

"We gotta fix our own problems." He's shutting the topic down. "We have all the intelligence we need here." He looks around at the busy warehouse as if that makes his point. I'm pretty sure he'd rather be doing something besides watching us. Maybe if I change the topic. "How long have you been in Portland?"

He looks wary, but he answers. "A long time. We moved here Before. My dad brought us all from Spokane when I was fourteen. I loved it from the time I saw it."

He must be forty now. "So you were here during the quakes?"

He nods. "I was married. We had a baby." His voice is thick. "Candy and Alicia were in California when the first quake hit, and they died. They were in one of the buildings that came down, at a doctor's." His eyes are all wet. "The baby had a cold."

"I'm sorry." I don't know what else to say. He's blinking his eyes, as if it were yesterday and not years ago. "Portland was still all right then, wasn't it?"

"Mostly." He has wide brown eyes, and even though he's guarding us, he reminds me of a prey animal, maybe a deer. "I worked for a company that built office buildings. So I lost my job early. There weren't any other jobs, but I didn't have anywhere to go so I stayed. After...after the quakes here and the way so many people died of the Tunisian Flu, after all that, I wandered around lost for a few years. Then Kevin found me."

"He helped you?"

"He gave me work in trade for food and a place in one of the tent cities. He's good," Jim says. "I know you probably don't think we're treating you right, but this is a new world. We have to do what's for the greater good."

Since mistrusting me is apparently for the greater good, I don't have anything to say to that. "What was it like in the quakes? I was so little I don't remember much of anything except my dad being scared."

"Where's your dad now?"

"Dead."

He doesn't ask how, so I don't tell him that he died of sickness. It doesn't matter anyway. What does matter is that Jim looks at me different now, like both of us having lost our family makes a bond between us.

"I'm sorry." That's all he says, although he seems to be sad. A muscle along his jawline twitches. He picks up a book and leans back and flips pages.

Monday is still reading, and it seems like she has gone to a different place.

Maybe they're smart. They're escaping while there's nothing else to do. There is a pile of books on the table. One is about Ghandi. Oskar has talked about him, and I leaf through the books and look at pictures of a thin East Indian man in a white loincloth. He doesn't look at all like I imagined him. He looks small and weak, even though he freed a whole country. I pick up another book that looks pretty well-thumbed and has a coffee stain on the front cover. It's titled "From Dictatorship to Democracy."

Jim notices and says, "That one's almost our bible. It's what we make choices by."

I sit down to read it. Right in the front I see a dedication from the freedom fighters in Egypt. Jim sees what I'm looking at and he says, "These things happened Before. Not here. Not in America. But in some places. This book helped people win in the Arab Spring. For a while."

I start reading. The book loses me pretty fast, so I pull out the fliers I had folded into my pocket from the bar and read those. They talk about people dying, about fighting, about a future. They have all of the passion I felt in the bar, that I feel all around me here. They make me want to be on the same side as these people even though we're kind of prisoners. I'm sure this is the side Justice would be on if he were here, maybe that he was on. I wish I knew that history, but I can't ask so I settle for studying Jim's face. He looks so tired and so kind and so sad I wish there was a way for me to help him.

A bigger burst of wind than the one that turned over the plane rattles the walls so loud we all jump. Cold air finds some new holes in the roof, whooshing down from above us and blowing my hair. The lights flicker three times and then go out.

At first everything is dark. I can hear Jim's breathing and people moving around. Then, one at a time, bits of light bloom in the darkness. Flashlights and candles and the light from cell phones bob around the hangar in multiple directions. None of the lights are bright and from time to time an eddy of wind blows a candle out. I can barely see the faces of people carrying them.

The wind sounds louder in the dark. I use Being Now to detect the difference between Monday's breathing which is deep and slow, and Jim's which has a little rattle. My own breathing is fast and shallow, and I slow it down. I can tell which direction footsteps are going in and out of the hangar, hear the quiet scrape of the door that's in the lee of the wind and is the only one people are using right now.

There is order in the way people move, and calm in the few voices that speak louder than whispers. They have a mission and the loss of power barely slows them down.

The wind smells of the city—it's dirtier than our wind near the garden, and wetter. Conversations carry and echo, but individual words refuse to separate. Frustration at being trapped derails me and I start Being Now again, lose it again.

To my surprise, I doze for a while.

I wake when the lights flash back on. Monday hisses, "Sage. Sage. Get up."

I struggle to sit up, so disoriented it takes a moment to remember where we are. I must have slept a while, maybe hours. The hangar around us is almost empty now. Footsteps draw my attention. Raj and Bryce are pelting toward us. Bryce takes my arm, whispering, "I'm so sorry. They sent us on a run for supplies, and we didn't get back until just before the lights went out. My dad told me what he did to you. Bastard was proud of himself. You're not spies. Come on, before you miss it."

I glance at Monday and grin. No point in getting left in an empty building.

Jim glares at Bryce. "You shouldn't."

Interesting. Not, "You can't."

Bryce ranks Jim. More to the point, Bryce ignores him. Monday ignores him, too, but I give him a smile and say, "Thanks for the sandwich." It doesn't seem to make him feel better, but apparently he's philosophical. He follows us out the door.

There's a white truck backed up close by with a big open back door and the engine running.

The cold bite has turned merely cool and the wind is a soft sough that no longer rattles metal on metal. The sky to the east is greying awake and three high clouds have orange underbellies. Most of the airport is dark and quiet, as if exhausted by the storm.

At least the truck isn't an open-bed truck with stakes, but still I stand there and laugh. Monday doesn't get it, since she looks at me like I might be losing it, but I think it's hysterical. We're going back into Portland the same way we came out. This truck is taller and was probably meant to be a long-hauling truck. It smells like cardboard and oil and some kind of fruit that rotted so long ago the smell is almost a sour ghost. Benches and seat belts line both sides of the inside of the back part. I end up between Raj and Bryce near the cab. Monday is on Raj's other side.

"Does your dad know we're coming?" I ask Bryce.

He shakes his head. "He's an asshole."

Dangerous ground, here. "He wasn't mean. Just firm."

Monday snorts.

"Right," he agrees more with Monday. He had looked so proud of his dad when he introduced us. Maybe every kid has challenges with authority.

A single dull bulb inside the windowless truck creates a dusky light. Signs and boxes lie in careful piles in the middle of the truck, tied down with bungees attached to metal hooks. A shelf above the cab has been stuffed with more signs. People sit along both sides. About half the room on the bench is taken now. "So what are we doing?" Monday asks. "I mean, I'm glad to be along for the ride, but I'd sure like to know if I'm riding into Hell."

"We're massing."

Right. Bryce must have been able to tell from the blank look on my face that I don't have a clue what he means. He adds, "That's a big demonstration designed to shut the city down. It gets Storm's goons out there and his people will hurt our people and we'll get pictures and broadcast them."

Monday leans forward, looking interested.

The idea makes me a little lightheaded. It must be dangerous. Everything is dangerous out here, and being afraid is what I fled from. I swallow deeply and make myself sit up straight and go back to the planes. "What about the reporters?"

"They're here to witness. They take our stories away, and they post them while they can. They have better equipment than most of us, and satellite phones, and they send stories up and out to the major cities."

"Why outsiders?" Monday asks. "The Internet works here, right? Can't they get the stories from us?"

"It's okay on Storm's side of the river. Off and on," Bryce says. "Mostly on."

Raj elaborates, his small, animated hands drawing circles and lines in the near-dark of the windowless truck. "Think of it as an island of mostly okay connectivity. Inside the network here, you can get all kinds of traffic around. Talk to anybody in Portland using PDXNET. Most of the time." He points to a box full of black boxes and antennae and wires. "We keep it going, not Storm. So we can talk to each other."

“That was the electronics on the bench?” I ask him.

Yes.” He gestures with his hands. “But the point-to-point connections—like between cities—are broken or monitored or metered or hacked. I mean, sure, sometimes shit gets through. But you can’t count on it.”

I like how he’s always willing to explain things, and the way he’s always got good energy. Bryce is reserved, steady, except maybe about his dad. Raj is always busy, always happy. Cute.

The truck is full now, and the back door is closed. The latch makes a metallic click as it closes in place. I wish we were in the stake-bed truck after all. It feels like there’s no air in here, like I can barely breathe.

When it pulls away we all lean a bit and then find our balance, legs working to keep our backs against the truck walls. There’s no real engine sound. “It’s electric,” Bryce tells us even though we didn’t ask. He looks really proud of that.

I smile at him and then ask Raj, “So the people from different places take the story back to the networks in their towns?”

“Yeah. That’s why the small planes.”

“Who pays for them?” Monday asks.

“Some rich guy. I don’t know who.”

“So these people just fly around and find stories?”

“When they come, we learn more about what’s going on other places, too. Boston and what’s left of New York and DC are all still run by the old government, but more military. Chicago is run by the mob, but Kevin says it was always run by the mob. The Canadians are doing fine; they all help each other and have great big co-ops. That’s what Kevin wants for Portland.”

I don’t remember Kevin letting anyone else have any say in his decisions, but I decide to watch a while.

Monday interrupts. “Tell us more about the massing.”

Raj nods and his voice firms. “We don’t hurt anyone. That’s rule one. Don’t hurt anyone. Ever.”

He sounds like he’s talking to a six-year-old. It’s a little grating since I don’t want to hurt anyone.

“Even if someone tries to beat you up, don’t hurt them. You can run away, or you can defend yourself.”

“I get it,” I tell him.

Monday listens but stays quiet. Her expression is guarded and I suspect she's going to want to slip away from these people as soon as we get out of the truck. Which will leave us in Portland without passes.

Raj is still going on about rules. "If you get beat up, and you're okay, find a camera. Or use the cameras in your cell phones."

Monday frowns. "We don't have any battery."

"Well, I have a camera. Stick with me, then."

This sounds so crazy I don't promise Raj anything. I can't tell how dangerous this is, but my stomach feels light and I'm a little dizzy. The air in the truck smells worse as time goes on, and I wish I could see out and tell where we are. The truck slows, but doesn't stop, and it feels like we are only going a few inches at a time, lurching. There is a noise like chanting and maybe singing outside, but I can't separate individual words from chaos.

Chapter Seventeen

THE TRUCK DOOR OPENS, SPILLING LIGHT AND SOUND AND GLORIOUS fresh air in to displace the stale, sweaty air in the back of the truck. The other riders perk up and slap each other's hands. "Go get them," Bryce says, "This is our day!" He looks proud and happy, and a bit anxious.

"This is our day!" the others call back to him.

Raj bounces on his seat as we all wait for the people nearest the back of the truck to get off. They start climbing out and the people in the middle hand signs and boxes down to them.

The nuances of people's voices vary widely. Anger and anxiety, elation and weariness. "No! No! Storm must Go!" contrasts with a group of people singing a song about letting the sun shine. There's some yelling but it's not close and I can't make out the words.

We wait for the people nearest the door to climb out, and then a hand helps Monday through the big door. Monday is the first of us outside of the truck. I climb down next to her. The rising sun limns the buildings closest to us in haloes of light. The sky is nearly cloudless and there's almost no wind left. Except for the destruction, the giant storm might have simply never happened. Nearby, two large trees have fallen, the root balls sticking up in tangled webs with mud clinging to them. Shards of glass litter the streets.

Someone tries to hand a sign to Monday and she refuses to take it. Raj takes the same sign and hands it to me. It has blue words painted on material and sewn onto a metal square with a wooden handle. "Free Portland."

I'm a little torn, since Monday refused to take the sign, but Raj's look is so expectant that I can't disappoint him. It's lighter than I expected but it occupies at least one hand all the time.

Raj takes his own sign, but Bryce is like Monday and keeps both hands free.

Around us it's noisy and crowded. Light touches puddles and the grass we're walking on is so boggy it's like walking on a sponge.

We're near the same park we passed on the way to the bookstore. We're not close enough to Burnside to tell if the street is blocked, but the two thinner streets that border the park are choked with people.

We walk, keeping on the edge of the swelling crowd. We pass a girl handing out scratched plastic bottles filled with water. Bryce takes one for each of us. The girl with the water looks like she's handing it to a god. Now both of my hands are full. Monday hisses at me. "Give the sign to someone else."

I hold it out to Bryce, and he takes it and passes it over his head to someone pressing into the crowd we're edging. They call out "Thanks," with a big grin.

Bryce starts talking to the air and I'm a bit confused until I realize he's using an earbud and a phone I can't see. I imagine he's talking to his dad.

I almost trip over a man sitting on a blanket filled with spoons and forks bent in funny ways to make jewelry. Bryce steadies me with one hand and talks loud enough for all four of us to hear. "Over thirty thousand now, and getting bigger. There's a riot squad marching down Burnside. No injuries yet."

Raj looks that direction, the look so longing I think he wants to run toward whatever a riot squad is.

"The streets around City Hall are blocked and they're not letting anyone near there. A broken water main in the Pearl district is flooding Quimby. A bunch of trees are down."

"This is why you were waiting for a storm?"

"If they ignore the water main and the trees it'll make the people that support Storm mad at him."

Monday says, "Won't that just make them mad at you?"

"We didn't make the wind or the rain." He smiles. "Revolution is messy." A minute later, like an afterthought, "It's handy for us to have the street blocked anyway."

So non-violence only means directly to people. I need to think about that; Oskar and Kelley always mourned destruction. Of anything.

The crowd thickens around us, presses. Bryce carves a path, using his voice and his body and what I can only describe as a sense of presence to get us through.

We pass a circle of singing monks. Each one wears a brown robe with yellow or orange or silver tied around their waists. Their heads are bare and they're chanting low, the sound seeming to come from their feet. They stand in a circle holding hands, looking across at each other. When protestors jostle them, they stand firm, maintaining a bit of openness, a bit of green grass. A few have tears in their eyes.

I've met them before on the road—not necessarily these particular ones. On the interstate they were in a band of about twenty, walking in a half-circle, chanting a round so magical that I followed them for most of an afternoon just to hear it. This group sounds as good; their voices blend like eagle-flight one moment and butterflies in a field the next.

Bryce pushes us past them.

I want to stop and listen.

I'm willing to bet they would be standing in the same spot chanting whether there was a protest going on or not.

Raj tugs on my arm. "Don't get lost."

We get near the end of the park where stair-stepped seats rise from near the ground to pretty high. An American flag flies from each corner, faded but whole. A plain blue flag flies between them, almost the color of the paint on the sign I gave away. The material is new and it snaps a bit in the wind.

The seats are filling up, and people in blue vests are choosing who gets to go up and who doesn't. Blue seems to be a color that fights the green, although it's not as consistent. I look around for Kevin but I don't see him. Jim—our watcher from last night—is there in a dirty yellow vest. He looks happy to hand us both up the stairs, like now he's done his job and we're contained again.

In spite of that, I like him. I tell him thank you, and he looks surprised, and smiles before he reaches for the next hand in line. For just a moment, I feel bonded to him again. Two people without any family.

At least I have Monday, who is watching to be sure I get up safely and has saved room for us to sit together. Raj goes with us but Bryce stays near the bottom. He stands with his head bowed, one hand over the ear with the speaker in it.

"What happens now?" I ask.

"Bryce will talk to people, tell them what's going on."

"So, like he's a mouth for his father?" Monday asks.

Raj stiffens but he says, "More like a speaker for Free Portland."

From up here there are heads and signs bobbing as far as I can see in front of me, and the noise is a blur. It's almost as much like insects as people. "Did Kevin organize this whole thing?"

"Kevin and a few others." Raj waves a hand expansively across the crowded streets. "There's more than just Free Portland, too. There's really a bunch of groups that don't all agree with each other, except they all want Storm out of here. Everybody has lost people."

Monday's eyes narrow. "Lost people?"

Raj swallows. "People disappear. If they fight Storm too hard. Or if they get effective. That's why Kevin never comes to this side any more unless he's in a big group."

"Where do people disappear to?" I have to speak louder since the noise of so many people crowds out my own voice.

"Mostly they just kick people out, like they kicked you out. But the people who really threaten them? There's jail, there's the river, god knows what else."

He's telling me people get killed. I remember the woman in purple they found in the river. And that we're here with no passes. "Tell me about the other groups? Besides Free Portland?"

"There's Sunshine Now—they want to ban all technology. They say that's why the world fell apart. There's a group that thinks we need more tech—Geeks for Good. The Libertarians want no government. I guess that makes us the moderates."

"So what do you want?" Monday challenges him.

"Good government. Order. To rebuild." He's kind of babbling, and I squeeze his hand to calm him. "To get rid of fear." He squeezes back, but then pulls his hand away.

I wish he had left it; it was warm and I liked how it felt in mine. "Does everyone want you to win?"

"No." He points to his left and after looking closely I see that there is a knot of people in green with green words on the signs. I can only read one of the signs, and it says, "Peace through Order."

"That's not very many people." Monday is looking around, squinting, as if she's trying to see as far as she can. "We could take them," she says calmly.

"No." He reaches for her but she leans away. "These are sympathizers. Not Storm's real power, not the ones who work *for* him." He points past everything we see. "All around the outside, there are greens. Storm troopers. That's what he calls them, as if they were from Star Wars. But we're winning. If Storm has any sense he'll step down."

"Why doesn't he?"

"He's afraid of what we'll do to him."

"What will you do?" Monday asks.

Raj shakes his head. "I don't know. I guess put him in jail."

Monday frowns and I remember that she has killed two men. At least two men.

The bleachers fill in front of us and it feels almost like being stuck in the truck. So many people. My backpack straps cut into my shoulders but I'm afraid to take it off. If anything gets stolen here it could be gone forever in a breath.

I spot Alex on the far side of the top of the bleachers, the same level we're on, but not close enough talk to. I catch her attention with a wave. She hesitates a second, then smiles and returns the wave with her free hand. The other one is full of camera. She snaps a photo of us and then turns her attention back to the stage.

I'm jealous of her.

I would like a life that is all about gathering information. Except maybe it's lonely. Which is not that different from me. I don't know that this fight of Raj's and Kevin's is mine, but I don't belong in the garden anymore.

Maybe I'd be the perfect reporter. If it means flying on planes, seeing where else they go, I'm good with it.

Raj is between me and Monday, looking right and left like a small excited bird. He loves this.

Bryce does, too, but he's more controlled, although right now he's pacing on the stage.

A tall woman who's maybe twenty-five with long blonde hair stands up and takes the microphone. She starts singing, and I poke Monday. "That's the girl from the lookout. The night we got here." She's singing 'The Star Spangled Banner'. The Board plays it at meetings once a month; they have three versions they rotate through with different singers. Both Raj and the man on my other side start singing and so I do, too. By the second verse, the people in the bleachers and a lot of the others around them have started singing. Everything feels together now instead of fractured like it felt a few minutes ago. I feel connected to the protesters for the first time.

Maybe there is some good in crowds.

The singing fades away, and then the woman says, "Good morning."

People respond. "Good morning."

She says it again, and the mass of people repeats it to her.

"I'm Aisha." Her voice is so confident I imagine screaming, "I'm Sage" in front of a group of people and wonder how it would feel.

She makes a demand on the audience. "Who are you?"

"Free Portland."

"Who are you?"

"Free Portland!"

"Today. We. Take. Portland. Back."

The crowd returns the same words to her, matching her cadence. A few rounds go by, Aisha turning so she is not only addressing us on the bleachers but also the people behind her. Her voice is louder each time and so is the crowd. It feels like the chant is spreading out from her, from the stage, from us, and seeping through the whole city. Raj stands and waves his fist and then we're standing with everyone else, like being caught in water and having to go the way the water goes.

There's yelling and screaming to the left. I can see back and forth movement in the crowd but I can't tell what's going on. Raj is looking, too.

Below us, Aisha announces, "Please welcome Bryce Lord," and the crowd claps and hoots and whistles.

He's preening, running a hand through his hair and coming up to the front of the stage. The clapping slows, becomes scattered.

I hadn't realized Raj has a phone but he gets it out and starts talking fast, something about a disturbance.

Bryce says, "Thank you for being here." He pauses and waits for the clapping to stop, comfortable being on stage.

Almost everyone is watching him. It's gone silent nearby although chants and singing and shouting still surround the perimeter, making a cacophonous, uneven background. I glance in the direction Raj is looking again, but I still can't tell what's happening. Sunshine makes stars on metal, but it might be eyeglasses or buttons or anything.

It might not be weapons.

"Today, we have the biggest protest in the history of Portland. There are almost forty thousand of us. We are peaceful protesters." He pauses.

Jim, standing below us, cups his ear like Raj.

I whisper to Raj. "I thought he said thirty thousand?"

Raj laughs. "No way to count."

"We are an army of peace!" Bryce yells.

A few people repeat him.

"What are we?" Bryce yells.

"An army of peace." The crowd is yelling back at him and they sound more excited and anxious than peaceful. There's a lot of energy in all these people, in all this focus.

Guns go off.

Without hesitating, Bryce shouts, "Hold your ground. Those are warning shots."

More guns and a woman's cry rises above all other sounds. The grief in the single wailing voice cuts into me. The bleachers grow quieter, as if we're all listening to the woman screaming from her soul. The sound is visceral, deep. Pain, stopping me from even breathing for a moment.

"Stay where you are," Bryce yells, the control in his voice drowning out the mourning cry with order. "There are more of us than there are of them."

Smoke starts to rise from a few hundred feet away. It billows up over heads and protest signs like black mist.

Bryce takes command. "Cover your mouths and come down slowly. We'll march toward the 405 bridge."

People seem to expect the smoke. Some of them pull out handkerchiefs and tie them around their mouths and noses. Monday and I slide the collars of our shirts up over our noses like everyone else who doesn't have anything. The stink of smoke has stained the air and is catching in our throats by the time we start down the metal steps of the bleachers. It's blinding and the pain makes me afraid I'll fall.

Everyone escaping with us hurries, and Monday is pushed into me once and in front of us a woman goes down and someone steps on her arm. We're clotted and caught like snared animals until a man helps her up.

In the crowd, there is more yelling, mostly anger.

Nothing else like that wail of grief.

We make it all the way to the ground. Neither Bryce nor Jim is close to us.

"Come on," Raj says. "Let's find a camera." He scans the crowd, spots Alex behind us, waves.

Alex is shooting the whole area, but she stops and focuses on us for at least a few pictures.

We're being pushed by people from the side and behind.

Monday pulls on my arm and I lean back. Her breath is hot against my cheek as she whispers, "Good time to run."

My first instinct is to pull away from her and toward Raj.

"Come on," she hisses. "Stay safe!"

There is a long second of decision. These are our friends but it's not really our fight. I see Monday holding the gun after she shot Jack. She has that look again, the one that's stubbornness covering fear. She is beautiful. Fierce. Strong.

There is no way I can resist that look.

She pulls me three steps and turns. I'm following her. People are going all directions, so it's like trying to swim through a whirlpool. Smoke clings to us.

A man passes us with a bloody face and bloody hands and blood on his shirt.

I catch a glimpse of Raj on tiptoe, squinting in a different direction than the one Monday chose, but probably looking for us. He's not really tall, not like Bryce, and he's swallowed by a small crowd in moments.

I regret leaving him. Somehow, I know he will worry.

Monday looks spooked.

I've never seen so many people and they're all confused. Some angry, some desperate.

Trapped animals.

Getting away from people becomes the only thing I care about, that and not losing Monday. I grip her shirt. She leads us through the smoke.

I point out a whole line of people dressed in green. We turn, walking quickly the other way, then running, then seeing two more and turning again. A single boy in green—maybe our age if that—steps in front of us. "Stop!" he says.

Monday reaches behind her and pulls the gun out. She points it at him and says, "No." He skids to a stop, his eyes wide and full of fear; predator turned to prey by a hunk of metal and a girl. He doesn't move, doesn't look around.

Her voice is calm and slow as she says, "Go the other way."

He turns and runs and we duck in the opposite direction, the gun disappearing again into the small of Monday's back.

All around us it feels like panic.

I hear three shots, close. A man falls down, maybe fifty feet in front of us, the air going out of him in a huff so big I hear it at this distance even with the shot ringing in my ear. He's not bleeding, just on the ground. Someone helps him up and he's able to stand although he's limping now and one hand covers the front of his right thigh.

I overhear someone say, "Rubber bullets," and I understand it's more like Kelley's taser than Monday's gun. He's hurt, but not dead.

We push past him since he has a crowd around him, and we keep going until we find room to breathe and to take two or three steps at a time before we have to dodge someone.

Two big black dogs on leashes whine at us, and I shake my head. Not a good place for pets or kids, although I realize I see a few of each, and also some old people in the crowd. One man has a parrot on his shoulder. The parrot looks completely panicked but apparently it can't fly; it tries, spreading its wings and standing tall. But it gets no lift, settles and then tries again.

The crowd thins further and we're in an area full of blocky, red-brick buildings. One has fallen down, as if the earthquakes just shook it to rubble. There is a fence around the rubble, and holes in the fence. Other buildings nearby look lived-in. A few trees are budding out.

"Stop." I'm so winded and shaky I'm surprised my voice comes out big enough for Monday to hear.

"I'll find a place." She doesn't even slow down.

I manage to keep up, although by the time she stops in the middle of a park I have no words left inside me and my knees are rubber. We pluck off our packs and collapse onto the concrete side of a wide street planter with nothing but moss and rocks and trash in it.

I turn to Monday just in time to see her face collapse into tears. She leans into me. She's sobbing, her hand clutching my waist from behind. "The boy," she gasps out. "The boy."

I put an arm around her and let her cry, patting her head from time to time.

An older man walking along the sidewalk gives us a wide berth. His shoes look homemade, like they've been knitted onto his feet. He walks slowly and deliberately and wears a green tie.

The noise of the protest is a low rumble from here, background like a river.

Green trucks drive by—gasoline-powered trucks that make noise and smell horrible. They are full of men dressed in green and a few have guns.

Monday is making soft whiffling noises into my chest. I've never seen anyone cry so hard, never felt so much pain go through a person. It reminds me of the wail from the minute the violence started. The woman.

There are shots far off in the distance, maybe twelve coming fast, then another short burst. Monday stiffens at the sound but keeps crying.

A group of five men run down the middle of the road. They're in street clothes, their tennis shoes slapping on the pavement. They look like they're being chased, but no one follows them.

I hate it that she's crying. The only thing I can do for her is let her do it. I hate it when people tell me everything will be okay. That's a lie.

A stray dog with loose jugs from having puppies recently scuttles across the street. She's white with brown spots and one brown ear. I call to her, but she merely looks back and keeps trotting away.

Monday sits up, and I dig into my pack for one of my dirty shirts and hand it to her to wipe her face with. This is becoming a habit—sacrificing shirts for Monday. Her face is blotchy and her dark hair sticks to her cheeks. Her eyes look like Oskar's after he's been smoking pot. I don't say anything; I have no idea what to say.

She hands me back the shirt. "I was so sacred I'd shoot that boy. I kept seeing his blood spraying all over."

"You didn't."

"I shot Jack."

"We would be dead if you hadn't."

"Are you sure?" She sounds like a five year old.

"I'm sure. I'm glad you did that."

She sniffs a few more times. "Thank you," she says. "Thank you for being my friend."

"Thank you for only shooting the people who need to be shot," I say as simply as I can.

She smiles.

We sit that way, still and quiet in our own thoughts but together. Screams and chaos come from all directions, but it's all a bit distant.

My stomach has become a hole in my middle. It's such a big hole that it is more important than the fact that my life has gone from boring to something I hope is a dream I'll wake up from. "Let's eat something."

We share a cold can of chili. It's good. Spicy. It feels oddly normal to be eating cold chili out of a can. I finish the water Bryce gave me earlier and save the bottle.

"We need to charge the phones."

She nods.

"So Just Robyn can get data from PDXNET by satellite? Can we call them?"

Monday closes up her pack. "Just data. We're supposed to log on to PDXNET and say something about where we are that will tell them we're safe. That's all I know."

"You know more than me."

"What good are you?" She's smiling.

"I have a lot of shirts."

That gets her laughing.

We stand. The protest is close enough to hear, the street right around us is almost empty, and we smell like sweat and smoke. Monday's face is stained by soot where she hasn't cried, and I'm sure I look no better. "We need to find someplace safe," she says.

She looks little after all the crying, younger and more vulnerable. "Let's try Powell's again."

I've had my airplanes. She can have her empty bookstore. Maybe there are still books in there. "Do you know which way to go?" I ask her.

"Yeah, if we go back there." She jerks her head toward the protest.

"Is the protest near it?"

"It's everywhere. I'll find us a way." She takes off, walking south. We cross Glisan Street, which has a thin trail of protesters on it, some going toward the crowd and some away. There's no greens, but I keep looking for them, afraid to be asked for passes. We're on Eleventh Street when we see the sign for Powell's. We're coming at it from a different angle, and there is a door that isn't boarded up. The door is intact, and it looks like it can open. Right now it's closed. Monday jogs across the street and tugs on it to no avail.

I close my eyes. I don't pray. I know people who do though, and I pretend I'm one of them and I pray for the door to open for Monday.

Chapter Eighteen

WE'RE ON OUR SECOND CIRCUIT ALL THE WAY AROUND THE POWELL'S bookstore building before Monday stops and just stares at it. I don't want her to cry again, and I don't want to start crying for her; we have to be strong. From the corner we're on—Burnside and tenth—we can see the crowd's ragged edge just two blocks down.

"We need to find a place to spend the night," I tell Monday's stiff back. This is like a re-do—the same place we were a few days ago at the same time of day. Except closer to the closed-up store.

She's still staring at the locked door. "I came here when I was about five. My mother brought me. Portland was still sort of okay. The quakes had started. Starving had started. We'd lost my little brother to the flu the year before."

I stand still, transfixed. Monday has never talked about her family.

"I loved it here. I bought a whole armload of books, and we took them back to the house on the beach, where we were living then. My friends and I swapped out the books over and over. One was 'A Wrinkle in Time,' by Madeline L'Engle. I remember that because one of my friends was named Maddie."

I take her hand and squeeze it, like I did with Raj earlier. As I let go, I say, "I'm sorry."

"I can get you inside."

I step backward, not sure where the low voice is coming from. Male. Just louder than a whisper, almost like my imagination.

Monday gets right to the point. "I can't see you."

"Look down."

I squint into a dark shadow. A white rag resolves into a long white beard that hangs over a man's distended belly. He's dressed in dark clothes that blend with shadows, and clutches a dark blanket that drapes his shoulders.

I'd thought he was trash. Some observer I am.

"Can you get us into the bookstore?" Monday asks.

"Maybe."

"Are there still books in there?"

"Many." There is a smile in his eyes. "Tell me what you want to do there."

She blinks at him like he's speaking nonsense. "I love to read. You heard me. I came here when I was little and it was the best place in the world and I want to go back."

He holds out a hand to her. She takes it, helping him up. He's a foot taller than either of us, but weighs less. He looks like a beggar from a storybook illustration, except for the way his belly sticks out, which makes him look even worse. He's bundled up, so I can't see details, but the shoulders of his stained sweatshirt hang over his bones. His cheeks are sunken and his eyebrows big and white, like rabbit's tails stuck onto a face that is almost a skeleton.

"I'm Tom," he says. "Just Tom."

"And I'm Monday and this is Sage. We *would* like to get in. We can help you with some food or something."

"Do you have anything to stop pain?" His voice is so soft I can hardly hear it.

I can't imagine why he thought we would, even though we do. He must need something badly. Monday nods. "We do. We'll give you some if you help us into the bookstore."

The protest has swelled a quarter of a block closer. In an hour we will be inside it, even if we just stand still.

"I need help to walk."

This old guy can't hurt us, and I want to trust him. "Are there other people in there?" I ask him.

He glances down the street. "I think they're all down there. But they'll come back when it's over."

"Is this going to be over tonight?" I press.

He laughs, chiding. "Been going on for years. But maybe. Always maybe."

Monday furrows her brows and glances between the closed door and Tom. Then she nods and hands me her pack. "You take this. I'll help him."

Tom ignores the doors that are right behind him. We walk down Burnside in front of the bookstore, around the corner and down Couch Street until we've almost done a half-circle around the bookstore. He moves slowly even with Monday taking most of his weight, and it looks like every step hurts.

It hurts me to watch him, and I want to give him the aspirin now, but I also want to make sure Monday gets into the bookstore.

I had thought *we* didn't have anything, but we have our packs and we don't hurt. Every step Tom takes drives the pain lines deeper into his face, like his eyes are river otters swimming in a river of pain.

There is a little doorway three quarters of the way down this side, right next to the parking garage. We know it's locked; we tried it. Twice.

Tom looks both ways. A group of protestors walks down the street. He whispers, "Wait."

When they are gone, Tom uses a key that's tied to his belt loop on a long string and lets us in.

Past the threshold, it is almost completely dark even though we came in from daylight.

Monday leans back against me, hesitating.

Everything is dark except a knife of light shining in a patch of window that's above the board over the door. I try to extend my senses as far as I can, to Be Now. I don't hear anything I don't trust, and the air smells like dust and old books and stale coffee.

Tom pulls a flashlight out of his right pants pocket and shines it in front of us, showing us the aisles between stacks of books. Books fill shelves taller than my head, real physical books made out of paper. More than I thought existed in the whole world. He speaks slowly. "This is the Orange Room. Gardening and business." A pause while he waves the light around, illuminating the spines of books, and here and there, old faded posters.

I go in front, Monday behind me with the old man leaning on her. The stacks of books loom eerie in the faint light, filling shelves two deep and shoved across other books and into every corner. There are quite a few books and tattered magazines in the garden but I only read them on bad-weather days when I couldn't garden or sneak out. I like this place, but Monday must be in heaven.

We go up a wide flight of stairs. Tom does them one step—other foot to the same step—one more step. It's hard for him. There are windows in this level that aren't boarded over and faint light illuminates even more books, although the stacks are so high that almost everything is in shadow. Ladders lean against shelves and stand in corners.

"This is the Red Room." Tom leads us to a table near the window, a metal and plastic flat space that probably once held books. Mismatched chairs surround it. He collapses into a stuffed brown chair, his long legs bowing out and a look of pained relief crinkling his brow. He looks even worse in this light than he did outside. He holds out a hand.

I dig out the first-aid kit that Kelley packed for me, and find the little bottle of aspirin. I take out four, and drop them into his hand.

He stares at the bottle hungrily.

"I can't give you all of them," I say. I don't like withholding from him, but the pills might be like money, at least here. We might need them. We need a safe, quiet place pretty bad. I need to be away from crowds, and this big building with three of us in it feels good.

Tom pulls a water flask off his belt and takes the pills. He looks better right away even though they don't work that fast. It must be anticipation.

"Thank you." He looks at Monday. "We can't turn on lights here, not now. Don't want attention. But we can see well enough not to fall. When the others come back you'll meet them and they can take you around more."

"What kind of books are in here?" she asks.

"Religion, travel." He wheezes. "Books written in other languages."

Monday doesn't look really happy about this, but she disappears immediately behind shelves.

"Is there power?" I ask him. "We have some phones to charge."

He nods. "When we go down for dinner."

I really want to find it now, but I'm not sure he can walk any distance at all.

Tom sleeps with his head on his hands on the table. He is so pale and skeletal, I keep looking to be sure he is breathing.

Monday peers back to check on me from time to time, but stays immersed in the shelves.

The quiet drives me to nap beside Tom, my cheek against my knuckles.

I wake when footsteps rush up the stairs. There's three women, all middle-aged. "There he is." The one who points at Tom looks oriental. She is neat and thin with dark hair pulled back in a bun and fixed with two sticks, and slanted dark eyes. "We were worried."

Tom's head comes up off of the table and he says, "Hey."

The oriental woman holds out a hand to me. "I'm Mei."

Her hand is cool and dry. Before I can get a word out Mei nods toward a thin woman who is light brown everywhere—brown hair, tan clothes, sepia skin—a multi-colored scarf that's brown with a tiny bit of faded yellow. "This is Rebecca."

The woman nods, silent and otherwise unmoving.

Mei points to the third woman who has russet hair streaked with grey at the front and intense blue eyes that almost match the turquoise jewelry that looks like it should weight her down. "Ida."

Ida looks us up and down. "And you are?"

"Sage and Monday," I answer her.

"Monday wanted something to read," Tom says.

Ida favors him with a look like the ones Kelley used to give me when I came back from a forbidden trip outside.

"They're okay," Tom says. "They gave me aspirin."

Mei looks pleased at that. "Good." She pats him on the back, her touch protective. She addresses me and Monday. "We have enough dinner to share with you. Then we're going back out. You can come with us."

Monday stirs herself enough to answer. "I'd like to see the rest of the store."

Mei laughs. "It's no store these days. More like a home for wayward books. We trade for services and food. There's work for you. We've got a great big sorting project on the lower floor."

"In the middle of all this fighting?" I ask.

Mei laughs, a light laugh that brightens the room. "If we stopped for this, we would have died of hunger years ago."

I guess I can see that. "Happy to." I realize my belly hurts for food. "Can I help with dinner?"

She nods. "You both can."

I can see from the look on Monday's face that she's more starved for books than food. She grabs three she has put in a pile and carries them down, leading the way as if she owns the place. Mei follows her, and I follow Mei.

Before we're even partway down the stairs I hear Ida's voice letting into Tom. She mentions vagrants. I'm sure she means us. Mei leans over and whispers, "Don't worry. Ida's fear comes out like bitchiness. Tom has learned to ignore her."

"Do you all live here?"

"Now." Mei's walk is more like a glide, even going down stairs, her hips swishing back and forth and her head barely bobbing at all. "Tom was the store manager, and I managed the returns. Ida and Rebecca were clerks. There's five more of us still here; everyone who lives here worked in the store."

Before I can ask more questions, we're in a big kitchen. "This used to be called the coffee room," Mei explains. "We added some parts and now it can feed a lot of people. Part of what we're doing is making food for the protesters. Kevin helps us keep our power on in trade for our cooking skills. Brings us generators and fuel and batteries."

"What about Storm?" Monday asks. "Does he try to stop you?"

Mei shakes her head. "Most of Portland loves us. I think that's the reason we're safe."

Two men and a woman work in the kitchen, cutting up bags of potatoes and adding them to something that smells of pepper and broth.

"Can I plug in phones?" I ask.

Mei waves at a wall with two outlets in it. I start with the two Kevin tried to steal. I notice one of the men watching me closely, and decide to pocket the other four phones instead of leaving them in my backpack.

I wash lettuce and Monday cuts up carrots. A man shreds about half a chicken into a big bowl.

"Where did you get the chicken?" I ask the man. He is thin with sunken cheeks and a slight beard.

"Lots of readers in Portland." He gestures for me to sit down. Ida and Tom have returned, Tom looking cowed and Ida frustrated. "We got three today—two and a half are in tonight's soup."

I sit between Tom and Ida.

Three people from the kitchen bring out cups of hot tea for everyone.

"Mint." Ida announces the obvious as if I had no nose.

The tea and salad taste like food from home. The bread is dry but filling. We don't get any of the soup even though the smell fills the room.

"So you were at the protests?" I ask Mei, who sits across from me, sipping tea from a chipped cup with colorful butterflies painted on it.

She grimaces. "It was awful today. A woman got shot and her husband carried her like a baby, her blood leaving a trail like a stream on the road." She shivers, and purses her lips primly. "It was down past Park, just five blocks from here."

"Were you there?" Ida asks me. "At the protests today?"

"In the morning. We were with Bryce Lord, and he was talking to a bunch of us, and then there was smoke and gunshots and we left."

Ida's eyes go wide and I hear Rebecca's voice for the first time. It's soft and deep. "Too bad about his father."

"What?"

"Bryce's father." She sounds like we should know this. "Storm took him."

Monday starts paying attention. "What about Bryce?" she asks.

"I don't know."

"So the protest failed?" I think of Raj.

"Maybe not." Mei puts down her butterfly teacup. "Stupid of Storm to lock Kevin up. It could bring him down."

My stomach knots and curls and I picture a bigger, angrier crowd and then Raj in jail or dead and I must have made a sound because Mei gives me a sweet smile and pats my hand. "You met Kevin?" she asks.

"Yeah." Monday sounds bored but I think she's acting again, like she did around Jack.

Mei leans forward. "What's he like in person?" Her eyes are shining as if he's bigger than life.

"He's intense." I watch Monday since this isn't a good time to say he doesn't trust us. She's just staring, jaw locked. Good enough.

Mei sounds wistful. "I only met him once. All this time, all this protesting, and I've only talked to him once. Heard him talk a few times. You're very lucky."

Monday's voice is even and controlled as she says, "He has a sense of presence."

Ida stares at us. "What does he look like?"

Ida must know that. She's testing us. I imitate Monday's calm boredom even though I'm getting angry with Ida. I describe Kevin, and then for good measure I describe Bryce.

Monday interrupts. "What about a man named Justice?" She looks close at Mei and Tom, as if willing one of them to answer. "Do you know Justice?"

Tom nods.

"He's dead," Ida snaps.

Mei just smiles softly. "Justice has not been around for a long time."

Ida interrupts. "You can only stay here for two days. While we have that whole pile of new books to move."

I like Ida less than Kevin. Maybe cities are full of people who don't trust you. Maybe so many people shouldn't live together.

Maybe we shouldn't have come in here after all.

Mei speaks softly to me. "Maybe you should go find Bryce tomorrow. If the Freer's win, you could get a job with them. Make a living. That's hard here."

"Freers?" Monday asks.

"The Free Portlanders," Ida says. "Us."

I need a break from her. "Excuse us a minute?" I gesture to Monday and we peel the phones off the wall and start two more charging. We sit at a table in the corner. The room is big enough to achieve a bit of privacy.

We use the phones to look at PDXNET. After poking around a bit we open the right windows for sending information. Monday's phone is the one set to what we think is Justice's ID and she posts, "Portland is full of people. Yesterday was Stormy."

I laugh and wonder what Kevin will think of that if he sees it. Or Justice, for that matter. She did capitalize the "s" in Storm. I post, "The wind was scary last night and sunshine came out today." Nonsense, and who knows how many days it will take for Just Robyn to pick up the messages. But it will tell them we are safe so far. The nuances will have to wait. Maybe Justice will get word to Kelley. I feel a lot better now that we've sent a message out into the world, like maybe we aren't as alone as I feel.

We browse the information on PDXNET. It tells us that Bryce got away, but Kevin is in jail. I have trouble picturing him in jail, especially since my imagination is running toward dungeons from fairy tales. I know that's not right, but it kind of feels right, anyway.

The phones stop working. Not the phones, the ability for them to access information. Monday shuts hers and sighs. "Network's down."

A man I haven't met calls from the kitchen, "Soup's packed up."

"Ready?" Mei asks us all.

Chapter Nineteen

WE STREAM OUT THE SAME DOOR THAT WE CAME IN, A KNOT OF PEOPLE wrestling two sturdy carts with shelves and outsized wheels into a dark side street. The street is almost empty; a few people are walking on the other side. They ignore us. Ida and three men pull one of the carts down the street the same way the walkers were going.

Mei, Rebecca, Monday, and I push the other cart uphill, the savory smell of the chicken soup steaming around our faces. Jugs of water and chipped coffee cups fill the rest of the top shelf. An empty plastic bin sits on the bottom.

We lean into the work. The cart is unwieldy and one of the wheels squeaks and tries to pull us all to the right. My pack is heavy, and I think of Monday loaded down with her new books as well. But it's not as if we'd leave our stuff behind. Monday and I live like turtles.

Tom walks beside us, two old men on either side of him. At the corner, Tom stops to watch by the door where we found him. He looks directly at Monday. "Come back tonight. I'll wait for you."

She lets go of the cart with one hand and gives him a brief hug, the first time I've seen her hug a man since Justice. Tom looks like he regrets not being able to come with us, but he turns obediently when one of the men takes his hand and pulls. They are all old, but the other two are strong enough to help Tom walk in spite of their wrinkled, sunken faces.

From the outside, Powell's looks empty and shuttered.

Burnside is busier than the side street and by the time we've gone no more than a block toward the bridges there are people sitting on the sidewalk in groups, talking. On one corner about a dozen people sing and a nearby crowd cheers as a man uses two sticks to juggle a third stick with balls of flame on each end.

Mei and Monday ladle soup into cups while Rebecca and I hand them into the crowd. People nod and say thank you, and we keep going until all the cups have been handed out, working just one side of the street. There are so many people that there will not be enough soup, but Mei and Rebecca seem unfazed by this. Rebecca is largely silent but Mei greets almost everyone, many by name.

Once a man hands them three books in trade for soup, and Mei places the books on the bottom of the cart.

Empty cups begin to come back to us, filling the bin on the bottom. It all feels like a familiar ritual, like the carts and the booksellers were expected. It feels good, too. Helping.

We pour water into containers people already have, or back into soup cups when people hold them out to us.

Someone taps me on the back and I turn to find Alex. "Have you seen Bryce or Aisha?" she asks. "Or Tam?"

I'm really happy to see her and I hand her a cup of soup.

She looks startled at the food in her hands, then grins. "Thanks."

"We left right after the smoke. What happened next?"

"Bryce started leading people up here. I lost him."

"Is it true Kevin's in jail?"

She nods, her mouth full. She's so thin she looks like she needs more than one cup of soup, so I slide an extra to her, making sure no one else can see. But she returns it, and the empty cup. "Gotta go. Thanks."

I want her to stay so I can ask her more, but she's already lost in the crowd. In some ways I feel like a reporter, like I'm here to watch and report back to someone. But I can't imagine the Board being interested, although I can picture Oskar squatting while he pulls up tiny weeds and asks questions about why people here are fighting each other, questions I can only answer a little so far.

Justice and Robyn will be interested. So will Kelley. So those three are my audience, and of course, me. This is what I came for, and as I'm helping ladle out soup I feel like I'm part of something active, something that's an adventure.

The supplies last for two blocks. As dark finishes filling the street, candles come out of pockets and in a few places, fires dance in portable fireplaces or even just on the street.

Mei smiles tiredly. "Thank you."

"You're welcome." I don't tell her that I liked helping, since I don't know what I think of these people yet. I like Tom, don't like Ida, and Mei is too perfect.

Mei smiles, and even her teeth are perfect. "Do you have a watch?"

We don't but our phones tell time.

"Tom will be there until midnight or so," Mei tells us. "Don't be late."

That gives us three hours.

"Do come back and help with the sorting. We'll do that in the morning."

"Okay."

She turns to go back, and people make room for her. Maybe Portland does love Powell's.

As soon as we're alone, I turn to Monday. "I want to find Raj."

"You're crazy," she says. "There's thousands of people here."

Burnside is growing more crowded. We pass a group with signs that say, "Free Lord," and two of the signs say, "Free our Lord."

"We should leave," Monday says. "Now. I don't like it here."

A group of singing monks walks near us, going the same way, not singing at the moment, but picking up trash from the street. They do this reverently in the midst of all the noise, like the trash matters more than the people. Or maybe the absence of trash matters more than the presence of people. I do like it here. I like the sense of purpose, and the monks and the families and the slight hint of danger. "I don't want to leave the airplanes."

She gives me a look of daggers but doesn't say anything. For a moment, I'm utterly afraid that she'll leave me, but then she smiles and I think she won't.

As we get closer to what feels like the center of the protest, people sound angrier. The look on Monday's face reminds me she hates this, so much I almost feel guilty. I want to make sure Raj is okay; that's the only thing I can really think about. I understand it's probably futile, but I don't care.

We search up and down crowded streets, the night air chilling. Two men in thick coats whistle at us and we drop our heads and weave a bit through the crowd until we lose them. A woman with a tiny brown dog clutched to her breast lets us pet it, and all the while its big eyes scan the crowd and its ears stick straight up.

We hit a knot of people too thick to go through easily, and Monday pulls me aside. "Stop for a minute," she says.

We find room to sit in a doorway. A child who can't be much more than four years old squeals as his father tickles him in a makeshift camp to our right. They have a battery-operated lantern that throws bright light up to show us the faces of people passing by.

Monday says, "I don't like Kevin Lord, and I don't like Ida."

"What about Raj and Bryce?" I ask her. "What about this whole thing? Isn't this what Justice sent us to find out about?"

"Maybe. But we don't belong here. We could die." In the darkness her expression is hard to read. "Maybe I don't belong anywhere."

I can't go back now; Portland has made the garden even smaller. Four people walk by arguing about something loudly, but I can see they're friends in spite of the loud words, or maybe family. "I feel like I'm doing something good. Like I matter now. That's what I left home to do."

"How do either of us matter?" Monday mutters, keeping her voice soft. "This is so big."

"Do you have anything else you want to do?" I ask her.

Three people go by on bicycles wearing white shirts. "Let's go to Seattle. We could get bicycles and ride there."

I laugh. "I do want to go back tonight."

"Why?"

"To give Tom his aspirin. Because we said we would."

She shakes her head at me again. "You're such a bleeding heart."

"Oskar always said it's the little things that matter. I didn't used to believe him."

"Oskar and Robyn would get along," Monday snaps.

"We can go to Seattle after this is over."

A man walks by with a homemade torch, the light so bright I can't see anything for a moment. The little boy from the camp screeches, "Light!" and his mother laughs and tells him "Yes, yes, there is light in the world." She sounds happy.

After the torch passes, Monday sighs. "Okay. So we keep looking for the head do-gooders and the center of the danger. Then what?"

"We find some way to help."

"Like sing?"

I can't stand it that we're arguing. I take a deep breath and tell her, "You sing better than me."

Even in the near dark I can see the smile bloom on her face, and it feels like it's just me and her again, like we are the most important things in each other's world. This has never been true for me before. I need her, and say so. "I don't want to lose track of you."

She holds my hand. Her hand is warm, and strong, a little bigger than mine. We sit that way for quite a while, watching people go by, listening to singing and chanting and talk and laughter and complaints. Ever since we left Powell's there has been no gunfire and no screaming. We could almost be at a party the size of Portland except for the way people look carefully around them and the laughter that sounds too loud and too forced.

Monday looks disappointed when I ask if she's ready to keep going. We search through the crowds, not stopping, just walking and pushing and avoiding. Looking out for Bryce or Raj, listening for words or phrases that will tell us something. We gather that Kevin in still in jail, that the protest is getting bigger because of it. We are nearly back to the bleachers and stage when I spot a familiar face.

She is moving away from us, a little faster than we are, but headed in the same direction. "Tam!" I call out.

She turns, stops, and stares at us.

"Sage and Monday," I remind her. "I heard about Kevin. I'm looking for Raj."

She looks angry. She chews on her lip. "Raj doesn't think you did it. I'm not so sure."

"Did what?" Monday I ask in concert.

"Betrayed Kevin. Raj told me they brought you along."

Monday's face looks angry now, too. "We didn't know where Kevin was. The man was leading a protest. So he was visible to anyone." She isn't done. She's almost bouncing and she's getting loud. "Do you people just blame strangers for fun? You invited us into the hangar. Raj and Bryce came to find us and bring us coffee the morning after we met them. We're not stalking you."

Tam holds up her hands. They're empty, and she carries no belongings. There's fear on her face as well as anger and it feels like the three of us could end up fighting or she could abandon us, and take any clue to where Raj is with her.

I hold my hands up, too, looking at Monday until she also complies. "We don't mean you any harm. We just got here. We didn't even come for the protests."

She stares at us with suspicion.

"Really," I continue. "We were with Bryce and Raj and Aisha and there was smoke and gunfire and we left. We're looking for you. Why would I have called you if I betrayed you?"

This last sentence gets to her although she still doesn't exactly look ready to trust us. But she nods, and turns and walks off. For the second time in two days we're following Tam.

She walks almost as fast as she moved on her bicycle. We're out of breath by the time she leads us to Raj, Bryce, Alicia, Jim, and a few other faces that look familiar from the hanger. They're sprawled on the grass talking amongst themselves. Raj's face is in profile at this angle, the light of a candle flickering on his cheeks. I'm surprised at how good it feels to have found them.

The others notice us, and their faces all change. Bryce looks uncertain, and like he hasn't slept, but then of course he hasn't. It seems like days since this morning, but it's not even a whole day. We still have more than two hours before we have to be back.

I don't want them to question us. I just go into the circle and sit beside Raj. Jim, across from me, gives me a welcome smile that eases some of my worry that we aren't trusted.

"Where did you go?" Raj asks me.

"Powell's." When he doesn't respond immediately, I remind him, "We told you that's where we were going. Before we got caught in the bar."

He laughs. "Yeah, you did." He pauses, glances at Aisha. "I hoped you'd stay with us."

"We came back to find you."

Aisha hesitates. "We're talking strategy."

She doesn't want us around for it. I think about staying anyway, but when I look at Raj he knows it, too, and I can tell he wants to go. He tugs on my arm. "Let's take a break. I need to think anyway."

"Don't do anything stupid," Aisha warns him, looking at me. She sounds dismissive, like maybe Raj is about to jump off a bridge or something.

"We're just going to take a walk," he says. "I won't be out of sight."

"Fifteen minutes." She stands and stretches. "Maybe we should all move. Bryce?"

She and Bryce stand and go together just out of earshot. Raj and I go in a different direction. "We should take Monday," I tell Raj.

"They're talking."

True enough. Monday and Tam are engaged in a fast-paced conversation, Tam's arms waving and Monday's crossed over her chest. Jim looks at Raj and says, "I'll keep an eye on her."

I bet she'll love that. But I do want to talk to Raj. And he looks like he wants to talk to me. "Thanks, Jim. We won't go far."

In spite of the occasional flashlight and candle, it's dark enough that I feel separated from Monday after only a few steps.

A torch flies up from the midst of a small crowd in front of us, light turning circles against the dark. "What's that?" I ask.

"A fire juggler."

This one is throwing far bigger fire than the one we saw on the street. The crowd blocks our sight of anything except the flame going up and coming down. There isn't really anything good to climb on, so we stand and watch from a distance. "Are you okay?" I ask him. "I'm sorry about Kevin. Do you know what happened?"

"Not really. He was a few blocks down Burnside by Chinatown at the main stage when he was overwhelmed. We don't think he was hurt. But we haven't had any new information for hours. The nets are all down now."

"Where are they keeping him?"

"Storm's new jail downtown." Raj's face is cold and hard, a look I'm not used to thinking about when I think of him. "He keeps it full."

"Have you been there?"

"No." He looks around, reminding me a little bit of the brown dog. Alert. "It's supposed to be very modern. Runs on solar power with backup generators. Biggest thing the city's built Post. A goddamn jail. And Storm got a lot of people liking it, told everyone it would keep them safe from looters."

Raj sounds so bitter I feel sorry for him. It's not the voice he usually uses. "Has Kevin been caught before?"

"No."

"So are Bryce and Aisha the leaders now?"

"There's a lot of leaders left. It's a problem."

"Are you worried?"

"I feel better now that I've found you." He puts his arm around me, and he's warm and smells like sweat and smoke and coffee. "I know you didn't betray us."

"How?"

He laughs. "You don't know enough."

That stings but it's also a relief, like a deep worry I hadn't known was eating me lifts. I slide my arm around his waist, feeling what it's like to hold and be held. I like it. "What are you going to do next?"

The muscles in his side tense under my hand. "Bryce is afraid that if we fight, they'll kill Kevin."

I think back to the book from the hangar. "You don't believe in violence."

"Three protestors died today."

The flame shoots up and twirls again, the crowd clapping. Even though I'm worried and I'm watching for greens, it still feels more like a party than a fight. "What do you want to happen next?"

"Kevin doesn't allow violence anymore. So if you see some, it's not Free Portland. He'd want us to use sheer numbers to own the streets until there's no room for Storm or his trucks full of greens." Raj lets me go and steps away to stand up on tiptoe and look around.

"What are you looking for?"

"Danger. Greens."

"Is it okay?"

"It's too dark to tell." He slides his arm back and I'm warm again. "We can't be like Storm, but it's hard to stay peaceful when I'm so mad."

"I met a man on the road who said to be polite, but then don't miss when that doesn't work. He helped me get part of the way here." Raj tenses so I quickly add, "He and his family. We walked together for hours, but then I had to help Monday and I lost track of him."

"I thought this would be over yesterday. It takes so long."

I don't have anything to say to that so I just squeeze him a little, kind of startled at my audacity. It's a big step for me, this being so close to a boy and touching him. He smells good, he feels good. Solid. Even though nothing in this new world is solid. I've traded boring for new, and the new in this moment is good. It hasn't all been good, it's been scary and bloody and uncertain, and this is new and uncertain, but I'm really content in this small moment. Everything since I left the garden is more intense, the colors, the feelings, the noises. Like being fully alive.

"Do you have a place to stay?"

I nod. "Powell's."

"Really? I heard no one gets in there unless they have books. There's an old man who guards the only glass door left with a gun."

I laugh while I try to imagine where Tom would keep a gun. "He's enchanted with Monday. She's a reader."

"She's a puzzle," he muses. "Tough."

Some of it's really fear, but I'm pretty sure she wouldn't want me to say that. "She's brave."

"So are you."

I laugh at that, since it isn't true.

He continues, "I thought I liked Monday best, but you're easier to be friends with."

This makes my cheeks hot.

I look over at Monday and she's not there anymore. It's all wrong, in fact. Screwed up. There is a hole in the crowd, people moving away from the center of an ever-widening circle. In the middle, three greens struggle with Aisha. Her blonde hair is the only way I'm even sure it's her since they are so much bigger.

"Run." I let go of him and grab for his hand. "Greens." Although he's craned his head and seen them, too.

"No." He traps me in his arms. "Draw no attention." He's still looking, and I make myself hold still even though it's hard. I search for Monday's black hair and oval face, and she's nowhere. Tam either.

"We're going to look weird because we're standing still."

He shakes his head, keeps looking. The crowd seems to have decided as one that they are all far enough away, and some push toward the edges while others keep moving; the front of the line seems to bubble.

There's nothing to see, no way to get a big enough picture. I squeeze Raj's hand so hard it hurts my hand. Finally, he looks down at me, and his face is soft. "Walk carefully away. Be slow."

We walk together, our strides matched, his arm back around my waist.

"I need to know if Monday got away."

"Did you see Bryce?" he asks.

"No."

Soon we're at the edges of the crowd around the fire juggler. The clapping and calling keeps us from talking. Raj pushes us politely and firmly in where three people have just left, and in another moment we slide in a few feet more. There are people behind us now, all around. It feels tight, almost like being on the stake truck. Even the bleachers earlier weren't this bad. People I don't know are so close they have to touch me.

I'm glad of Raj and worried about Monday and Bryce and Aisha and even Jim.

We're close enough to see details about the juggler. He's a small man, sweaty and bare-chested. His hair sticks to his cheeks and his eyes look as bright as the fire, as if he is mesmerized by it or has sent himself into some altered state to deal with the heat. I can feel it even from this distance. He throws the wand of flame up to spin and turn against the dark sky. The crowd steps back like a single beast and then forward as he catches the end of the brand that isn't burning.

A little girl sitting on her father's shoulders claps and squeals.

We keep moving forward until we're near the front. The heat of the brands is so intense that I touch my hair to make sure it's not burning. I turn my head from time to time, checking to be sure there are no greens pushing after us. There *is* a man in a green shirt on the far side. Like us, he is watching the juggler. I am careful not to catch his eye.

Three more throws and I'm shaking now from the crowd pressing in. "I need to see Monday." It's become the only thing I can think about, like finding Raj was earlier.

The juggler throws particularly high, and this time as the brand comes down, Raj starts us moving back. He's good at this, at maneuvering through so many people. In another throw we're out and walking. "Hold me close," he says. "Look like two lovers. They might not expect that."

I feel like the other day when I had the glass of beer and it made me excited and a little ill and all funny. We fall in with a crowd of people heading toward Burnside, walking like we're with them, my arm tight around his waist and my hand riding his hip. We get near where we left the others, and Aisha is gone, the greens too. There is no sign of Monday or Tam or Jim. I stare at the places I want them to be as if that will make them appear. "Maybe we should try the bar," I suggest.

"They'll be watching it."

"Monday might go to Powell's."

"I should take you there anyway. Then at least I know you're safe."

When we get to Burnside the group breaks up and people go every which way.

A gun goes off somewhere close, making me duck and flinch.

Raj pulls me into a doorway, maybe the same doorway where Monday and I sat earlier. I can't quite tell with the light different. There is no family camped to the side.

He leans me against the wall. He is breathing hard and I guess I am, too. Fear. Adrenaline. Worry.

He puts a hand on the back of my neck.

He looks down at me, his face hard to see in the shadows, just dark eyes and a dark face, momentarily illuminated by a flashlight and then dark again. He comes close to me and whispers. "Thank you for finding me."

"Yes." We've already said this, of course.

"I want you to stay safe." His breath tickles my cheek. "I want to take you to the bookstore and I want you to go in whether we find Monday or not. I'll look for her if she's not there."

For the first time in my life, someone trying to tell me what to do feels sweet. I'm not willing to promise him. "I can't stay if she's not there. She wouldn't abandon me."

He seems to like it that I won't do what he says. His mouth finds mine, and for the first time ever I am being kissed. He is gentle and hungry all at once. His breath and my breath mingle. He tastes different than I expected, spicy and warm.

I like the kiss, love the kiss, fall into it. I understand why books and movies say the first kiss matters.

His heartbeat pulses beneath my palm, which is on his chest.

He takes my hand and pulls it away from his heart and steps in so we are even closer together, touching almost everywhere. He is hot and I'm tingling at being so close to him, like all my nerves have gone off at once.

His hand caresses the back of my hair and we become one being sharing a single skin.

It almost hurts when he lets me go.

"Come on. Let's get to the bookstore." His voice shatters a spell and I breathe deeply for the first time since he pulled me in here, starved and shaking.

I have become a different person. Transformed. In an instant.

We return to the street and I feel so light I barely think about the protest or the lights even as we're surrounded again by people and noise and the hot emotions of the crowd. It is as if the kiss formed a bubble around me.

Chapter Twenty

I KEEP SCANNING FACES FOR MONDAY. OR, FOR THAT MATTER, FOR TAM or Aisha or anyone. But mostly for Monday. Not seeing her makes me feel guilty about the kiss, for not taking her to Seattle. A hot and confusing guilt.

Engines start. Headlights make bright spears in the dark of the street, brighter than anything people are carrying, making the candles and hand-crank flashlights look like dim stars fighting suns for dominance.

A gun fires.

The lights are attached to trucks. Raj pulls me to the side of the street, enveloped in a crowd of people. The trucks are open-beds with green shirts kneeling in them. The lights of trucks behind them illuminate faces peering at us and glint on the metal stocks of handguns and rifles.

We stand very still, watching. Three trucks, four, five. A string so long it might stretch all the way to the bridge.

Raj starts chanting next to me. "End the storm. Bring the light. End the storm. Bring the light."

He might be praying.

His voice grows louder, and I chant with him, and then the people next to us, as if the shock of the trucks has helped us find our voices.

The trucks pass us slowly, as if showing they don't care that we're here.

They stop.

Lights swirl from the tops of the vehicles, flashes of yellow that force us to look away. The lights silence some of the crowd but drive Raj's voice louder. Up the street toward Powell's the red and white and blue light beams of a police bar add an ominous overtone to the show.

A motorcycle runs slowly alongside, outpacing the trucks, its engine low and powerful.

A man in the back of a white truck in front of us stands up and uses a microphone. I can't see him well, but his voice booms over us. "Clear the streets by order of Mayor Alexis Storm. Martial Law is in force and curfew begins in one hour. Effective tomorrow, curfew begins at dusk and holds until dawn."

The man stands there, as if waiting for us to scatter.

A few fade back, although no one runs. Most stand. I'm proud and scared to be right here next to Raj in the lead.

Raj has not stopped chanting and I start in again. He looks fierce and I can feel his breath, and his voice thrums inside me like an instrument. His determination infects me with his touch, and I chant louder and my voice sounds strong and sure. Only a few others take the chanting back up before the man begins to repeat his statement.

Three people in black clothes sidle close to the truck and the men in the bed brandish weapons at them. The three stop. Two of the greens yell at once, "Keep your distance!" and "No closer!" on top of each other. One of the men fires his gun, a quick action, barely aimed. A man back in the crowd screams in pain and the wails of women follow.

The three still stand. They back off, toward a man throwing cuss words at the truck. Other angry voices join in, although no one approaches closer to the vehicle. Whatever happened isn't visible to us, just the street where the line of headlights illuminates the open ground between the trucks and the crowds lining the road, and dark silhouettes of people moving in the crowd, indistinct and almost seething.

Raj lets go of me and sprints toward the place the shot went. I follow, blood pounding, worried about Raj. What if he gets shot?

It's only a little ways and Raj is running just on the outside of the crowd, between them and the trucks.

I follow.

An engine revs.

The curfew message is being repeated in the area we just left. People push forward in mass argument, faces illuminated by headlights, white and scared and determined.

Raj holds his arms out, as if he can hold back the crowd. "No violence!" he screams.

Another gunshot cracks the air.

Raj doesn't fall.

No one screams. Maybe no one is hit.

Some people hold their ground, even move forward, but others dip back and people begin to tangle and two collapse onto the ground and for a moment I worry they'll be trampled.

Cuss words fill the air. Screaming. Peace signs—two fingers up in victory.

Figures huddle in silhouette just off the street against a boarded store window covered with orange and blue spray paint. Flashes of yellow from the trucks' overhead lights sweep across the crowd, making everything look staccato.

Raj pulls me behind him, using his voice and body to get through. I marvel at how he shows no fear of the angry men and women, no fear of the trucks and the guns.

"Sage!"

Monday, yelling my name.

I am light and happy, so relieved she is okay that I run faster, intending to hug her, except the look on her face and the direction of her gaze stop me cold.

A man on the ground rolls and holds his stomach, moaning. A black pool spreads below him. Monday is right beside him, Tam protecting her, and holding back the crowd. Most people seem frozen in place anyway, transfixed and immovable. Monday doesn't come toward me, but leaves her hand on the man's shoulder, whispers to him.

Raj has gotten us close enough for me to see that it's Jim bleeding onto the sidewalk, his head rolling back and forth and his teeth clenched. He's writhing so hard I can't tell exactly what's happened to him, but dark blood covers his fingers and the belly of his shirt, stains the top of his jeans.

Raj falls to Jim's far side, face shocked, hands touching his friend, trying to lift his arms. This is the wrong thing to do since it will let the blood flow out even faster, but there isn't any point in doing anything about it, it won't matter. The blood is coming too fast. I've watched eagles and hawks and coyote hunt.

I know death.

I'm on my knees by Jim's head, whispering to him. Oskar always told us that death was only life, and that the dead should look forward and go out loved. I have never seen a human die except Jack, and that only took a second.

Jim takes longer, and I whisper in his ear, using words Oskar might have said. "Go peacefully. Thank you for being on the earth, accept."

He seems to hear me. He turns his face toward me for a moment, his eyes bright with tears and pain.

The disbelief in his gaze stops my voice.

His eyes narrow, reacting perhaps to whatever I must look like in that moment.

I say the same thing again.

He nods once at me and then doubles over harder, his head now turned away and his face scrunched tight. I can't think of any new words, so I say the simplest part over and over: *go peacefully, go peacefully, go well, go loved, go peacefully.*

Jim stops writhing. He seems past the pain, and I feel his body stop fighting and his eyes turn back toward me, Raj, and then me, and so I say the words again and again until life flees every part of him, its last stop a single rattling breath followed by a slow exhale.

Raj and Monday are both looking at me like I've done something fabulous, but I'm just tired and sore and shocked.

Chapter Twenty-One

Jim's body is on the ground, wrapped up in a sheet someone must have had with them. Monday and I lean against the wall. I'm so tired and confused I can't imagine leaving the sturdy support of the bricks. All of this fighting seems like a waste, but for the first time I know—know deep—that Raj and Bryce and Kevin are on the right side. I have not seen them hit or hurt or kill anyone. They have not abducted anyone. Kevin had us watched when he didn't trust us, and now our watcher is dead at my feet and I feel so sad for him I don't think I can speak any more than I can walk. It is all I can do to feel my backpack bunched between me and the wall, and to stay on my feet.

Raj and Tam talk into phones, their voices too hushed to hear. The trucks have gone on. They have probably done more damage than this. The street is again full of people, but the chanting and the singing is uncertain, rising and falling in fits.

It has to be almost midnight. Maybe it is midnight.

Raj knows this, too. He comes over to us and he says, "Go to Powell's. You won't want to be out after the curfew. They'll be back, and it'll be dangerous."

I don't want to leave him out here. But I can't imagine doing anything else. At least at Powell's we'll be safe.

Raj pulls me away from the wall, maybe the only force that could pull me away at this moment. His lips brush the top of my head. Briefly. I want more, but Monday and Tam are watching. "Go," he whispers.

I turn and gesture to Monday. She holds her hand out, and I peel her from the wall, and start toward Powell's.

There are so many milling people in front of Powell's it takes a moment to spot Tom, slumped in the shadows with his head leaning against the wall. His eyes are closed, and he's so still and pale that he looks dead. It is only when we're really close that I see he's breathing. His brow is drawn down, and sweat beads his face.

It's too cold for sweat.

We sit, one on each side of him, and I dig aspirin and water out of my pack. "Tom," I whisper.

He groans but doesn't move.

"Aspirin?"

He nods, and a gnarled hand emerges from a thin, gray blanket that covers him. He has trouble swallowing, but he manages. "Thanks," he whispers. "Give me some time."

My phone tells me its ten minutes to midnight. It will take Tom that long to get around to the small door. But we give him five minutes anyway; they can't enforce the curfew everywhere at once, and he looks so weak.

I take a lot of deep breaths, struggling to control my reaction to Jim being killed. Murdered.

If I die here no one will know except Monday. Kelley and Oskar might never hear of it. If Raj dies he will never kiss me again. If Monday dies I will be alone in this city except for Raj who seems to love danger. I need them both; they keep me balanced. Raj, a pacifist who throws himself into the path of bullets and Monday, a fighter who tries to avoid trouble.

Tom groans, pulling me out of myself and back into blinking at the cold, dark street full of strangers. It takes me and Monday working together to get Tom standing. All three of us are exhausted. Tom clutches his blanket tight with one hand and I support his elbow while Monday holds his other hand. We must look like we've gotten into someone's beer. It's hard to walk upright.

More headlights appear in the street beyond us.

Dark shapes of people are haloed in light then gone, followed by more. I can't tell what's happening and after Jim, I don't want to know.

Trucks roll slowly toward us. A rock pings hard on the metal side. That's wrong. This is non-violent. Supposed to be non-violent.

A voice yells commands from the truck. "Go inside or go to jail."

Tom mumbles, "Keep going." He can't walk faster. Maybe he won't even be able to walk far enough.

A group of men with guns—not in green, but armed—heads away from the trucks, passing us.

We turn downhill, and headlights shine where we just were. There are no street lights here, and almost no light leaks out of the book store. Darkness feels safer. Tom is walking wrapped in his blanket and Monday and I are wearing dark clothes and we're walking away from Burnside. No one in the trucks notices us, although I keep my head down and I'm half-expecting to be shot in the back while we walk. I feel like a rabbit frozen by a dog's bark or a deer with a flashlight in the face. I should be bounding away but instead I'm slow and steady and a target.

Ida and Mei come out of the store and take Tom from us. The door closes behind us.

"Upstairs," Mei says. "Lights out in ten minutes. Third floor. You get the hallway."

We rush to the bathroom. I throw water on my face and give up on my hair. It doesn't matter.

Somewhere outside the staccato of gunshots pings against something metal. The walls of the old building muffle the noise so it sounds like popcorn but it makes me cringe. Raj and Tam are out there somewhere, and maybe Bryce.

A pile of old towels sits by the sink and I pick one up and scrub at my face. "They got Aisha. We saw that. What about Bryce?"

Monday shrugs. "I think he's still out there. Tam spotted them before I saw them, and she and I ran. He ran, too. In a different direction. Aisha was too busy being brave to notice she should run."

The door opens and Mei comes in. "Help Tom?" she asks.

We trade with Mei and Ida and take Tom's weight one step at a time.

At the top of the stairs, sheets hang from the ceiling in a room labeled, "Art Gallery." The sheets create makeshift flowered and stained white walls, with blankets and pillows and tables and chairs making small narrow rooms, one for each person.

Mei stops and says, "Take what you want from the pile," which turns out to mean choose from a pile of blankets and pillows that are all thin and overused. There are enough of them to set up nests next to each other just outside the door to the gallery.

Inside the gallery, people are playing cards and board games. The absurdity of games in the face of the death outside hits me like a punch in the stomach. Tom is stretched out by the far wall, already sleeping. Every once in a while he snores, an uneven and painful sob of breath.

"Two minutes," Mei says with authority, and people set down books and put away games, obedient.

A dark figure shuffles over to us. Ida. She hands us an old tablet PC. It's got a big screen. On the screen there is a close-up of us with the headline, "Have you seen these girls?" It has to be one of the pictures Alex took of us this morning. Me and Raj and Monday are all standing together, and the air is smoky. Behind us, a little wedge of the bleacher steps verifies the location. I use my finger to scroll down the page.

"Anyone with information on the whereabouts of these two women is encouraged to provide it to Alexis Storm. A reward will be provided."

There's more to the article, but Ida takes the pad back. "Why do they want to find you?" she demands. "What aren't you telling us?"

"Nothing." I protest. "We told you we were with Bryce. That's a picture from this morning. That doesn't make us matter."

"Yes it does." Ida waves her hand around at the building. "Storm and his goons want this building. If he takes it, it would be like losing Portland's history."

"We didn't do anything," I say. "We didn't come here to protest. We came to meet people and to see what's happening here and report back home."

Ida stares at us like we must be lying and I stare back at her. Deep wrinkles almost hide her steely eyes, and she gives away nothing.

I fish around in my pack and find the aspirin bottle and hand Ida four. "These are for Tom. For the morning."

She takes them, looking puzzled that I've just offered. She also looks hungrily at the bottle as I put it back, and I decide to hide at least half of them somewhere else in my pack. "We have something here," she says. "A library. We matter to the community. I will do anything to protect that. Anything."

Monday's voice comes out the gloom near me, impatient. "Your enemies are looking for us. Doesn't that make us your friends?"

"What did you do?"

"Nothing." I'm tired and Ida grilling us makes me even more tired. "We aren't important."

She looks at me for a long time then says, "If you're lying I will kill you myself."

Wow. "We're not," I stutter.

She goes away again. We didn't have time to read the whole article. When she's gone I whisper, "I'm tired of no one trusting us."

My eyes have finally adjusted enough to the dark to see Monday nod. "Tam's okay now," she says. "I set her straight. Look, we need a plan. What if we set up our own PDXNET accounts? Then we can follow each other and if Storm and his goons take you, I can come save you. And vice versa."

We have saved each other so far, but breaking in and out of jail is a bit much. Still, I sit up and dig quietly into my pack for my phone while Monday finds hers. Every sound we make seems loud.

We lean so we can see each other's phones and hide the light from them with our bodies.

The network is up, although everything loads slowly.

It takes a few tries to come up with names, Monday becomes WednesdayMorn, and laughs at that. I name myself SalalGal. We talk about how to post so Just Robyn will find us, but can't think of anything except following the usernames we think are Justice and Robyn. I'm not too sure how these networks work, and I don't want to get caught being stupid. I mean, clearly people are looking for us now. Maybe Justice and Robyn will guess who we are, maybe not, but we want to stay secret from the greens and the Freers. And we don't want to lead anyone to Justice and Robyn, either. So we follow a bunch of other people, too, a bit randomly. We learn that six people died today. One was a seven-year-old girl. "Why would anybody bring a little kid to a protest?" I whisper.

Monday whispers back. "Lots of kids these days."

Yeah. No birth control any more.

Monday continues, "They arrested more than Kevin. They arrested twenty people, and Storm says they were all leaders of the Free Portland Movement. Almost every place else says they're heroes."

I accidentally come across the same article Ida shoved at us on the tablet. It's hard to read on such a small screen and our names aren't there. It calls us dangerous. "This isn't fair," I hiss.

"Nothing's fair," Monday whispers. "Use your backpack for a pillow."

"Yeah, I will."

"Put your hand through a strap."

I do.

"Did you ever have a boyfriend?" I ask her.

"Go to sleep," she says. I know she's been raped, and that she's nervous around a lot of men. Kelley has always warned me about that, too. That men are dangerous to girls. But she and Oskar have both talked about love in good ways. Not just family love like we *do* have, but being in love. Nobody in the garden seemed to be in love, but Justice and Robyn look like how lovers in movies looked. Was Raj's kiss love?

My hand is still tangled in the strap hours later when Monday shakes my shoulder. "It's getting light." Her voice is really low. "I want to leave before they turn us in for nothing."

I must have slept all night. I feel better than I have in a few days. "We promised we'd help with books."

Tom pokes his head out of the gallery. He looks a lot better than he did last night. "You girls up?"

Monday glares at me, but I shrug.

I try to sound perky. "Hi Tom." So much for sneaking out this morning.

"Let's get breakfast and then I'll show you what we need moved. I bet you find a few books you want, and I'm sure nobody will mind if you slip them in your packs." He sounds like he's still trying to be a manager, even though he looks like he might lie down and never get up. His face is pale, although his gaze is strong and friendly and full of trust. Kind of like the Board back home getting old in their jobs, not really knowing that everything has changed. Still, Powell's is running in some small way, and the garden has saved seeds and plants.

Stubbornness is a survival trait.

We help Tom get down to the coffee room and he makes us bitter coffee. I plug in the phones, and top them off while we drink the coffee, then plug in two more.

I'm starting to like coffee.

Mei and Ida and two others join us. Ida cuts up tomatoes and makes toast. She doesn't say anything about the pictures or the article or anything. She clears our plates and brings us extra cups of coffee, like she's trying to tell us she's sorry.

Because of the boarded-up windows, time inside Powell's City of Books passes strangely, but by the time we get up to go stack books and earn our keep it looks like day outside even though there is no sun shining directly in. The thin views show a sky that looks like it's all just one big cloud of grey.

I make sure I have all the phones and that we have our packs.

The pile of books Tom points at must be hundreds of books big. Maybe even thousands. It's deep and wide, like an ocean of ideas and stories. We can see the tops, and along one side the spines. Many are faded or wrinkled or stained. "Where did these come from?" I ask.

"From out there." He waves his hand at Portland. "We have people who scavenge houses for them and bring them to us in trade for other books or for credit to borrow books from us later."

If that's how they got them, there must be fifty houses worth of books on the floor. We sort them into stacks by the colors of the rooms in the bookstore. There's a crumpled paper map that helps. Red for bibles, rose for dogs and science, gold for horror. It's dark in this part of the store, almost like night. We work by the big doors that are closest to the small one we came in—the first doors we tried yesterday. We use small battery-powered lanterns to read the most difficult titles. When we can't tell what stack a book belongs to, Tom always knows. He looked good this morning when he woke up but already his hands shake when we hand him books. He's wearing a small flashlight strapped to his head which he points right at books to read the insides.

My shoulders are sore by the time we take a break. Monday scores two more books and looks pleased enough that maybe she's forgiven me for not just coming quietly with her this morning and being gone from here by now. Like maybe already on our way to Seattle.

Monday still wants to be gone. I can feel it, like a wall of thick, unresolved energy between us.

I daydream about Raj and kisses and worry about him and bullets.

I see a bunch of books I'd like to bring back to the garden, but they're heavy. Oskar would love a big one I see about Japanese gardens which is full of color pictures. Heck, I want it, too. I want to be home, flipping through the book with Oskar and talking about how to take care of bonsai and whether or not we should add another bridge to the stroll garden. I set it on a counter and ask Tom to keep it for me and he raises one bushy white eyebrow. "A gardener?"

"Yes."

"You can take a book or two with you if you want."

"No." Too heavy.

Someone knocks on the door.

Ida walks over and opens it.

Three men in green uniforms stand outside, holding guns and peering curiously into the store.

Ida points to us. Her face is a stone mask, her eyes hard.

All of the others stop. Mei looks furious. She steps on Ida's foot and jostles her so she almost falls down. One of the men I don't know pulls Mei aside.

I tense, ready to run. I catch Monday's eye and she shakes her head. She's right. Where would we go? Deeper inside? These people would find us.

Tom takes my hand. Not to keep me here, because I could pull away from him easily. He's offering warmth. "I'm sorry," he says. "I told her no. She used to listen to me."

He looks so sad that I lean down and kiss him on his papery cheek. His eyebrows tickle and he smells like sour sweat and age. I can't bear to think he knew Ida would do this.

The greens stand in the doorway, impatient. I put my pack on and walk over, my blood running fast and my stomach light and unhappy. But I smile and hold my hand out, try to sound upbeat. "Hello. I'm Sage."

"Come with us," the shortest and widest of the men says.

"Why?" I ask.

"Orders," is all he says. He looks at Monday. "You too."

We go quietly except that Monday spits as she passes Ida.

Ida looks down at her shoe but she doesn't react otherwise. I'm sure she made the deal, but maybe some of the others are in on it. I guess we're not as important as Powell's pretending to be a library for another few weeks.

Fuck. I don't use that word, except right now it's the only word I can think of.

We are ushered into a truck with the City of Portland logo on the door. I should just develop a deep allergy for trucks. I shouldn't ever get in another one.

This one has a front seat and a back seat and a back bed littered with dirt and a few pieces of trash, and I spot the dull brass of shell casings.

Monday and I are in the back seat with a mesh wall between the three greens and us. I take her hand, and the truck starts up. Our backpacks are squished beside us on the seat, but I'm willing to bet Monday has the gun in the back of her pants like usual, just the way the man she killed used to carry it. It's no bigger than a fist. I actually run my hand along her back and feel for it. It's there, hard but oddly warm when I expected it to be cold. Must be her body heat.

She gives me a sideways glance and one of the greens spits words behind us. "No girl on girl in our truck!" He's actually leering as he says this, and I drop my arm and sit so I'm not touching Monday.

Chapter Twenty-Two

The greens who take us from Powell's yell at people to clear out of the path of the truck twice. Otherwise they are silent, serious, and grim. I press my face to the cool window and hope that Alex or someone will notice me in here.

All I see is a blur of faces either looking away from the truck or glaring at it.

I expect the jail to be dark and dirty and crowded, but only the crowded part turns out to be true. It's a square building with black bricks up to the second floor and then it touches the sky, all white and shiny like a cloud. I had admired it from a distance, clueless about its purpose.

At the top of the roof, twenty or so stories up, I spot greenhouses. A sign on the wall by the door says something about solar paint, but there's no time to read it before a green tugs me toward the doors, his hand on my arm bruising. I'm certain the building isn't entirely Post. Someone started it while there was more stuff still being made in factories.

Our captors shove us through an imposing metal door that slides open with help from a stern man in a spotless green uniform. The driver comes in with us, and another man in a clean uniform holds out his hand. He demands our packs. Handing mine over makes me feel naked.

Two more greens come in off the street with a tall, bearded man between them. He doesn't have anything to give up and he smells like vomit. The outer door closes, and when it clicks the inner door opens. The three of us are led out by the two people in clean uniforms, one in front and one behind. They have guns at their sides, although they don't point them at us.

Monday still has her gun. I can't see it, but I know it's there.

After what the men in the truck said, I don't touch her although I want to.

The click of the door closing behind us makes me shiver.

Because it seems better than crying, I focus down on the sounds of the elevator (almost silent), the way the one guard watches us all, but watches the bearded man more than us. There are deep circles under the guard's eyes and his shoulders droop. The bearded man looks comfortable, like he's been here before.

Monday has gone cold and silent, like she's hidden inside herself.

We're escorted off at the fifth floor and driven through another set of airlock-style doors. Our packs get piled inside the two doors, on top of a torn duffle bag with a towel and underwear sticking out, another pack that looks neat and almost new, and a big bulky coat.

Even though I'm scared and I feel small, I'm still pissed off—the word *Fuck* is still in my head, but it's smaller now and not as angry, more like fear. Like *fuckfuckfuckfuckfuckfuck.* I try to make it stop but the word likes being in my head. I don't like the word so I try replacing it with *breathebreathebreathe breathe breathe b r e a t h e.* The breath in my belly stops me from shaking although my stomach is a pit of sourness.

We stop. I count ten doors, five on each side of a wide hallway. A bold, nasty light illuminates everything. It's brighter than I've ever seen, so bright I blink and blink to adjust to it. The floor and the walls are clean although there are a few scratches in them.

One guard pulls the man into one of the back cells and pushes him in. We're left standing on the concrete under the lights. We can see into some of the cells and the people in them watch us.

Right there in public, where the people in the closest cells can see, the men roam our bodies with their hands. They could have done this in the elevator or inside the airlock doors, but they do it here. I don't like the feel of fingers running up and down my inner thighs and my calves, and along my sides up to my armpits. Especially since the tired one who is searching me is slow about it and squeezes my calves and runs his thumbs up the inside seam of my pants. It feels creepy but I'm not giving him the satisfaction of knowing I hate what he's doing to me.

Monday is twisting beside me. She's almost teasing the man with his hands on her, sliding her behind one way and then the other, standing a bit on tiptoe. He reaches toward her back and she twists just a little, shoving her rear into his hand as if she likes it there.

I know what she's doing. She's keeping his hand from the small of her back. He can't see her face, but I can, and it doesn't look at all lined up with her body. Her eyes are wide and flat, her teeth clamped onto her lower lip.

The radio on the belt of the bastard who's hand is full of Monday crackles and he squeezes her so hard she gasps, and then lets her go and reaches for the radio. He listens with a cocked head.

The guard touching my thigh jams his hand where it isn't supposed to go and I clamp my legs shut, squeezing him away from me, giving a little angry cry in spite of myself.

"Enough," the guy who is on Monday says, and then steps back a pace from her. Good thing since she's shaking all over and I don't know what she'll do if she loses it.

"Get 'em into cells. We've got more." He sounds frustrated, but whether it's at leaving us or having more prisoners, I can't say.

A hand slaps my butt and I'm sure my face looks like Monday's and I barely manage not to cry out. My cheeks are hot with mortification.

At least they didn't find Monday's gun.

I'm jerked by the elbow, dragged. The third man holds a cell door open and the man who pawed me shoves me into the room. The door clicks closed with an electronic sound that's way too soft for what it means. I turn and press my face between two bars as they shove Monday in another cell, across the hall and up two. I can only see into the tiniest corner of where they put her.

I glare at the guards as they leave, shutting the outer door behind them with a *click* as close to silent as the one that locked me in here.

"It's you."

I turn around and Aisha is in my cell, sitting on one of the beds with her legs crossed and her blonde hair falling down her sides like a cape. She has a bruise under one eye. "At least we found you," I babble. "Are you all right?"

Her nose wrinkles in disgust. She is on one bunk and there are two other women on the other bunk. One has short spiked blue hair and is my age, give or take a few years. The other is old enough to be her mother.

I stick my hand out. "I'm Sage."

The blue-haired one is Trill, and the older woman is Shelley.

One of those awful silences which feels like an enemy in the room falls over us.

I fidget.

Aisha hums.

Trill picks at her fingernails.

I catch Shelley's eye, since it's pretty clear Aisha isn't going to talk to me. "Is Kevin here? In this building?"

She glances toward the door and then nods and points up the way they took Monday.

"What happened last night?" Shelley asks.

"When Storm captured Kevin it made the protests bigger so Storm called a curfew." I look at Aisha. "I didn't see Bryce, but Monday thinks he got away. Raj did, too. At least as of midnight."

Aisha looks a tiny bit relieved. "Bastard loves curfews."

"Was anyone hurt?" Shelley asks.

I think about the seven-year-old girl. "People were killed." And then I remember the worst part. "The greens killed Jim."

Aisha closes her eyes and it feels like some vital energy is temporarily gone from her. After a while a tear runs down her face, streaking across the bruise. Only one.

The sound of breathing is loud in the silence.

Eventually, Shelley whispers, "What happened?"

I tell them what I know, and about the trucks and the lights.

Aisha's jaw tightens but she doesn't react otherwise. Almost every other time I've seen her she's been talking. She runs things, she directs. She doesn't just sit and cry.

The guards return with three other people. Aisha looks up and there's recognition in her eyes, but she doesn't move or call out. All three of these people—one woman Aisha's age and two young men—get the body search treatment we got before they're thrown into cells.

I feel desperate. There's no real reason for it except the bars and the lock, and the idea that I can't move. This isn't like being banished to the stroll garden by Kelley or watched over by Jim in the hangar. Kevin having us watched felt like a threat, but this is a trap that's been sprung, real and cold and hard. It makes me angry in every bone.

I can imagine someone standing outside the cell and shooting us. We'd have no place to run, no place to go. A fire would consume us. An earthquake would send us to our deaths with the building.

I wish we were together. Monday and me. I wish she was here and could hold my hand. I haven't even told her about kissing Raj.

Aisha looks up and drags me out of my worry-brain, pinning my attention with both an intense gaze and a hiss to her words. "Kevin doesn't trust you."

I'm really tired of this. I can hear the F-word in my head again, and I'm not that person. "We're on your side."

"How did you end up in here?" Her voice is almost accusatory.

I just lose it. Words start pouring out of my mouth like water out of a hose. "I ended up in here because I left my safe house in the woods and came to town because it looked like civilization was coming back and I wanted to join it. I have been chased and threatened and my friend was almost raped. I thought I found a safe place in the airplane hangar with Bryce and Raj, then a stranger in a wheelchair accused me of being some kind of spy. Bryce and Raj took us to the protest anyway. People threw smoke bombs at us and there were guns going off. We hide in a bookstore and then this morning we get sold to three goons in green by a librarian." I am almost yelling. Maybe Kevin can hear me. I kind of like that idea so I do talk louder. "I didn't do anything except exist and have bad luck. I've never met Storm, only seen him from a distance—once—while I was picking through a whole city's worth of scrap to earn a cold dinner. If this is his jail, I don't want to meet him, either. I just want to go home."

I didn't expect to say that I want to go home. But I do. Right now, I want to be home more than anything in the world. I want Oskar. I want Kelley and the taser she used to keep me safe. I will never call the garden a prison again.

What if I never see it again?

I'm shaking and I feel weak. My eyes are wet and I will not cry in front of these women. I will not do it.

Aisha says the same thing Raj said to me earlier. "Revolution is messy."

I really, really want to hit her.

Instead I sit down in the corner. Aisha and Shelley are whispering. Two men I can't see are talking in another cell.

Deep breath.

I look for Monday but I don't see her.

I focus on that, on one breath in and one out. One in and one out.

The others all leave me alone. There is maybe five feet between me and the three of them. The floor is concrete and cold and the walls are concrete and cold. The cold leeches out my anger and I'm just cold, as if I've been turned hollow. They must hate this as much as I do. That's what the near-silence is about. Like the jail has locked up our hearts.

The circles under Aisha's eyes are so deep they look like stains above her cheeks. Trill looks pissed. Shelley looks resolute, blank.

Apparently no one trusts us. Me and Monday shouldn't be important. We're not worth putting in jail. It has to be because of Justice and Robyn. I mean, really. Monday and I haven't done anything but defend ourselves. No one seems to know about Jack or the yellow house, so it can't be that.

Footsteps.

The heavy doors bang open and three men come in. Two bodyguard-sized men stand a tiny bit behind the man in the middle. I recognize him from the scrap heap.

Storm.

He looks like he's just stepped out of a gym. Muscles bunch under a green shirt with the arms torn off. His hair is a little wild. He wears a belt that supports two handguns and two knives.

Storm.

I wonder if he has come to do something to Kevin.

His boots tap loudly as he stalks up and down the walkway between the rows of cells, his gaze swinging from cell to cell. His eyes promise that he will remember every pore in our faces. He stops even longer just opposite the cell where they put Monday.

There is hatred in Aisha's eyes. It's deep. Everything about her is tense. The others don't like him either, but Aisha looks like a cornered mother bear.

She knows him. He's hurt her and people she loves. I can see it in the set of her body.

He walks up and down three times, looking us all over and over and over. He stops and stares at Aisha.

She stares back at him.

They know each other.

"Aisha." He says her name like a whip and she jerks but keeps looking at him while he says, "See what your pride got you."

She brushes the hair from her face, the gesture steady and in control. "We will win."

He stares at Trill and Shelley and then me.

It's different to see him this close. The day we were picking through trash, he was too far away to see details, and he sounded and looked like he was in control. Like everyone would do whatever he wanted forever. But he hadn't sounded cruel.

The man in front of me is a different man. I feel like a bug or a specimen of Oskar's or something. Less than human.

Storm's eyes are incredible. They're green with purplish irises, almost too pretty to be natural. He has a scar from his right eye to his right ear, like he's been grazed by a bullet or the blade of a knife.

He speaks to Aisha again. "What will you win? It won't be safety or security. But then, you don't want those, do you?"

"We want freedom."

"Freedom to die?"

"To choose how to live."

"You want chaos, little bird. Be careful what you wish for." He laughs at her, and she flinches but holds her ground as well as anybody could in a jail cell with a monster staring at her. He is a monster, I can feel it.

She's very brave.

Maybe Aisha is like Kevin. A force that you follow even if he's wary of you, a force for right and good.

He turns to me. "You. You know where Justice is."

It's a statement. I don't have to answer a statement. My head shakes. "No."

"Yes, you do. I heard you have Justice's phone."

Who could have told him that? I try to imitate Aisha and stand up as straight as I can and take a deep breath. "I don't know what you're talking about."

He steps so close that if I reached through the bars I could touch him. I feel the heat of his breath as he says, "Tell Justice I've won here. Tell him if he comes back, he's dead. Tell him you'll be waiting right here, since this is where I'm keeping you until he comes back or I finish rooting out these rebels." His gaze flicks to Aisha, and again it looks like more than a casual acquaintance.

"I don't know Justice," I say. "We're just passing through."

He laughs. "You're stuck now. You had your chance to stay out."

So he knows they deported us once.

When I don't say anything more, he stalks up and down the row of cells once more and then leaves.

Chapter Twenty-Three

THE SILENCE AFTER STORM LEAVES IS THICK AND HEAVY. MY VOICE sounds small in it. "Aisha?"

"What?"

"I need some history. Tell me about Justice."

She shakes her head. "Maybe you should tell me what you know." She sounds tired and almost bored. "Or tell me more about where you're from."

"I have people to protect, just like you." I stare at her, trying to make her believe it.

"This is the best place in the world to put spies."

"Would the greens have put their dirty hands all over spies?"

A look that might be doubt crosses her face. "Maybe."

Trill watches us, her eyes wide, but she doesn't say anything. Shelley stares out through the bars and might be listening. I work harder. "You saw me with Raj and Bryce at the massing. We weren't doing anything but sitting and watching."

"I barely noticed you," she says. "I was busy."

"So how—if I'm not a spy—do I convince you I'm not a spy?"

Aisha shrugs. "Why do I care? If I don't tell you anything, it won't hurt us."

"I'm not asking you about now. Not about your plans. Just about the past. It might not even be *your* past. But Kevin doesn't trust me because we had these phones set up with two ID's that he says were his friends. JustinTime and SignsofSpring. That's all Kevin has against us. He told us they were old leaders. Like maybe his leaders. Were they?"

Silence as Aisha regards me. Her eyes are bright blue. Even dirty and bruised she has that fragile blonde beauty I see in old ads and pictures of Before. Almost like she's not real.

"Give her a break," Trill finally speaks up. "I believe her. No one makes up feeling that pissed off and that confused. Besides, it's old news."

"You never knew them," Aisha says to Trill.

Trill blinks at her, not cowed in the least. "So tell *me* a story about them."

There is a long silence. Murmurs of conversation come from the other cells and the too-bright lights make little humming noises from time to time. A toilet flushes somewhere on a floor above us and water runs through a pipe over our heads.

Aisha begins to rock and the springs on the bed under her squeak. She closes her eyes. "There used to be a lot of powerful people in Portland. There was Storm in the central city, where we are now. Up on the hill, near 24th Street, there was an intentional community that started to promote businesses, like getting people to shop and walk the art galleries. Then they started to do more as stuff got worse, organizing food and meetings.

"Justice and Robyn were already feeding people and giving people work when the quakes hit. They knew Kevin. Knew the Commissioners. Knew all the city people. They worked with them."

She stops rocking and opens her eyes. "During. That's what we say about those first awful weeks after the quakes when we were finding the dead. During. That's when Storm first took power. It seemed like he was a leader along with Justice and Robyn and Kevin and one of the Commissioners, a woman named Doris Dufrau. He cleaned up the dead and took away the worst of the rubble and set up stations for water and food."

She looks like she's not here.

"They worked together. Storm was the strongest, had control over most of the city proper—the downtown core and the Pearl—and that was okay. He kept order, which everyone wanted then. When the world is falling apart you want order.

"Storm liked power and he started talking about setting up elections. No one else wanted them, but he managed to get a vote about having a vote. That backed everyone else into it, of course.

"He didn't have any authority to call a vote or to count a vote. But he had all the media except PDXNET and some blogs. He used paper for the vote—the net was even worse During and right Post, before we started re-building it..." Her voice trails off, goes silent, and then she swallows and starts again. "Storm still controls everything but the net, and he keeps getting pieces of that. The thing is, we're better than the city IT people he has, and no hackers have gone over to him. The television stations are his, and he still puts out a newspaper whenever there's paper." She's in full story mode, and everyone in the cell listens to her now.

"So everyone campaigned. That's when I met them all. I was only twenty and I wanted the world to be a better place again. I wanted to be safe. Even though I should have known better, even though people told me I should have known better, I believed in the elections like I used to believe in fairy tales or the tooth fairy."

She pauses for breath, and Shelley adds, "I worked for Storm that first time. Going door to door and telling people they needed him." She sounds pissed off. "I was stupid."

Trill is quiet, listening like me. But even if she was in Portland then, she would have been a kid. If only I were old enough to remember Before and all its glories.

Aisha takes up the story again. "He stole the first election. Lied. Owned the people who counted the ballots. We did our own straw polls, since we didn't believe it. Almost nobody we talked to voted for him." She sounds bitter. "Not that it mattered. He told them they voted for him and they believed him. Stupid." She pauses, switches positions, combs her fingers through her hair, and I can almost feel the stress pouring off of her. Old anger. "He appointed his own people for all the districts, as if that was all it took to put Justice and Robyn and everybody out of business. People that didn't have any support, that no one wanted to work for. They took money for favors and jobs.

"A fight started all this. Seven years ago, when Doris DuFrau got shot. Killed. A woman. Kevin got shot through the spine, which is how he ended up in a wheelchair. Justice and Robyn nursed him. Within two years there was enough going on in the city that most people who loved Storm stopped and switched to support Kevin and Justice and Robyn." She pauses, purses her lips, leans her head back, and then starts over. "Not everybody changed sides. Some people still love Storm since he brings order." Her voice has a little edge of anger. "Sheep."

She's talking some for me, telling the story to someone who didn't live it. Maybe she has a heart after all.

Trill asks my next question. "So where did Justice and Robyn go?"

The big door opens and there is a scuffle as greens bring in new people. Six. Two of them are women and they get pushed into our cell; no one searches them. The men get taken further up. The greens move fast and they look like they've been fighting; they're sweaty and one of them bleeds from a cut on his arm. Their voices sound rushed.

We're all quiet until they leave. Shelly and Aisha know the women, who are Louise and Lisa. I'm pretty sure I won't be able to keep them apart—they're both about forty and have brown hair and names that start with L.

"What's happening?" Aisha demands. "How did you get caught?"

"It was a vigil. For Kevin. By the fountain downtown. They just picked us at random." The woman shivers. "At least they didn't shoot us."

"Who did they shoot?" Trill's voice is laced with irony.

"A kid. Younger'n you. In the legs. And two men. I didn't know them, but I heard one of them read poetry at a vigil a few weeks ago." Her words stop coming out in long strings and she is clearly trying not to cry as she bursts out short sentences. "He was really good. It made a lot of us cry. His poetry. They killed him."

"Shit," Aisha says. "Greg. Must have been Greg."

No one confirms or denies.

Shelley is almost wailing. "Why doesn't the rest of the world help?"

"Sheep. It's the same everywhere," Aisha says, starting pissed off and then stopping. Moving into command. "No easy way to get around like there used to be. There's just us. That's all we got. Look—they're thin. They have to be. I can see it in their eyes."

"What about the reporters?" I ask. "Like Alex?"

"Fucking watchers. They never help." Aisha sounds bitter about it, too. Then her face brightens. "So who has weapons? I'm getting out next time they open the door."

I think of Monday's gun, but otherwise I can't imagine how anyone else could have weapons. But I'm wrong.

Between us we have a kitchen knife that has just been sharpened; one of the L-women produces it from the shoulders of her jacket while explaining how she's designed the hidden sheath. She looks so proud of herself I'm proud of her. Two nail files emerge from Aisha's shoes. Trill has nothing, but she holds up her fingernails, which are long and sharp. "I know how to fight," she says, and the way she says it, I believe her.

Aisha hands me one of the nail files, and I decide to interpret that as acceptance.

Aisha starts singing.

Chapter Twenty-Four

THE WHOLE CELLBLOCK SINGS. THE SONGS ARE ABOUT SUNSHINE AND revolution and freedom. We even do the national anthem once, and it's the loudest of them all. Singing makes me feel stronger and more connected to the others here. Like the whole cellblock is a string of people and no one's alone when we sing.

There is a little sink but we don't have anything to drink from, so from time to time we cup our hands under the faucet and sip out what we can. It is barely enough. Monday's voice is unique enough to identify, and beautiful. I am glad to hear her.

The singing drives away some of my physical hunger.

The doors open.

We don't stop singing.

Four men are pushed into the corridor, surrounded by four greens. There's blood on one of the green's shirts and blood on two of the captives. No one is fighting at this moment but they all look like they have just stopped and feel like they could start again at any moment.

"Stay ready," Aisha hisses. She reminds me of a lynx.

The elevator isn't finished disgorging people. It spits out a young woman being held by a small older woman in a torn green uniform. The green is fierce and pulls the meeker woman along, handling her harder than she needs to. The captive is thin almost to illness and her hair hangs over her face in long greasy strings.

"Back," the green yells at us, staring into our cell. She acts like we're dogs and not people. "Back!" She gestures with one arm.

We step away from the door, still singing, although softer.

Aisha's gaze narrows and her lips thin. She feels like a cat ready to spring. She and I are beside each other and close to the door when it clicks open and the green uses one hand to open it wide. She is watching us closely the whole time. We hold our hands open and at our side and stare back at her. The nail file is a hard sliver in my back pocket.

I don't feel ready for whatever Aisha thinks we're about to do, but I try and look ready. I don't want to let her down.

The green starts to push her captive in front of her and the girl looks up and locks both of her hands together and twirls on her feet so fast I can barely follow the movement. It looks like she's setting up to hit a volleyball and she takes the smaller woman on the chin, snapping her head back.

The cell door starts to close.

Aisha and I step forward and push, keeping it open.

It keeps trying to close in spite of us; something automated. Shelley grabs it, too, and the three of us can stop it, although our arms shake. "Out!" Aisha hisses.

Trill leaps forward and out, smacking into the green while she's focusing on the messy-haired girl. The green stumbles. She's not really any bigger that Trill, but she hits Trill with her fist and Trill falls onto her butt. A surprised look fills her face.

The stringy-haired captive uses the moment to plant a kick that sends the green sprawling. The two L-women are out the door and then Aisha hisses at Shelley and inches around the door, keeping her weight on it so it can't close. I'm next, Aisha last. The moment we're all on the far side we leap back and the door closes.

While we were focusing on getting out, Trill has scrambled to the downed green, searching her pockets. I expect keys, but there's something like a remote control in Trill's slender hand as she stands up, looking pleased.

The men who passed us earlier have seen the commotion. The four of them fill the corridor between the cells, a wall of green shirts bearing down on us.

Trill points the remote at the greens as if they were game characters. They don't fall, of course. They just keep coming, ignoring Trill, most of them with eyes on me. Their running footsteps are like slaps on the metal floor.

I pull out the nail file, shaking, keeping my eyes on the man closest to me.

"Stop!"

It's Monday yelling from behind them. They ignore her; maybe don't hear her. I catch a quick glimpse. Her arm is extended, the gun out. She shoots, the bullet going high over them but then bouncing off the wall and coming back toward them. It lodges in one of their thighs.

The man screams and falls, and the other two hesitate, bend to help their comrade.

"Don't." Someone is giving orders from behind her. "Don't shoot. No guns." I recognize the voice yelling at Monday. Kevin. "Bullets ricochet."

She could have hit any of us. She keeps her gun on the men, who have stopped, the one she hit down on the floor. This explains why they haven't been using their guns to control us. She's shaking, and she snaps out words. "Not if I hit them before I hit a wall."

Kevin emerges from the crowd, wheeling between Monday and a man we saw in the airplane hangar. The look he gives Monday is both angry and proud at once. He says something, but it's too low for me to hear and Monday lowers her gun hand. Two of the greens that stopped when her gun went off start toward us.

I rush at them.

They stop and stare, not at me, but behind me.

I hear the doors opening. We'll be caught and thrown back for sure, but I can't stop watching the men in front of me. Their faces display fear and confusion.

I dodge sideways and gain enough distance from the greens to turn and see people racing into the jail. Our people.

I start toward Monday. There is so much noise and movement it's hard to tell what's happening. Cell doors spring open up and down the corridor.

I watch as the four greens—even the man Monday shot in the leg—are stripped of anything they could communicate with and locked into the cell we were in.

I get close to Monday. She's shaking. She gasps out, "I thought they were going to hurt you. I thought you'd be killed." We stand next to each other and away from all the cells. She pushes back from me a step and her gaze is really intense. "You okay?"

"Yeah." I'm scared but I am okay. "You?"

She nods and then she's holding onto me and kissing my hair softly. It feels so good I melt into her and for a breath, all of the chaos around us is gone and there is just the smell of her hair and sweat and the feel of her hand against my back. She lifts my chin and kisses me on the lips. It feels just like Raj's kiss. It makes me shiver.

I push away from her, suddenly awkward. When I look in her eyes I see she is hungry for me. I've known this on some level for a while, and I feel it for her. But this is the first time it's out in the open, the first time I have to really acknowledge it.

There's no time to think about it.

I brush her cheek with my lips, a promise to think about it later, but no more. I pull away but take her hand, not willing to lose her or lose myself in her. Justice told me to take care of her, and I have to do that first, get her out.

There is a jostling chaos between us and the open doors as people make an aisle for Kevin's chair.

He rolls through the doors. Monday and I follow just behind Aisha and Trill and the small woman who has now drug her hair off her face and exposed a scar from eye to chin. We make it down the elevator in the same tight group, all of us crammed in close to Kevin, the elevator barely able to contain so much jubilation.

It's still light outside and the sky is brilliant with the early evening sun painting high clouds gold and red and orange and, in a few spots, a trace of magenta. The streets themselves are shadowed by skyscrapers. Lights snap on.

Cameras point at us. Phones. Flashes, calls, and questions come at us like the wind. I look for Alex, find her close to us, totally intent on her job. She smiles and snaps a picture of me and Monday, then re-focuses on Kevin and Aisha. Aisha is grinning as if the whole world is perfect and Kevin's arm is in the air, his hand making a victory sign.

I am smiling wider than I recall ever smiling. The goodness of the feeling of freedom is as overwhelming as the terror of losing it.

We wait on the steps and in the street, letting all of the people in the jail come out. There's more than were held on our floor, many more. Maybe hundreds. Reunions happen all around us.

Monday and I keep holding hands. There's too much noise to talk. We are slowly pushed a little away from the center of the crowd.

It is fully dark by the time the jail is emptied and we start down the street as a group. The skies have cleared; here and there an early star shines.

Cameras follow Kevin more than any of us. He is the story. His fist pumps in the air as he rolls along, grinning wide, looking like he has all of the energy in the world.

People wave protest signs on both sides of the street.

We clot up for a moment, the street too full for any forward progress. People yell, "Make way," and, "Let them through," but the crowd is a confused, triumphant beast and we stand still while it figures out how to open.

Raj runs up to me and grabs me tight, turning me so my hand slips free of Monday's. He smells like sweat and stress and happiness all at once, tangy and alive. I remember that I need a bath and the last time I washed my hair was just after Monday shot Jack, and that I can't smell any better than Raj. I probably smell worse. But we're all here together. He leans down for a kiss and I let him have a brief one. His lips crush mine with a promise of more if I want more. This is a new language I'm learning, and to have it from two people at once is like being split.

I can't have them both.

Raj steps over to hug Monday, but she steps back, a hurt look on her face.

Raj turns from me and swings Trill up in the air and then puts her down, and they immediately get into an animated conversation that I can hear the intense tone of, but not the words.

Monday is backing away from me. I go to her. I'm not deciding between her and Raj right now. I'm pissed because I have to, but I'm also not willing to lose either of them.

This minute, I just want to be happy I'm free and that we've won.

The crowd finishes sorting itself out enough for us to move.

Monday looks at me and I say, "Just keep going," but she's still hesitating. "Please?" I say, and her face softens.

We walk, swinging a little closer to the crowd around Kevin. We don't hold hands again, but we swing our arms and sometimes our hips or our shoulders touch.

Bryce is talking to his dad, then he falls back, walking until he's beside me. He has a funny look on his face. "Dad sent me to make sure you're all right."

Monday laughs at this.

"I think he likes you," Bryce adds.

"No shit," she says. Then, "I'm thirsty."

Bryce produces half a bottle of water and Monday and I finish it in a few gulps each. I feel a lot better, like the water is a battery charge.

Cameras are still snapping. People yell questions and answers back and forth. The feeling is buoyant. We're down along the waterfront now. The grass is jammed with people, but the sidewalk is kept clear for Kevin's wheelchair, and we're only a little way behind him.

Bryce starts dancing, doing it up for the crowd. Aisha appears from nowhere at his side. They are a pair, both natural performers. They are beautiful, in fact. They don't appear to know how well they move together, their focus outward on the crowd, yet each very aware of where the other is.

She's older but it's not the first time I think they're lovers. Sensuality surrounds us all, heightening the sounds, the rush of blood in my veins, the bump of Monday's hips against mine, the flash of Raj's smile.

I dance a few steps and look from side to side at Raj and Monday. They aren't dancing so I take both of their hands and pump them up and down and move my feet. "Come on!" I call. "We're free."

I hope all of Portland is dancing with us.

Monday tells me, "You're crazy." In spite of her words, she starts to dance a little, and then her free hand reaches for a man behind me who was in her cell. Soon the whole line of jailbirds are dancing and the people in the streets are dancing with us.

Sparks rise into the sky from fires lit in trashcans and makeshift fire rings along the street. Candles burn bravely in glass jars that keep the wind from eating their small flames. Flashlights sweep across the line of dancers.

We dance and walk and chant and dance and walk the whole way along the river and come to the part of it where we can see the train station. The train tracks haven't been fixed Post and there's no trains except for a few single cars that have been there a long time and have graffiti all over them. A working streetlight shines on tall grass between the trestles.

The station windows aren't boarded up. Light spills out of them, welcoming and warm, almost like I imagine things looked Before.

The crowd surrounding the station is huge, and fires in the parking lot brighten some areas enough to see faces. Everything beyond the station is dark.

Kevin rolls along in front of us, and I think about how far we've gone and how he must be tired and yet he is still moving, still happy, still full of purpose even in his wheelchair.

I know why people follow him, and Aisha, and Bryce. They are all bright, as if they burn with more light than the rest of us.

We follow Kevin into a huge half-circle parking lot where he stops in front of a tower with the words, "Go By Train" almost disappearing into the blackness of the sky up above.

He sits for a moment, talking into a cell phone, a series of unreadable emotions playing across his face. Bryce and Aisha are bent down beside him, part of the same conversation, heads cocked at the phone. When he snaps it closed the look on his face is pleased.

Someone shoves a microphone into Kevin's hand and he blows into it once, so it emits a high crackle. People become still around him. He calls, "Hello!" and the silence spreads and he does it a second time and the whole big parking lot is quiet except for the sounds of fire and shifting feet. He says, "It's good to be free."

The crowd cheers. They cheer for a long time, clapping and yelling so loud I think all of Portland must be able to hear it.

"You did this!" Kevin proclaims. "You freed those of us they locked up. You released us from tyranny. You did it!"

More clapping.

"And tonight?"

Silence.

"Tonight, tonight we will take back the rest of the city. We own the streets. So many people will join us after this that we can force Storm out and exile him forever from Portland."

Raj and Bryce are still nearby. "I thought we already won," I whisper to Raj, heavy with the idea that it's not over, suddenly exhausted from the jail and the walk and the dance. "It should be over."

Chapter Twenty-Five

THE CROWD KNOWS STORM IS STILL OUT THERE. I TRY TO CATCH THE adrenaline I see on their faces, to feel like fighting on, to be brave. It's hard.

I thought it was over.

Kevin exhorts the crowd and the crowd responds with yells and hoots and claps. It keeps growing, as if all of Portland is coming together in this one place, in spite of the dark, in spite of the windstorm, in spite of anything about this moment.

Fireworks blaze overhead. Just three of them, three big umbrellas of bright red fire like streamers. They are impossible, a thing that can't exist, but they do and they're so beautiful my chest fills with heat. Another thing I've always wanted to see, another little dream that still lives in the real world.

I'm hungry and thirsty and cold. But the afterimage of the fireworks leaves me a little brighter inside, a little lighter. I can go on. Beside me, Monday looks exhausted. "Are you okay?" I ask her.

"Yes." She turns and looks at me. "This has endured for years. Why would we think it could end tonight?"

"The crowd believes it. They've been here all along."

She reaches a hand out to put it across my shoulders, and I lean into her, and we watch the sky for more fireworks, but there aren't any more.

Kevin hands the microphone to Aisha. Bryce stands by her side. Aisha starts the same songs she took us through in jail, the microphone carries her voice out across the crowd to join her. Monday and I sing, too, almost a reflex. Aisha sings, we sing.

The doors of the train station open. A small army pours through them with pitchers and cups of water, with dried apples and bottles of soda and big canisters with pumps on them. A young girl in braids serves me two fingers of coffee from one of the canisters in a small paper cup and even though I haven't gotten any food yet the coffee helps. Eventually I snag a soft, tasteless apple and a cup of water.

Raj leads me and Monday into the station. Four big men with serious faces control the entrance, but being with Raj is apparently enough. They step aside.

I spot the unique blue of Trill's hair and a few of the other people from the march, and more faces I remember from the hangar. There's also a lot of people I don't know, and I take a deep breath, remind myself that I'm getting used to crowds.

Raj spots someone he wants to talk to and turns to us. "I'll see you in a few minutes." Then he's gone.

Monday and I head to the bathroom. There is a small half-used bar of soap by the sink. At the moment, the soap looks like a miracle.

"I never thought I'd get jailed for doing good," Monday mutters while I fill a bottle I'd saved with water from the sink. "They could jail me now. I shot that guy."

I remember how she felt about the boy she didn't shoot. "He deserved it, and you didn't kill him." I start pouring the bottle over her head, slowly so it's not a shock to her.

"I want to throw the gun away but I can't."

"I wouldn't mind if you did."

She purses her lips in a way that tells me she isn't going to do it. Her hair is so thick it's not wet through yet, so I refill the bottle.

"Were you in the same cell with Kevin?"

She nods.

"How was he?"

She sighs. "He didn't apologize. Not even after they threw me in jail with him. I think being in a wheelchair and running all this has made him stubborn."

Did she shoot the guard to prove something to Kevin? I don't know how to ask her that, so I fill the bottle again and let the warm water out slowly through my fingers and massage her scalp. Her hair feels coarser than mine. Must be the Indian blood.

I remember how she looked at me in the jail, full of need.

If she wasn't a girl, I'd know how to react. Maybe I don't know the difference between friendship and love. I worry about her when I'm not near her. Actually, I worry about her when I am near her. I keep rubbing her scalp, keep my hands busy doing something they won't get in trouble doing.

"What about Seattle?" she asks, the question so casual it gives away how much she wants to leave.

I place the bar of soap into her hand and start wetting my own hair, sighing at the warmth of the water. I don't know why some things work here and some don't; why there is warm water in a train station. Some piece of renewable energy built from Before, like solar panels on the roof. But I don't need to know. I've accepted stranger things on this trip. "We're in this now."

Her face falls a little. "I thought this was over for a while."

"I know. At least no one thinks we're spies anymore."

She nods, her hair slick with soap that smells of mint. "It feels dangerous." She doesn't say this like she minds.

"Everywhere is dangerous."

She snorts.

"Seattle is a few hundred more miles of I-5."

"This sucks, too."

I don't argue. Everything is dangerous except the garden, and maybe Just Robyn. In fact, now that I know what's out here, those places don't feel safe either. I understand more about why the Board was always scared, although I still think it's the wrong choice. But I might die here, and that's not the best choice either. "Maybe after we win, this will be a good place to be."

Monday doesn't answer, and she doesn't agree. She holds her hand out for the empty water bottle and I give it to her and start rubbing soap into my hair.

"I feel like this is my fight now. If we leave Portland like this—under Storm—then maybe someone like him will want to run Just Robyn and the garden someday. Maybe they're already there. Maybe Seattle has its own Storm."

"Justice could take Storm." Monday fills the bottle again.

"I heard he tried once." I take the bottle from her and start pouring a rinse into her hair. As I tell her the story I got from Aisha, Monday shifts her head under my hand and I take the hint and scrub at her scalp and she whimpers a little.

"Now I know why he sent me here," she says.

"Really?"

"I bet he wanted to know what's here. And he knew there were good people here." She smiles. "Maybe he wanted to send me someplace safe after all."

"We might have died on the way here."

She touches me with a wet hand, withdraws it again.

I'm confused by how close she feels. Telling her about Raj and his kisses seems wrong and right, both, and in the end the words don't come out of my mouth. This feels a bit messed up. Still, I do a good job helping her finish washing and lean my head back so she can rinse the soap from my hair. Her hands are strong.

Three women I don't know walk in, ruining our quiet moment. We're as clean as we are going to get in a small public bathroom. There is no way to dry our hair so we leave it soaked and dripping.

I'm ready. When this is over I can think about what to do next, and I can think about how Monday makes me feel, and whether or not to go to Seattle.

Outside, Raj is waiting for us. This makes me smile, and I feel both better and more torn. "Now what?" I ask him.

He looks rather pleased with himself, like he has some great secret. My stomach hopes he is going to surprise us with an excellent meal.

Instead, he swings his arms around from behind him, and he has a phone for each of us.

"Cool." Monday says, flipping the one he hands her open to be sure it works. It's pretty banged up on the outside, but its display lights up and looks cheerful.

"Clean and with communications ability restored," I say. "What more could a girl want?"

Raj smiles and continues to look entirely too pleased with himself.

He leads us to a huge room in the train station with benches and a ticket counter and a lot of open space. This must have been where people waited to take the train Before. Best of all, there is a sense of space since no more than twenty people occupy a room designed for many more.

Kevin's wheelchair is on the far side of the room, near where people would board the trains. Leaning on the counter where the conductor must have stood to take tickets, I spot the beautiful ebony of Robyn's skin, and beside her, the bulk of Justice.

Monday looks as shocked as I feel, and then she gets a broad smile and looks like someone gave her presents.

I would be that happy if it was Oskar or Kelley. In a way, this is even better. Justice is right for this place, fierce and a bit feral. Robyn appears exotic in contrast to Aisha's ethereally pale skin.

Monday starts forward. I put a hand on her arm and say, "I want to know what they're talking about."

We walk as quietly as we can and sit down on benches near them. Aisha and Bryce notice us, but the other three are deep in conversation, focused only on each other. There's so much tension in the air it stops us.

We catch the end of a sentence by Kevin. "...now. This late. You can't swoop in from outside."

Robyn's voice is high and full of anger. "Justice got you out of jail. He came the day after you got locked up and he's been running logistics and ops out of here for twenty-four hours straight."

Justice says nothing.

Kevin nods, which I suppose is acknowledgement of Justice's role, although it's perfunctory. He doesn't even look grateful.

There is a lot of silence.

Aisha and Bryce stand still, gaping, like they're shocked to see Justice and Robyn here, too. Kevin sees us, although Justice and Robyn haven't yet. He doesn't say anything, but his eyes meet mine for a minute and pass on.

Damn him. Monday just shot a man for him.

Kevin is still looking at Justice, looking up since he's in the chair. "Why now? Why not last year or the year before?"

Justice speaks so quietly I can hardly hear him. "We're not going to stay, Kevin. We have another life, now."

"So why did you come back?" Kevin asks. "Why now?" He points at us. "Because of them?"

Justice and Robyn swing around, and both of them look ecstatic to see us. Robyn comes toward us, stands beside Monday. Justice turns back to Kevin. "I came for a lot of reasons. Not half of which was to help you finish this."

Kevin shakes his head, not believing.

This feels like the way they didn't trust us, and it makes me angry with Kevin all over again. I like him and I don't; he is my enemy and my friend. I hate it that I don't know how to feel about him, or about Raj versus Monday for that matter.

My stomach is clawing my backbone for food and I'm tired of people acting stupid. This is all inside me, demanding to get out until my feet start moving almost all by themselves.

I stalk over to Kevin.

As soon as he looks at me, I half-kneel by his chair and look him straight in the eyes. He looks back, curious and maybe a bit annoyed.

"It's always about trust Kevin."

No response.

"It turned out that you could trust us. Does it really matter why Justice is here? Isn't it good?"

Kevin gives me a long look. He doesn't want to respond. I can see it in him, this inner fight that shows in his eyes and the way he grips the arms of his chair and in the short sharpness of his breath.

Aisha senses how important the moment is, and comes over and puts a hand on my shoulder. I touch her fingers and let go, but keep looking at Kevin.

It feels like there is a ball of silence around us.

Kevin actually shakes a little.

"We're on your side," I say. "And I bet Justice can help. Winning the battle matters more than anything, and Justice and Robyn can help."

Kevin swallows, looks away, looks back. His eyes are damp and his face struggles to decide what expression to wear. I turn my head away so that he can fight his own fight, and after a few breaths I hear him say, "Okay. Let's go free Portland."

Justice smiles and says, "Together."

That breaks all of the silences between us. Monday is in Justice's arms and I'm asking Robyn if they saw the things we posted on PDXNET, and she says, "Yes," and that makes me feel pretty good.

Raj is watching and Bryce is talking to his dad quietly.

Pretty much everyone needs to hug everyone, which feels awkward but also like it has to happen.

A half an hour later, we're all standing just inside the doorway to the parking lot, checking phones. Everyone else has phones and earbuds. With some fiddling, they all work and we all have contacts for each other and a way to get texts to and from each other as a group.

Kevin must see the irony in this because he gives me a soft wink before he leads us back out to the half-circle, to the thousands of his supporters that are waiting for him to lead them to freedom. We're all bundled up but my damp hair still makes me feel cold. And I'm still hungry, damn it.

Justice and Robyn walk beside Kevin, with Bryce and Aisha behind. Raj walks with us, and a few of the reporters, including Alex. I'm always pleased when I see that she's still alive.

Collectively, this third line that has me and Raj and Monday in it forms a half-circle of protection for the leaders. I'm holding Raj's hand and Monday's hand, and there is no tension in this moment. Only resolve. This is a big family out for a big fight.

Chapter Twenty-Six

I ENJOY WALKING WITH THE LEADERS, ALTHOUGH IT FEELS STRANGE TO have so many people looking my direction. A slightly over-important pair of young men keeps the way clear for Kevin's wheelchair, and thus for us. People watch us go by, their faces hopeful. Alex is always near, her tall, skinny form feeling almost like a guardian.

I'm with these people because we joined a fire circle one night on our way into the city. I mean, I am smart enough to know that I didn't earn this, that I'm not even part of Portland.

Perhaps I am becoming part of it. I let that sit a bit. It's a new thought. I promised Monday I'd go to Seattle with her, but maybe she'll stay here now, since she made up with Justice and Robyn.

I'm still holding her hand, and Raj's hand. We're chanting. My love for both of them feels so real, they're filling me with as much energy as the chant does. Maybe more. Definitely more.

Raj is excited, in his element, like there is no place he would rather be. He even looks taller, regardless of the fact that he's really not much taller than me. Monday looks pretty damned magnificent with her long dark hair, clean and dry enough to catch breezes now, her chin up, her eyes focused. It's like Justice and Robyn coming here has energized her all over again.

Raj stops chanting long enough to lean down and half-shout into my ear. "That was great!"

"What?"

"What you did. Talking to Kevin. Making him forgive Justice." He really does look proud of me.

"I was just pissed off."

He laughs. "I like it that you always know what to say in an emergency."

"I don't."

"You did. There and with Jim."

This line of talk feels creepy. "Why did Justice and Robyn leave? When I met them, they didn't say anything about Portland."

Bryce falls back to talk to Raj for a minute, interrupting the flow of the conversation. We're getting closer to City Hall; the streets are even more crowded. I feel like I need to be more aware of my surroundings. More ready. Like I need to do Justice's exercise all the time if I want to stay safe.

It's hard in a crowd.

Trying to really separate sounds and pull meaning from them with so much going on is almost impossible. Engines. Dogs barking. Snips of conversation. A loud yell. A chant. A prayer. The sharp scent of fires. Shadows from the tall buildings.

The day before yesterday, Portland felt like part protest and part party. The parrot preening on the man's shoulder, the singing monks, the booksellers handing out soup, the shots, a man I know dying.

This feels more serious the further we get from the train station, shifting into all-protest and desperation and excitement. Tension settles on me, palpable, as cold and dark as the night is becoming.

Hats and gloves and scarves cover skin, mostly in browns and blues and blacks, so we look like bears walking to war. Some people swing lanterns and some clutch candles in glass jars. The way the small flames illuminate the protesters' faces from below make them all look like angels or paintings.

People watch us as we go by. Some call out for Justice and Robyn, others for Bryce or Kevin or Aisha. They all wave, even Justice. Whatever ruined his enthusiasm for this, it's back. He looks keyed up and in control.

He looks, in fact, rather impressive.

Bryce takes Aisha's hand and they wave with their free hands. Monday gives me a squeeze and whispers, "I need to talk to Justice."

Like that, she's too far away for me to reply. Whatever candle I am for her, Justice is a bonfire.

Raj finally returns to my question about Justice leaving, talking loudly and near my ear so I can catch the words. "Kevin wanted to take down Storm no matter what."

We slow, knotting up, waiting for some people to let us through.

A tall man slips out of the crowd and high-fives Justice. Justice returns it, the slap of their hands audible, both giving a sharp cry of victory. More people notice him. They all look happy, some almost delirious, to see Justice.

Monday trails behind the returned hero, all "look at me," in an almost desperate way, like his acknowledgement will feed her.

I understand why Kevin didn't want him here. The people love Kevin, but they love Justice in a different way. It's visceral.

Raj puts an arm around me as the crowd closes in. "Justice didn't want to fight. He said we had to take the city without violence. Kevin said as long as Storm was killing, we might have to kill. Kevin won the argument; being peaceful took too long."

I agree. I'm hungry and my feet hurt and it feels like I've been protesting for days, which for me means like two days. Years *would* be impossible.

Raj continues, "Bryce saw a bad fight between his dad and Justice. After everyone made up, Justice helped Kevin organize the biggest protest they'd done so far. Kevin made sure at least some protestors had guns and Molotov cocktails. I was there that night. Not at the protest itself—I was too young. But when they were preparing. Justice was there, too. Giving out guns and hand-made bombs, his face hard and dark. He scared me."

I can't imagine Raj being scared of anything. Not even when he was a kid. I can imagine Justice being scary.

"It was like a little war. A hundred and seven people died, some of them Justice's friends. He wished Kevin good luck and he left. This is the first we've seen of him since then."

Wow. And now Monday is carrying a gun tucked into her pants, and more like Kevin than Justice in some ways, no matter that her reasons are easy to understand.

I wonder if I should tell Justice about the gun, decide it's for Monday to tell. I am pretty sure she's why Justice and Robyn came back. For Monday. I saw the relief in his eyes when he saw her and the way he held her. He's ignoring her right now, but I'm not sure he knows she's behind him. I'm still sure there's a secret there—he pushed her away but then he came after her. But he clearly loves Robyn, so it's not seduction, not on his part. Maybe it's just guilt.

Maybe it's Kevin, too, but when Justice looks at Kevin there is love and respect and complicated things that look like worry. When he looks at Monday there is love and hope.

Maybe it's partly even Portland. People do things for places. After all, I would die to protect the garden.

Emotions make my head hurt. "Hey, Raj?"

"Yes?"

"Does Kevin have weapons tonight?"

"No. He never fought like that again. I don't think he could bear it."

That drives me silent for a whole block. We shuffle more than walk, the streets thick with people, the voices around us dripping with jubilation, with determination, with fury, hope, and a few with fear. About half the people are singing with Aisha who is just ahead of us, so loud she's not even in tune any more. I join in.

The total group of us, Kevin and his followers, is maybe twenty or twenty-five and the crowd parts in front of us, slowly, and then re-joins behind us.

And then we stop.

Instead of protestors, lines of vehicles block the street.

Trucks, of course. There have to be trucks. In this case, there are even fire trucks. There are also cars with the city logo on them, and a few larger yellow vehicles that look like awful metal insects poised to strike down at us.

They are all silent and still and cold.

I expect some attack by all of these cars and trucks and farm trucks and fire trucks.

But they don't move.

We don't move, either. We settle in, and mill, frustrated and full of energy. Vehicles loom over us, dark hulking shapes that blot out the tops of buildings and the stars and the reflection of light on clouds.

Robyn puts an arm around Monday's shoulders and talks to her in a voice so soft I can't hear it.

No greens come rushing out from the cars with guns drawn.

No Freers rush through the vehicles.

After a while two things became clear to me. Something else is going to have to happen. And whatever it is, it isn't happening in the next few minutes. This isn't calming; it's worry. Waiting for something that's sure to be scary and painful is hard, especially when you don't know exactly what it is.

Storm is not going to just walk away, even though he should. Bryce calls Raj, and I am left standing alone. It feels both strange and liberating. I don't really feel alone—I feel like I'm part of something. This is why I left the garden.

I chant pretty loudly. Listen. Chant some more. I love the way my voice mixes in with everyone else's voice. I feel strong and tough.

Someone comes and stands near me. Even before I look, I know it's neither Monday nor Raj. I smile when I see it's Alex.

She's so tall my head just comes to her shoulder. "Hello intrepid," I say.

"Intrepid?"

"Intrepid reporter. Isn't that you?"

She laughs. She actually laughs pretty hard, harder than my over-perky greeting should have made her laugh. When she stops and catches her breath she gasps out. "Thanks. I needed that."

"I'm not sure why it was so funny."

She laughs again, but only a short bark. "I don't know either. At least you have a sense of humor. Not many around here do."

"So you've been collecting all of our stories. What do you do with them?"

"I haven't got your story yet."

"Not much to mine. I followed your airplanes, and here I am."

"I never did thank you for helping us get them tied down in the windstorm."

"I'd do anything for an airplane."

"Really?" Her face lights up a little. "What do they mean to you?"

"Hope." No reason not to tell her more, as long as I'm careful. "I didn't come from here. I came from a place that isn't a city. And the planes flying over convinced me there's life out here."

Even though it's dark, there is enough flickering light from a fire someone started nearby that I can see the look on Alex's face. She understands. "That's pretty cool."

A man walks right in front of us swinging a lantern and I'm momentarily blinded. When I can see again, Bryce is kneeling down in front of us. "We can hear people moving behind the vehicles. Be ready."

I feel a bit of regret. I would have liked to talk to Alex more.

A hand taps my shoulder. Raj. I let him pull me up. He puts a hand on my waist and one on my shoulder so he's standing in front of me, looking at me. His hands are warm and I feel hot everywhere that his hands touch me. "Are you sure you want to do this? You could go someplace safe. It's not your fight."

"They jailed me for this fight." It's offensive that he doubts me; I am sincere about this now. I hadn't expected this when I left home, but it was why I left. To get away from isolation and to face the world. "It's for everyone, isn't it? Can I run away from the Storms of the world?"

Bryce shakes his head. "Wherever Justice found you, he did a good job."

Raj pulls me in for a hug. I hold him. He's solid, and he feels good in my arms, and he confuses me like Monday does, maybe more. But this is also why I left home.

Engines start. All of them at once, the trucks, the cars, the deep thrum of tractors. Sirens scream. I remember Storm walking through the jail and I shudder as I turn to face the oncoming headlights.

Chapter Twenty-Seven

HEADLIGHTS SNAP ON AND ILLUMINATE US ALL, TURNING THE PEOPLE standing in front of me into silhouettes.

Moments blur together. People press each other out of the street and onto the sidewalk. Aisha's voice, loud, trying to lead a song. Screams. Vehicles moving directly at us, splitting the crowd.

Justice grabs my hand and pulls me though a knot of people, leaning down and saying, "You did good."

The praise feels good. "Thanks."

He stops me near Monday. "You two take care of each other. Keep your phones."

I nod. Monday looks spooked, like a deer about to run. She stares at Justice.

He sees her, reaches out and touches her shoulder. "Don't do anything stupid. It will be okay. I promise."

Then he turns and he's three people away, then five, then hard to make out in the crowd.

"You either," Monday whispers into empty air.

"What is it with you two?" I tease.

"He saw me kill a man."

She told me about that in the hangar, how she had killed a man who raped her. "And then he kicked you out?"

She shakes her head. "I did something else stupid."

"What?"

"I tried to hurt Robyn. A week later, while I was still crazy from the rape and guilty for being a murderer and half the people in town weren't talking to me. I wanted to make her leave so I could have him."

"But Robyn loves you."

Monday whispers, "I know," and her eyes are wet.

I take her hand. "We can do this," I say. Not that I know that. I have no idea what the plan is except stay alive and take down Storm, although that won't be our job.

The tractor nearest us has a tall arm, thicker than three people, with a bucket on the end of it. It swings back and forth over the street, metal screeching against metal as if it's being moved too fast. Three men brace themselves in the bucket, awkward. They laugh as we scatter away.

Protestors duck and scream even though the bucket is four feet above their heads. Monday and I twitch and lean when it comes our way.

It passes us.

Two police cars roll slowly behind it, sirens and lights hurting our ears and stealing our vision.

Now that there is action, it should be faster but it's slow and almost stately, a little surreal. I feel like I'm moving through syrup.

Three men clamber onto the tractor's big tires, reaching for door handles or the edges of windows or headlights. A shot pings off of metal and two men jump off, one falls. One of the men on the ground crawls in and out of light, pulling another man behind him. The third crawls on hands and knees, head down. Then there are more than three, a circle of people bundled up with just their faces showing, advancing on the big machine.

"It's like a parade of doom," Monday says. A trash can fire backlights her hair so it looks like she is wearing light into the darkness. Her face is shadowed and her eyes black in the dark of her cheeks.

Behind the tractor and the police car there are trucks.

We have no vehicles. We are people against metal.

But there are a lot of us.

"Come on." I pull Monday and she follows, although I have to lean into the job of taking her with me. We keep our hands together, stalking the lines of people, holding the peace by marching between the trucks and the crowd. She is beautiful, smiling, fisting the air and almost prancing.

We pass Raj once, and he is a dark warrior who slaps my outstretched hand in solidarity, leaving my palm stinging. His focus darts from the line of vehicles to the line of people and back.

We will win. There are more of us. But I want to win without more death. The thought of creating peace feels like a shot of adrenaline, a last hill to climb.

People join hands with us until a line of people stands in the street between the crowd and the greens in the cars. I feel exposed on both sides. No one shoots at us. We are three groups: a line of trucks in the middle moving slowly, full of power, then a line of people between the trucks, and a mob on the other side. It is hard to see the depth of the crowd in detail but easy to hear and feel. Like a pack, or a herd, or a bit of both. Predator and prey. It goes on forever, like it's all of Portland.

Surely Storm feels this? He can't win. No way. There are too many of us.

The trucks and cars are packed with people in green, with guns that are pointed at us or at the sky or down. Some of the faces in the vehicles are as scared as we are.

Maybe the trucks will just keep going. Maybe they'll drive out of the city in a long line.

There are enough other people holding the lines that I can pull Monday to a stop so we can catch our breath. Even in the cold, sweat trickles down my back and shines on Monday's forehead. She could get sick from this. I spot a few of the reporters who walked over here with us standing on fences or poised in high places. I don't see Alex anywhere.

My phone quivers in my pocket and I pull it out, see a message that the vehicles are turning, making a circle around us.

This isn't good news.

There are lights in the windows of buildings, and on top of at least one building. Candles and flashlights. Occasionally the brightness of lanterns or lamps in windows. Every light means people. It's like a night sky lit by close stars.

Thousands. The sheer number make me dizzy.

A yell rises above the street noise. The sound fills my bones as it's picked up by more voices, the noise a wave coming up the street toward us.

Something burning arcs up from the street toward the cars and trucks. It is as pretty as the fire juggler was but far more frightening.

The staccato of gunfire comes from further down the street and then from behind us.

The burning thing falls and explodes, searing the dark.

There is no way to tell who is firing at who.

I hate it. I want peace, not more death. I want to rest.

Monday pulls free of my hand. I turn to look and she's searching the street, the metal of her gun shining like a sliver of bright blood as it catches reflected firelight. I hadn't seen her pull it out. She hisses, "We have to do something. I can't let Justice get shot. Have to find him."

She means Justice. I agree.

She's running, darting through the crowd like a stag and I follow, twisting around a pair of men rushing toward a police car, leaping over a black dog that can't possibly belong here, twisting through people going two or three directions at once. I stay close, careful not to lose sight of her.

Justice told me to take care of her, both when we first left and again earlier today.

The staccato slap of gunfire burns my ears. We don't fall. I keep my eyes on Monday's black hair swinging as she dances around clots of people and trashcan fires and once, around a city truck with flat tires. She looks back from time to time. I don't dare look at anything except her. A single blink could leave me alone in all of these people. It is up to Monday to find Justice and me to stay with her.

The trucks and cars and tractors have all stopped. Just like back on Burnside, men with megaphones begin to talk. Only now I can't tell what they're saying. We're running. The crowd screams and pushes. It's all I can do to keep my feet.

Some people jump out of the trucks. One of them pulls off his green shirt and throws it onto a fire and races away.

Are they abandoning the symbols that make them green, that make them Storm's?

A man crosses right in front of Monday, arms extended, a handgun that must be four times the size of hers held out in front of him.

His gun is pointed directly at her chest.

Monday must see it.

She speeds up instead of slowing or dodging, barrels into him. He swings sideway, pulling the trigger. A scream as the bullet tears into someone.

I have to look. A woman down on the pavement, a baby being pulled from her arms. I can't take time to watch—I can't lose Monday—but the pitch of the screams tells me one of them is dead.

The man with the gun grabs Monday around the waist and I'm there, pushing him off balance. He falls. She leaps over him. A clump of people jump on him, the crowd a wall between me and Monday.

I can't lose her.

I knock a woman down to get through and stay with Monday.

Alex appears, running beside us, camera in hand.

There's a fire truck in front of us, the ladder so white it's easy to see even in the dark and the chaos. The ladder is raised part way, like half of the letter "V" on its side. A man is standing on it, dressed in a dirty yellow fire uniform. Men in yellow pants and green shirts hang onto the truck like insects. Most are armed.

Monday stops and stares. I almost bump into her.

"There he is," she hisses.

I look up. It's hard to tell who's there. People on the truck wear pieces of firefighter uniforms like boots or coats, but most of them don't fit right. Others are in street clothes with green shirts or hats or scarves. I can't make out faces.

I feel a hole where Monday just stood. She's leaping onto the truck, a hand on the silver railing, a foot kicking.

I glance back up, finally see what she saw.

Storm.

She wasn't looking for Justice at all.

She's on top of the truck, a hand on the ladder, shadowy. A green sees her and yells, flicks his wrist so a light illuminates her arm and then her face. She is fierce and determined, like a young female bobcat.

She hangs on with one hand; the gun is in her other hand. She shoots at the man in the light. He grabs his arm and falls backward, lands hard, still on the top of the truck, still close to her. He bounces a little as his back impacts a metal railing. Anger and pain sharpen his features.

The route she took is still open. I follow after her. Maybe to help, maybe to make her stop. I only know I need to be there, to be beside her.

I love her.

She's got a foot on the extended ladder, a hand on the ladder rail. The ladder is white so she's easy to see against it.

I'm barely up on the truck, one foot still on the running board, the other searching for purchase. My breath is fast and loud.

Storm still doesn't see her, doesn't look down. He's talking into his megaphone. "...fire. This is our city, your city."

No. No, it's mine. Bastard! The ball of my foot finds a valve. I use it to get good purchase, vault upward.

My hands curl around metal on the top of the truck, my body hangs over the edge.

The truck is huge. I'm already so far up a fall would cost at least an ankle. The ladder is long and wide, bigger from here. Like everything has become bigger than it should be, the world grown outsized.

Except Monday. Monday is small on the big ladder, pulling herself up one-handed.

The green who Monday knocked down is standing now, looking at me, holding his hurt arm. Blood leaks through his fingers.

Monday is three steps up the ladder. Storm is above her by a ways, maybe twenty feet. Her arm is extended. Her hair is flying behind her.

She looks like vengeance.

The man steps on my hand. It hurts like hell. I can't let go, can't fall, can't stop watching Monday.

She jerks. Something has hit her in the back and slammed her into the ladder.

I scream.

She grips the ladder tight, hugs it, uses it to steady her arm, pointing upward. She fires.

Her shot rips Storm off of the step he's on. He falls straight down onto the cab of the truck, the megaphone falling into the crowd.

More bullets slam into Monday, dancing her on the ladder.

The man's foot lifts from my hand and I pull myself the rest of the way up in one motion, reaching, just in time to stumble as Monday falls onto me. I go down and she's on top of me.

There is blood everywhere, blood on my hands, blood on the red of the truck. Blood in her hair.

Fuckfucfuckfuckfuckfuck....

Men racing for Storm leap over us.

I screech denial even though I know this is truth.

Monday looks at me. She can see death coming for her; it's reflected in her eyes, a darkness and a lightness mixed together, a narrowing of everything into just the moment. Now. She lifts a hand and smears blood on my cheek.

I take her hand and kiss it until it goes limp. I whisper to her, even though it's too late. *Go peacefully, go peacefully, go well, go loved, go peacefully.*

Oh god, don't go.

After a long while sound returns, yelling and movement and far off, cheering.

Alex is taking pictures.

Chapter Twenty-Eight

"THREE DAYS HAVE PASSED. IT'S TIME TO GO." ROBYN TELLS ME THIS AS she hands me a cup of coffee and a fresh roll. I don't know where the hell she got fresh bread but it smells so good. I'm hungry. Like my belly is just waking up and I realize I don't know if I've eaten anything since Monday died. I remember drinking water and crying and staring. I remember Raj coming in and sitting beside me more than once.

The bread is gone in just a few bites and I think of Monday when I take my first sip of the coffee. Maybe I'll have to learn to like it, for her sake.

Kelley won't like me liking coffee. It will mean less for her.

I shake my head. My thoughts still aren't clear. I can't go home. I've only been gone a few weeks, maybe less. At the moment, I can't count.

I'm on a hard bed in a small room. There's a light, and one chair. Robyn sits in the chair, the light falling on her face. Her eyes are red, although I don't know if it's from tears or exhaustion or both. Even tired and sad, she looks beautiful.

I watch her through a few sips of coffee. "Thanks."

She gives me a small smile.

"Is everyone else okay? Is it over?"

"It's over." She sounds like I feel. Like every word is being pulled through dirt.

I take another sip of coffee. My head is fuzzy but the coffee is a good thing. I can feel it seep into me.

"We're leaving this morning."

Oh. "I won't see you again?"

"We hope you'll come with us."

Oh. Oh! "What's happening out there?"

"If you get out of bed and get dressed you can see for yourself. Be ready in an hour."

I haven't been out of this room since I got carried here except to go to the bathroom. I didn't have the strength to move, not after...I swallow. After Monday.

After Monday died.

"I can't go home. I can't live there again. It's too small."

Her smile is soft. "You don't have to decide that now. One step. Come with us to Just Robyn."

I could do that. "All right."

The shower in the bathroom is broken, but the kitchen sink is deep enough for me to wash my hair. I don't notice how cold the water is until I'm shivering.

Robyn and Justice wait outside, talking. Like they know I need to be alone in the house for a bit, alone with myself. Not that I know what to say to myself. How to feel. Monday is a hole in my life, a place that's so empty it's dark and has almost no feeling at all unless I look at it directly and then it feels like it might kill me.

I walk around the house, touching things, breathing. Being Now. Eventually I'm ready and I open the door.

Outside, the sun is bright as hell. Life hurts my eyes.

We're in a neighborhood. The house across from us is boarded up and the one next to that has been burned out so it's just a chimney and English blackberries and opportunity grass. But the house next to that is lived in, with a garden started and a fence and a dog in the yard, following a woman while she tosses weeds into a red wheelbarrow.

There's a truck by the curb, idling. A white one with a city logo on it. But I guess it doesn't belong to Storm any more.

Nothing belongs to Storm any more.

"Good job, Monday," I whisper too quietly for anyone to hear. "He deserved your shot."

Justice is sitting behind the wheel, smiling at me.

Trucks. What is it about me and trucks and Portland?

Justice gets out and comes around and puts a hand on my shoulder. It's the first time I've seen him since...since it was over. Before I know it there are words blurting out. "I'm sorry. I didn't take care of her. I'm so sorry." And then I'm crying. This is the first time I've cried. A few memories stutter through me; someone strong carrying me down from the truck, me clinging to his neck. Not Justice. Someone I don't know. Robyn crying; me standing numb and covered with blood. A long walk to a shower I stood under naked while Robyn scrubbed Monday's blood from my face and hands. A drive here, stumbling in before dawn, thinking the night would last forever. A taste of bitter liquor, and then darkness. No tears. They're all coming out now. A flood of the damned things, rivers on my cheeks.

Justice and Robyn both hold me while I sob and shudder. They smell like soap and coffee and clean wind.

It takes a while before I'm ready to get into the truck. When I do, I feel empty and light. Not good, not happy, just like I'm light instead of heavy.

We go over the Burnside bridge. There's no one controlling who comes and goes any more, just a sign someone made by hand on cardboard that says, "Welcome to Portland."

Whether she had to or not, Monday bought us that sign.

Fuckfuckfuckfuckfuckfuck....

That word was never in my head in the garden. Never.

I blink and tell myself I'm not crying until it's true. Then I blow my nose and say, "We can't drive all the way to Just Robyn."

Justice laughs. "No."

I hold my breath then, willing to Be Now, to wait. The streets on this side of Portland look just like they did before we won. It's late morning and the flea markets are still up. People walk the streets, a few groups stand and play music. Children walk along a wall, balancing with their arms out.

It takes a while for me to understand we are going to the airport. Justice pulls the truck up almost all the way to one of the white planes.

There is a crowd around it, waiting for us. Raj. Alex. Even Kevin, sitting still in his wheelchair in front of the crowd.

Raj comes up to the side of the truck and helps me out. He pulls me close to him and brushes his lips across the top of my head. I could lean my face up to kiss him, but I can't do it. Not now. I can return the hug, feel grateful to be in his arms.

"You can stay," he says. "I'd like you to stay."

From the way he says it, I'm sure I'm getting onto the plane with Alex and Justice and Robyn. That's what they're offering. I pull back a little bit from Raj and look hard at him. "What are you going to do now? There's no Storm to fight."

He smiles. "I got assigned to help re-build. I'm going to work on schools."

I've never been around kids. But who knows? Right now, I feel like I can't decide anything. "Maybe I'll come back. No promises yet." Monday's sacrifice isn't the way I can choose Raj, not right now. Besides, I chose Monday. She's the one I followed through the protest. She's the one I chose to try and protect.

He touches my cheek with a finger. He looks more tentative than I've ever seen him, like he's lost.

"Thank you," I tell him. "Thank you for wanting me to come back."

"I do." Then he pulls me close to him. "I'm sorry about Monday."

I can't say her name out loud yet. I nod and pull away, turn.

On my way to the plane I smile at Kevin and take his offered hand. It's warm, and the look in his eyes is warm. He lets go and turns to Justice and I'm forgotten that fast. I can see it in his face.

Well, he has a city to run.

Alex is standing by the door. She boosts me in. I sit there, the only one inside the little plane, looking out of the window at the airport.

After a while, I hear Justice's and Robyn's voices outside. Alex puts a hand in. "Come on out."

But I want to fly! "Why?"

"We're going to put you in the co-pilot's seat."

I'm confused. "I can't fly."

"None of us can," Justice says. "But we thought maybe you'd be more help than we would."

Alex adds, "My usual co-pilot got shot. He'll recover, but he can't fly, not for a few weeks."

I hadn't even known a plane needed a co-pilot. I have no idea how to be one. "Where are we going?"

"Just Robyn. The main street's wide enough to use as an airfield."

I take Alex's hand and clamber out and back in. Now I'm feeling even more floaty. I have the presence of mind to turn around as soon as all three of us are in our seats. "Won't that tell people where you are? I mean, the town?"

"It will." He glances at Alex. "We've decided to let a reporter in. She promised not to report on where we are, but maybe the world should know we exist."

"Okay." I can't think very hard, but it's not my decision anyway. I stare at the blinking instruments.

The plane shudders once and then starts moving.

The quiet surprises me. It's quieter than a truck. More like a cat, purring.

We move slowly and I catch another glimpse of Kevin and Raj and the others. They are already going back by the hanger, chatting and talking as if we're not there, as if airplanes taking off is normal.

Not for me. I watch the whole process, the slow turn, the careful lining up along the runway. Alex points to the dashboard of the airplane. "That's the altimeter. Watch it after we take off and let me know when we get to 8,000 feet."

"Isn't that high?" I ask.

"No. We don't have far to go. It's just a half hour." The motorcycle gang, the nights out, Jack, the park. A half hour.

Wow.

Then the plane starts to move. It speeds up, the ground blurring, buildings flashing past. There's the slightest shudder and then we part from the ground and everything becomes smaller fast.

I have a job to do. I stare at the altimeter. By the time I tell Alex we're at 8,000 feet I'm glad to pull my eyes back to the window.

I expect to look down and see Portland, but we're over farms. I look behind, and the tallest buildings are there, sunshine reflecting on them so they seem to wink at me. Below, all the ground is green and the broken houses and the cracks in the roads are almost all too small to see.

From here, it almost looks like the world is whole.

About the Author

Brenda Cooper writes science fiction and fantasy novels and short stories, and sometimes, poetry. Her most recent novel is *Spear of Light* from Pyr, and her most recent story collection is *Cracking the Sky* from Fairwood Press. Brenda is a technology professional and a futurist, and publishes non-fiction on the environment and the future. Her non-fiction has appeared on Slate and Crosscut and her short fiction has appeared in Nature Magazine, among other venues.

See her website at www.brenda-cooper.com.

Brenda lives in the Pacific Northwest in a household with three people, three dogs, far more than three computers, and only one TV in it.

www.ingramcontent.com/pod-product-compliance
Ingram Content Group UK Ltd.
Pitfield, Milton Keynes, MK11 3LW, UK
UKHW041856190726
13854UKWH00002B/941

9 781942 990222